THE HOSTILE SHORE

Douglas Reeman joined the Navy in 1941. He did convoy duty in the Atlantic, the Arctic, and the North Sea, and later served in motor torpedo boats.

As he says, 'I am always asked to account for the perennial appeal of the sea story, and its enduring interest for the people of so many nationalities and cultures. It would seem that the eternal and sometimes elusive triangle of man, ship and ocean, particularly under the stress of war, produces the best qualities of courage and compassion, irrespective of the rights and wrongs of conflict . . . The sea has no understanding of righteous or unjust causes. It is the common enemy, respected by all who serve on it, ignored at their peril.'

Apart from the many novels he has written under his own name, he has also written more than twenty historical novels featuring Richard Bolitho, under the pseudonym of Alexander Kent.

D1338724

The Hostile Shore

Douglas Reeman

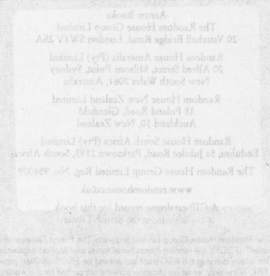

ARROW

Published by Arrow Books in 2003

5 7 9 10 8 6 4

Copyright © Douglas Reeman 1962

First published in the United Kingdom by Hutchinson in 1962

A CIP catalogue record for this book
is available from the British Library

The Random House Group Limited supports The Forest Stewardship Council® (FSC®), the leading international forest-certification organisation. Our books carrying the FSC label are printed on FSC®-certified paper. FSC is the only forest-certification scheme supported by the leading environmental organisations, including Greenpeace. Our paper procurement policy can be found at www.randomhouse.co.uk/environment

MIX
Paper from
responsible sources
FSC® C016897

ISBN 978 0 09 959149 8

Typeset by SX Composing DTP, Rayleigh, Essex
Printed and bound in Great Britain by Clays Ltd, St Ives plc

To My Mother and Father

I wish to express my thanks to the Office of the British Resident Commissioner, Port Vila, New Hebrides, for their help and co-operation.

D.R.

Andrew Grainger, Assistant to the British Resident Commissioner in the New Hebrides, dabbed wearily at his chin with his handkerchief and walked to the shadowed window to stare down at the island's natural harbour which was spread like an exaggerated tapestry below him. In the harsh forenoon sunlight Port Vila, the administrative centre of the archipelago, seemed to wilt and sway before his eyes, and even the lush green slopes of the jungle beyond the town shimmered in the relentless and searching heat.

The medical-cum-Customs launch curtsied fussily across the harbour, the twin white waves thrown back by its bows moving across the blue water to set the moored schooners, launches and luggers nodding and rolling uneasily at their anchors, and disturbing the dozing birds which sat hunched and dejected on buoys and slack cables.

Grainger blinked and turned back to the seemingly dark interior of the Residency. In the low ceiling a large fan turned with a slow, uneven squeak, and he made a mental note to have it fixed. He forgot the fan immediately as he let his gaze fall on the girl who occupied the cane chair by his desk.

Dressed in slim coral-coloured slacks and a white sleeveless blouse, through which he could see the line of her brassière against the tanned skin, she was lighting another cigarette, and appeared to be frowning above the sun-glasses as she brushed the short blonde hair from her forehead. Gillian Bligh, the much-travelled journalist from the *American Forecast*, swung one leg vaguely over the arm of the chair and kicked at her well-worn brief-case as it lay on the floor at her feet. The faint drone of a distant aircraft filled the humid air, and the girl cocked her head questioningly.

Grainger nodded. 'Right on time. That'll be the flying-boat bringing Major Blair from Cairns.'

She blew out the smoke very slowly, as if unwilling to part with it. 'God, what a place! It's so damned hot I feel I shall just about crack open!'

Grainger smiled gently. He had been in the tropics so long now he had not got the strength to argue about the climate. He stared at her instead. Gillian Bligh in his own office. It did not seem quite possible, but then none of this whole business did. He had often read her articles in the glossy New York magazine which reached him regularly a month out of date. 'Gillian Bligh meets the Pope' or 'Our globe-trotting girl sees British fall back in Cyprus'. Some of it was in rather bad taste, he had thought. But, nevertheless, she was extremely easy to look at. A very good figure, now well revealed by her thin garments, which, damp with perspiration, clung to her no matter how she adjusted her body. A rather wide mouth, which, unlike her photographs, rarely seemed to smile, but gave her the appearance of being very much on edge. But the hair, that was just like he had imagined it would be. Short, carelessly, but he guessed expensively, cut, it was so pale that against her tanned face it looked almost white. He put her age at thirty-two or -three.

He settled himself at his desk. 'You never did tell me how you came to get mixed up with this story, Miss Bligh?' His voice was smooth and polite. 'After all, it hardly seems to fit in with your more – er – political ventures!'

She smiled slightly and leaned back against the hard chair. The effort of movement stretched her blouse tightly against her damp skin, and she saw the man's eyes fall for the merest second, but she was just too weary to care any more.

'Briefly, it's like this.' Her voice was soft, but bored. 'As you know, this *Major* Blair is quite an important guy in England. He's head of one of the biggest bridge-building firms in Europe, and he has connections in other directions.' She lifted her leather-bound pad from the desk and flicked open the pages. 'He's thirty-nine years old, married, no children. Educated Eton and Sandhurst. Regular Army in good English country regiment.' The way she said it he might have served in prison, Grainger thought, but made no comment.

'Captured by the Japs in Burma and pretty badly treated. Has deformed right foot, but otherwise in good condition. However, the injury explains his leaving the army, but being of the "right set" his future was assured in other directions. Are you with me?'

She studied Grainger's pained expression from behind the safety of the dark lenses. 'My boss gave him some information a few months ago when he was over in the States. Some information which the Major had been after for twenty years.' She blew a thin jet of smoke into the fan and shook her head. 'Can you beat that? Twenty years? That gives you a real insight into what sort of a guy we have here!'

'I gather it was because of his family?' Grainger prompted carefully.

'Yes. During the British retreat from Singapore,' she saw him wince, 'Blair was there with his regiment, which, incidentally, was commanded by his old man, his father.' She shrugged. 'Well, you know how it was. All hell was let

3

loose, and they tried to evacuate the women and kids before the Japs broke through.' Her voice softened slightly. 'There was some old passenger launch, called the *Sigli*, which was one of the last to leave, and Blair managed to get his family aboard it.' She ticked them off on her slim fingers. 'There was the old man. He had been wounded in the fighting. Blair's mother and his sister. The girl was only about two years old, I gather. There were also some other women and a handful of wounded soldiers.' She slowly pulled off her glasses, and Grainger saw the wide grey eyes as they regarded him wearily.

'Well? What happened then?'

'The *Sigli* disappeared. It was never seen again. Major Blair just about turned the world upside down looking for it. Everyone said he was wasting his time or that he was crazy. Probably some sort of guilt-complex. Call it what you like, he never gave up. When he was in New York he met my boss. He, in turn, was able to drag up some employee who during the war had been an airline pilot on the Singapore run.' She leaned forward, some of her own curiosity showing in her voice. 'He actually saw this little launch being attacked by Jap carrier-borne aircraft right down here in the New Hebrides. Hundreds of miles off course, they should have been making for New Guinea, and then in sight of safety they had to be spotted by the Japs. Not content with that, the boat hit the reef and disappeared, this time for keeps!'

Grainger lifted his eyes to the long wall-map. 'Then, twenty years later, Blair stumbles on the one man who saw it all happen. Amazing!'

'Well, you know how it is. There were hundreds of ships being shot up at the time, and people were too worried to care much for the little *Sigli*. It just happened that this pilot knew her very well by sight, and was able to get a fix on the

4

wreck before he, too, was shot down. Still, he had other things on his mind from then on!'

She stood up and plucked the blouse away from her stomach. Through the window she could see the deep blue of the Pacific, like a sheet of unmoving plate glass. By moving herself slightly she could just see the waving line of white breakers where they met the long, curving edges of the island's beaches, and lapped even at the feet of the nodding palms which seemed to grow right down to the water's edge. It was a beautiful picture, and she felt vaguely moved.

She had arrived two days earlier, and had been nearly driven mad by the pathetic eagerness of the island's inhabitants to make her welcome. Traders, planters and a few of the old pearl fishers all seemed obsessed with the search for news. The English talked about the weather and the Australians about horse racing. The French merely looked grave and spoke of 'home'. All seemed to have lived in the New Hebrides for many years, some had been here, and yet none seemed to accept the islands as part of their lives.

She watched the Quantas flying-boat as it moved purposefully towards its moorings, and looked at the small fleet of launches and native boats which manoeuvred excitedly nearby, the distant occupants waving and shouting in spite of the heat. God, the heat! She felt completely sapped of all energy. But at the same time she was fully aware that the heat was not entirely to blame.

She idly watched the dark-skinned natives running down the dusty road to the harbour, between the corrugated iron roofs of the low buildings and the tall sheds which stank of copra. Her trained mind recorded the scene like all the others. Africa, Japan, India, what difference? Always the self-important little official, the pathetic natives and the leering male hiding behind each offer of help or friendship. She groped for a cigarette but changed her mind. She had seen Grainger feeling for his lighter, and that would necessitate more human contact. She felt that if she did not get away from this place and from everything normal she would indeed go raving mad.

She studied the schooners moodily, as they rolled their finely tapered masts on the flying-boat's wash. One of them was the *Queensland Pearl*, she supposed. Hired by this Major Blair to go looking for the wreck of the *Sigli*. It would be a change. It would give her time to think out what she was going to do with the rest of her life. The days of the celebrity journalist are numbered, she thought again. People don't want them any more. They get all the reassurance they need from the television. Nice, friendly, familiar personalities to do away with the necessity to think or form an opinion. She bit her lip and felt the needles behind her eyes. There I go again. Must concentrate on this assignment. Just this one. And then . . . She shook her head angrily. And then what?

She thought of her boss, Sigmund Meissberg. Small, dark and vital, sitting behind the big desk up in Madison Avenue. Get a human story, he had wired. A human story. He had become so twisted with cynicism that it was unlikely he would recognize one if he saw it. But she knew what he meant. Keep on top of the job, or . . .

Grainger was speaking again. 'I think you'll be comfortable on the schooner. The skipper is a good chap. An Australian, but sound enough. I've given him his instructions about the island you're going to. Vanua Santo. A charming name for a horrible place. As a matter of fact, it's one of the few places left in the New Hebrides for which we have to issue permits to people who wish to visit or land there.' He smiled 'Even on this island they were cannibals

6

fifty or sixty years ago, so it's not surprising that the more remote and less useful of the islands have fallen a bit behind.'

'You mean it doesn't pay off as much as the others?' She lifted her hand as his face creased into a frown. 'Forget it. I'm a bit weary of all the righteousness there is in colonial governments.' She hurried on. 'Are the natives a bit wild up there?'

He walked stiffly to the map. The islands were scattered from one corner to the other like a coral necklace. His finger paused at a tiny island near the top of the group. 'Pretty desolate place. No decent anchorage at all, and along the whole of the southern side we have the Phalarope Reef. It's invisible most of the time and one of the worst I know. It would have to be *that* island where the *Sigli* foundered!' He faced her squarely. 'I don't mind telling you, Miss Bligh, that I was surprised at the Commissioner allowing this enterprise. We have been carefully building up a friendly relationship with all the tribes on the islands. Missions, trade stores, medical help, all have been used to this end. But there are about forty-five thousand natives in the archipelago, and less than eight hundred of us. We simply can't afford any trouble. You must understand that in remote areas like Vanua Santo the natives are really savage, and apart from a few carefully encouraged visits to a small trade store they are left well alone for the present. Perhaps one day, when we are better equipped?' He spread his hands. 'But I hope you see the reasons for my surprise?'

'You don't imagine that Major Blair would start a war up there, do you?' The corners of her mouth twitched with amusement.

'Not at all. But if anything happened to you Her Majesty's Government would be bound to take some action

7

'– a punitive expedition maybe – and then all the carefully built-up relations would be smashed overnight.'

She watched the distant flying-boat. It was not too late to change her mind. She could be aboard the plane and on her way across the inviting water before she had time to weaken. She shuddered and picked up her case.

Grainger was watching her anxiously. 'Are you feeling quite well?'

'Yeah. Just tired. I'd like to go aboard the boat now, if you don't mind . . .'

'You'll not wait for Blair, then? I expect he'll be over from the flying-boat soon. The landing formalities are pretty brief.'

She waved her case vaguely. 'No. All this is enough for me at the moment.'

Grainger was suddenly unwilling to allow her to disappear from his sight. He could not somehow visualize this slim, nervous-looking girl aboard the schooner, with Vic Fraser and Blair as companions, to say nothing of the hazards which might arise on such a foolhardy venture. 'Could you not write your story from here?' he asked lamely. 'I mean, you might find the schooner a bit rough.'

She stiffened. 'And you would look after me, is that it? Don't you worry, friend, I've handled tougher propositions than this, and lived!" She studied the comic look of discomfort on the man's face. 'Bear up, junior! I'll write something really nice about you and your savages!'

Without another glance she strode through the door, and seemed to grow smaller as the white glare of the sun reached out to receive her.

The powerful launch skudded across the harbour, its engines throbbing confidently and making the varnished fittings rattle and vibrate in the long open cockpit. From the

8

short mast the Union Jack and French Tricolour flew side by side, while at bow and stern the neat native seamen frowned importantly at any local craft which were foolish enough to get too near to the launch's sharp stem.

The blue leather upholstery in the cockpit felt red hot, and Rupert Blair eased his body slightly nearer to the tiny canopy which covered the forward end. His well-cut khaki-drill suit was already crumpled in the heat, and he stared across at the slim shape of the moored schooner as if it was to be his final salvation. His taut features were finely cut, with a hint of arrogance, and but for the hard line of his mouth might have been handsome. His hair, dark brown but laced with grey, was thick and well groomed, and helped to retain the youth which the irritation in his expression was trying to destroy.

He watched the schooner with narrowed eyes. *Queensland Pearl* lay a little apart from the others, and by comparison seemed slightly bigger. Built at the height of the free-trading amongst the islands, just before the First World War, she had lost none of her proud lines, although her white-painted hull was well scarred by her forty-seven years of almost constant use. One hundred and ten feet over all, she had a gracefully high bow, the sides of which were decorated with large imitation oyster shells, and from which pointed the long finger of her tapering bowsprit. As the launch curved round her side, Blair could see the correspondingly high counter of her stern and raking tilt of the two graceful masts. He blinked away the sweat from his eyes and turned to his companion.

'Well, Myers, what d'you think of her, eh? Quite a museum-piece, don't you think?'

George Myers grinned and showed his small teeth. Round, plump and completely bald, it was hard to imagine him as a deep-water diver. He had been delighted at the prospect of a free holiday afloat, quite apart from the release it would bring from inspecting the underwater supports of bridges, blasting wrecks and the like. His eyes wrinkled happily. 'Never thought I'd see the like of 'er, sir. Wait till I write to the old woman abaht this!'

Grainger emerged from the launch's small saloon and handed a thick envelope to Blair. 'All your papers, Major. Not that you need them, really. But we must be systematic, even out here.'

Blair nodded briefly and tossed the envelope carelessly into an open travelling grip. 'More bloody red tape, I suppose! It's lucky that yours is a government department. If it had to make its own money I suspect it would be bankrupt by now!'

Myers began to whistle tunelessly and pretended not to listen.

'Now, look here,' Grainger retorted angrily, 'I hardly think you've got a right to make remarks like that, after all—' He checked himself as Blair turned his cold blue eyes towards him. They were ruthless eyes, he thought, completely devoid of pity.

'I have already explained my arrangements, Grainger, both to your head of department and to the people at home. I do not intend to discuss my private business with every damned busybody I may happen to meet along the route.' He smiled coldly. 'As you know, I want to put a diver down on the Phalarope Reef to look at that wreck. I've waited a long time for this moment, and I don't intend to be put off by a lot of nonsense about savage tribes, shark-infested waters and all that sort of nonsense. This is the twentieth century, remember?'

Grainger sighed. Blair's attitude had been the same from the moment he had collected him from the flying-boat. Uncompromising, almost desperate. He tried to imagine

10

how he would later describe Blair to his wife. He nodded to himself. Dedicated. That was the description which fitted him like a glove. Dedicated to this one strange mission which seemed to overrule all else.

'About the American journalist,' he began again cautiously, 'I hope she knows what she is getting into. This is not her normal sort of assignment.'

Blair smiled bitterly. 'No, I realize that. I've seen some of her work.' He turned to Grainger with sudden intentness. 'She represents the very worst type of do-gooder colonial experts in my opinion! People like this Bligh woman have done immeasurable harm by telling all these damned nignogs and what-have-you that freedom with a capital F is their right, rather than a privilege. I am surprised you allowed her in your little kingdom, Grainger!'

'She seems a very fine girl,' he answered gravely.

But Blair only laughed. 'I can see the next headline in that glossy, advert-stuffed rag of hers. "Gillian Bligh discovers Stone-Age Government under Union Jack! Headhunters are cute, she says!"' He laughed again. 'If it wasn't a form of debt I certainly shouldn't be taking her on this trip, I can tell you!'

The launch bumped alongside and two native seamen jumped down to take the head and stern ropes.

Blair stood up and swayed uncertainly on the small deck. Beneath the turn-up of his trouser leg the ugly, built-up wedge of his surgical shoe seemed to mock him, and he waved Grainger's steadying hand aside with a sudden anger. 'I can manage!' Then he seemed to relent. 'Nice to have met you. I shall write to the Commissioner and tell him how helpful you've been.' With unexpected charm he held out his hand. 'Thank you for putting me in the picture so well. You've been more use than you realize.'

Then, brushing aside the native boys, he swung himself over the schooner's low gunwale.

Myers winked at the perplexed Grainger. A small movement, but to Grainger, who still stood in the launch's cockpit as it idled clear of the old white ship, it explained a great deal.

Across the schooner's poop a small canopy had been rigged to provide a square island of shadow, beneath which, in a faded deck-chair, Vic Fraser, the captain, naked but for a pair of shorts, frowned in great concentration as he pulled a length of oiled rag through the barrel of an old British service rifle. Another similar rifle and two massive revolvers lay glistening on a piece of canvas, and with a final grunt he laid the weapon beside them. The rifles were essential on deck when sharks were about and should the divers be working below the surface, but the revolvers were for his personal satisfaction.

Even sitting down Fraser appeared as a big man. Broad of shoulders, and deep-chested, his skin was burned to the colour of the poop rail, and around his eyes the flesh had been pulled into a mass of tiny crow's-feet, the legacy of months at sea and staring into the sun to search for a reef. Normally, he lived an uncomplicated life. Uncomplicated by his standards, that is, and one that he was able to enjoy. But just lately things had started to go wrong. Trading had fallen off, and even more recently the local shell fishing had been prohibited because the waters had become 'fished out'. It was alleged to be a temporary measure, but he was not so confident.

To be hired for such a vast amount of easy money as offered by Rupert Blair's agent had seemed to be like a godsend. With the money he could carry out all the much-needed repairs on the schooner and lay the foundations for his next season of trading. He had been quite prepared to overlook the destination. Vanua Santo, or Hog Island as it was known by the natives, because of its pig-like shape, was reputedly a bad place, but he had no intention of finding out just how bad. They would cross the reef, do the diving and then sail home. It had seemed just as simple as that.

But then the American girl had come aboard and had demanded to be taken to her cabin. She had not yet reappeared. He rubbed his chest thoughtfully. It was a long time since he had seen such a pretty sheila, and certainly the only women passengers he had carried in the past had been the self-contained wives of missionaries. He ran his eye moodily along the spotless decks. In the small patches of shade provided by the rigging and slung boats the schooner's entire crew hovered unnecessarily, as they waited to see the rest of their passengers. The girl had been a wow. The thought brought a grin to Fraser's lips. The boys had clamoured around her to stare at her golden hair. She had won them over completely, if only because of her hair. He looked towards his crew with something like affection. Apart from Watute, the cabin boy, and assistant diver, and at thirteen the youngest one aboard, they had all be willed to him with the ship. His father, a great pearler in his day, who had squandered away everything but the ship and its crew, had solemnly handed them over to his son when Fraser had returned from the war, and with the practical manner in which he had lived out his eventful life went ashore for the last time and died.

There was Old Buka, the senior man. Short, grizzled and having only one eye, his ferocious appearance, already enhanced by an eye-patch of palm bark, was made complete by his teeth, which were filed into sharp points. Wabu and Yalla were the two Torres Island divers. Young,

13

and in the prime of condition, they could dive to eighty feet in search of trochus shell and ignore the constant dangers of sharks and the 'bends' alike.

Kari, a squat, scarred seaman, and Dinkila, the Malay cook, whose flat face was split into a constant grin, completed the crew, but for Fraser's mate, engineer and right-hand man Michel Tarrou.

Some of the annoyance and irritation he had felt earlier left him as he thought of Tarrou. He had picked him off the beach because of his eagerness and obvious intelligence, and had trained him to help run the schooner. He was able to overlook the man's vanity and the pathetic belief that he was French and not just another island half-caste. His father had certainly been French, although nobody could remember him, but his mother had been a plump Torres Islander who had died of some obscure disease, claimed, nevertheless, by the old-timers to have been a broken heart.

Tarrou climbed into view over the tiny engine-room coaming and stood blinking in the sunlight. He glanced quickly around him and then drew a white plastic comb through his sleek black hair and patted it into place. Then he pulled on a neat khaki-drill jacket and put his white-topped cap within easy reach.

'Has she come on deck again, Vic?' His deep black eyes looked eager, even nervous.

'Nah! She must have heard about you, sport!' Fraser grinned cheerfully.

Tarrou smiled automatically. He understood Fraser's rough humour at last, and was content with his lot. He dabbed a speck of grease from his jacket and frowned with great concentration. He had a broad, flat nose and rather thick loose lips, which outweighed the advantage given him by his skin, which was no darker than Fraser's.

'This trip is dangerous, Vic?'

'Nah! So long as we avoid the Motă tribesmen and the reef we shall be okay. It's the passengers I worry about.' He rasped his hands together. 'That bit of a girl, and a couple of Pommie bastards as well. I only hope we don't all get at each other's throats 'cause I need that charter money!'

Tarrou smiled gently. Fraser could do no wrong in his eyes. He had saved him from a miserable existence, and had made him someone of importance. A ship's officer! He put on a pair of cheap sun-glasses and folded his arms as he had seen Fraser do. It would make a change to have some other company aboard, all the same. Fraser's conversation was usually technical or rather coarse, and he was looking forward to seeing the American girl again, and also to speaking to a well-educated gentleman like this Major Blair was said to be. It was all rather wonderful to be happening to him.

Fraser stiffened. 'There's the launch! That'll be Blair now!' He pointed to the guns, and took a small key from around his neck. 'Go an' lock 'em up, Michel. Don't want to scare the poor bloke!'

He stepped forward to greet the other man, his big hand outstretched. 'You must be Major Blair. Welcome aboard.' He nodded to the second man who followed over the bulwark. That must be the diver. Typical Pommie, he thought.

Blair eyed him calmly. 'Are you ready for sea, as I instructed?' His voice was even, but carried a trace of impatience. 'Because after the rest of my gear is stowed I'd like to get moving.'

'Ready an' eager, Major! The sooner we leave the sooner we can get back!'

Blair ignored him. He was looking at the girl, who had come unnoticed on deck.

'Miss Bligh, I believe? I hope you won't change your

15

mind about this trip after we've sailed? It might be a little hard for a woman.'

Her eyes were invisible behind the glasses, but her mouth mocked him openly. 'That's not exactly a welcome, is it?'

His shoulders moved in a substitute for an apology. 'Of course, I forgot that you are used to this sort of thing.'

Tarrou appeared at his side, his face beaming. 'Major Blair, sir, this is an honour! It is very nice to meet another European out here!'

Blair stared at the wide grin and the outstretched hand with its purple-tinted nails. 'Another European?' His voice was cold and he made no move to shake hands. 'I should have thought—'

Fraser moved between them, his voice suddenly hard. 'This is Michel. He's *French*!'

Blair eyed the threatening Australian with amusement. 'He can be a Buddhist monk for all I care! Let's get started!'

Fraser clapped his hand across the half-caste's shoulder. 'Start up the engine, Michel, and get the hands up forrard to the anchor.'

The girl moved closer to Blair, and he faced her questioningly. She slowly lit a cigarette and blew out the smoke. 'I just wanted to study an English gentleman at close quarters,' she said calmly. 'It was quite an experience.'

The islanders on the jetty and on the slopes beyond the town watched the graceful schooner suddenly break free from the ground, and saw the dripping anchor black against her bows. Then there was a coughing roar from the ancient diesel engine, and a cloud of fine blue smoke hovered momentarily beneath her stern, followed by the upchurned froth from her hidden propeller.

Grainger sighed as the ship began to gather way through

16

the smooth water and moved past the green hump of Iririki Islet and pointed her bowsprit towards the open sea.

In spite of himself, he began to wish he had gone along too.

In Fraser's cabin, which had been put at his disposal for the voyage, Blair sat heavily in a canvas chair, his tired body swaying to the easy roll of the schooner as it lifted over the long Pacific rollers.

He felt washed out, yet nearer to complete satisfaction than he could remember. He studied his heavy shoe with hatred, and thought of his wife. Because of her constant entreaties he had suffered several agonizing operations on his foot, but to no avail. The Jap rifle-butts had done their work too well. Marcia, tall and poised. She had been half angry and half scornful when he had told her of his intended trip. He had watched her face reacting in her dressing-table mirror. 'Why don't you give up this stupid idea? Nobody cares what happened twenty years ago, Rupert! I'm sure *I* don't!' He had stared at her smooth white neck and tried to stop himself hating her. In his heart he knew that it might have been different had she not expected him to be the same carefree young subaltern when he was released from the prison camp. The picture of her which he had kept alive in his months of captivity and torment had proved as false as the defences of Singapore when he had put his family aboard the leaking, panic-ridden launch. Ironically, he and a handful of his men had been rescued by a minesweeper within minutes of the shameful surrender. He closed his eyes and saw again the great black pall of smoke over the dying city. The young skipper of the minesweeper had piloted them through sunken wrecks and screaming survivors and had laughed with the bitterness of his generation when Blair said, 'God help those left behind!'

He had replied, 'He doesn't care about us any more!'

Blair threw himself down on the bunk and tried to relax. Now at last, in spite of everything, he would know what happened to his family. It might in some inexplicable way make up for all his other disappointments.

2

Gillian Bligh awoke from her exhausted sleep, and for a long moment lay quite still and alert, her body tense and her eyes fixed on the white bulkhead at the foot of the bunk. Her aching mind wrestled with a feeling of uncertainty as she tried to remember her surroundings and to place what was different. The small cabin creaked about her, and she was aware of the pleasant gurgle of water against the timbered side, barely inches from her head, and she suddenly realized that the engine had stopped its incessant vibrations.

She groped overhead until her slim fingers encountered her cigarettes on the small shelf, and as she automatically clicked her lighter she propped herself on her elbows and surveyed the stacked luggage and the disordered garments around the cabin, and remembered how she had fallen on to the bunk, desperately eager for the sleep which of late had so often been denied her. Her pyjama jacket was open across her body, and although she could remember nothing, the bunk sheets were tangled and rumpled, mute evidence of another uneasy night.

There was a gentle knock on the door, and pulling her jacket across her, she called out: 'Okay! You can come in!' Fraser had warned her that the cabin boy, Watute, would be bringing her coffee in the morning, although from her watch she saw that it was barely six o'clock.

Watute sidled round the door, his dark eyes busy about the cabin, but his face split into a fixed grin.

'Morning, missy! Coffee bin fix on time.'

He laid the cup carefully on the small locker beside the bunk and stared shyly at the girl. Like the rest of the boys, he seemed fascinated by her blond hair, and Gillian smiled back at his small pug face.

'The engine has stopped,' she said. 'What is happening now?'

He watched her mouth carefully, like a deaf man. 'Sails all spread, missy.' He waved his hands vaguely to represent a wind, and puffed out his cheeks. 'We make through sea!'

He was wearing a long shirt, presumably discarded by Fraser, the tails of which hung about his thin legs like two flapping aprons. It appeared to be his only garment. She was aware of the sweet sickly smell which hung about him like an animal scent, and the complete lack of guile, or, for that matter, any expression she could place, on his black face. She nodded.

'Right, Watute, I'll be on deck shortly.'

He backed to the door. 'You gonna make wife for Captain?'

She laughed shortly. 'Hell, no! I'm a writer.' She shrugged helplessly. 'You know, make stories!'

He nodded, his face suddenly grave. 'Understand.' But disbelief shone from his eyes. As he turned to leave he added carefully, 'Captain say you make good woman for some joker!'

She lay back completely limp, not knowing whether to laugh or to allow this fresh bandied insult to add to her tension. She stubbed out the cigarette and swung her long legs over the edge of the bunk. She was immediately aware of the gentle rolling motion beneath her bare feet, and she saw her tousled reflection in the mirror. 'Good woman, eh? Another goddamned master-mind, it seems!'

She changed into a sleeveless shirt and drill slacks, and

with a final glance into the mirror prepared to meet the world outside. Immediately after the schooner had weighed anchor she had retired to her cabin, and after making a pretence at reading through her notes and instructions had turned in. She stepped into the narrow passage-way and walked unsteadily towards the steep ladder at the end. She paused, and looked up at the bright blue rectangle of the sky. Directly above the open hatch she saw the straddled legs of the old seaman called Buka. His bent, muscled back rippled and shone in the calm morning sunlight as he eased the spokes of the wheel with his thick fingers. As she mounted the ladder he stiffened, and without looking behind him bobbed his shaggy head and greeted her with his strange, grating voice.

'Mornin', missy. Plenty fine day, huh?'

She stepped carefully on to the deck, and saw that already it had been washed, and patches of dampness still showed along the dazzling lines of the planking. She stared with disbelief at the strange shapes of the huge sails which, controlled by the twin booms, swung across the lee rail like the wings of a giant bat.

Fraser lay on his camp bed watching her, a lazy smile on his lips. She noticed that his thick hair was plastered to his forehead and a pair of swimming trunks, very new, hung wetly from the companion hatch. For my benefit, no doubt, she thought.

'Sleep well?' He sat up slowly and scratched his chest. 'I never thought I'd have such a nice sight on the deck of the old *Pearl*!' There was something mocking in his voice again, or was it defensive? She eyed him for a second, then allowed her face to smile.

'Slept like a log.' She waved towards the sails. 'Can these things push us along okay?'

Fraser stood up and shook his cup over the rail. 'Like a

21

bird. Listen to her.' He cocked his head, and Gillian heard the warm breeze explore the billowing canvas and the accompanying orchestra of taut rigging and creaking spars.

She glanced along the deck to where the two divers sat cross-legged as they flaked down a mass of fine line.

'Say, where is everyone? Am I the first? What did you want me to get up so early for?'

She saw Fraser's smile fade slightly, but he forced a deep laugh and pointed across the starboard bow. 'Thought you'd like to see a bit of the islands.'

She followed his arm and saw a thin line of deep green etched against the shimmering blue sea. She was aware of many things at once, and was glad to be in this ship, and for an instant wished that this moment could go on for ever. She was not normally given to such vague thoughts, and it made her feel uneasy, but the sight of the distant land, any land, made the ship feel more of a refuge than merely transport, and she was all at once glad that she had accepted this assignment.

She was aware, too, that Fraser was watching her closely, his eyes puzzled. 'Thanks, but I prefer your boat.' She saw him grin, rather like a small boy. 'How come you're out here, anyway?'

Fraser frowned and leaned heavily on the rail, his shoulder touching her. 'Search me. I guess me an' the old *Pearl* are just about fit for this an' nothing else.' He turned suddenly and stared at her, his brown eyes searching. 'And what about you?'

'I've a job to do.' It sounded weak, and she felt the old caution creeping over her.

'Sure. I rather had the feeling you were running away from something.'

The shipboard noises faded away, and she was suddenly conscious of the sound of her own breathing. Running away? She had always been running away. But it had taken a big ignorant Australian to tell her to her face.

She turned on him angrily. 'Do you know what you're saying? D'you think I've got any personal feelings about coming on a crummy job like this? What d'you know about it, anyway?'

He held up his hand. 'Steady on there! It was just an idea I had.'

'Well, keep it to yourself! Just because I'm the only civilized being around here doesn't mean I'm peculiar!'

'Forget it.' He didn't apologize, but instead turned to Old Buka.

'Bring her round to the nor'west, damn you!'

The one-eyed helmsman grinned, and spun the spokes with casual ease.

'D'you always talk to them like that?'

'Who, the boongs?' Fraser looked perplexed.

'So that's what you call them.' She had regained her composure and met his stare calmly. 'One of these days Old Buka and his like will probably be in a position to call *you* names!'

'Hell! I don't understand you. Old Buka's a good joker, but I wouldn't exactly call him civilized!' Fraser looked across at the native affectionately.

'And are you? What have you done with your life?' It was amazing how safe she felt once she was controlling the conversation. Why did everyone have to spoil things?

'Nothing much, I suppose. Took over the boat from my old man when he died and carried on the trading, an' a bit of pearling when I get the chance.'

'Never been away from here, I suppose?'

Fraser frowned. 'Apart from the war, no. When that was on I went over to England an' joined up.' He laughed as if it was a huge joke.

'Why? What did you owe to England?'

His eyes narrowed. 'I owe nothing to anybody. But I went because I'm an Australian, an' that should be enough, even for a Yank!'

He stiffened suddenly and grasped her arm. For a moment she thought he was going to strike her, but his expression was completely absorbed. 'Look.' He pointed over the rail to where the water wallowed from beneath the counter. 'Look at that one!'

She looked down into the clear water, and for a while could see nothing but the shadow of the hull, and deep blue, which gave the sea the impression of having no bottom. Then a shape moved lazily near to the surface, and involuntarily she moved back. Long and greyish brown, with strange dark stripes across its body, the shark looked huge and terrifying. She heard Fraser mutter, 'That god-damned fool Blair should be here to see this.'

'What about it?' Her voice sounded small.

'It's a tiger shark, Miss Bligh.' He smiled, but his eyes were hard. 'The first I've seen this month. Blair didn't seem to think I knew what I was talking about, but by God I could set my watch by 'em!'

They watched in silence as the great beast swam easily in the shade of the schooner's shadow. Eighteen or twenty feet, she imagined, and each stroke of the powerful tail twisted the streamlined body slightly, so that she could see the small, cold eyes glittering from beneath the surface.

Fraser shivered. 'Jeez, I was over the rail swimming this morning!'

He looked so hurt that the girl laughed, and Fraser stared at her with surprise.

'So you *are* afraid of something! I think I'm beginning to like you after all!' She leaned back across the rail, and imagined the shark's eyes on her back. 'Suppose I fell in, Captain? What would you do?'

Fraser wiped his hand across his chin and studied her speculatively. 'I guess I'd nip over the side an' give the poor tiger a hand!'

Blair, shaving in his cabin, cocked his head to listen to the laughter on deck. He stood frowning until he saw the reflection of his half-lathered face, and then continued with his task, his eyes studying the set expression around his mouth.

He had slept very well, for the first time for some while, and as he towelled his lean, hard body he felt that once more there was some purpose in his life.

Watute entered his cabin and picked up his cup from beside the bunk. 'Captain say tiger shark alongside.' He grinned hugely. 'Think maybe you like him brought aboard!' He chuckled and reached over to tidy some of Blair's clothes.

Whether it was the implied jibe in Fraser's message, or whether it was a memory brought back by Watute's black head as he stooped over his possessions, Blair did not stop to think. He spun the boy round so that the cup clattered to the deck. He saw the expressions chase themselves across the boy's face. Surprise, fear and then that bitter glimpse of savage distrust, which he had seen on the faces of the Burmese villagers who had betrayed him so many years before.

'Keep your paws off my gear, see!' He shook the thin shoulder to emphasize his words. 'When I need your help I'll ask for it. Now get out!'

With a sob, Watute fled, and Blair forced himself to think calmly about what Fraser's message had meant. Sharks were about, but what did that mean? He pulled on a

25

clean shirt and combed his hair carelessly. The divers would be used to such risks, and Myers, too, was an experienced man. But in any case he would not concern himself with those troubles. He jerked out his charts and studied them carefully, although he knew them like old friends. He tried to picture the wreck lying on the reef. After all these years he was coming to put right a wrong, and dispense with fears and suspicions once and for all.

He limped along the passage-way and climbed up to the sunlight. He sniffed the clean sea air and stretched his shoulders. It was all at once good to be alive.

He greeted Fraser and the girl and pointed to the islands. 'What are those?'

'The Shepherd Group.' Fraser puffed on his blackened pipe. 'Another hundred and twenty miles to go for your reef.'

Blair walked to the rail and looked down at the shark. The cold, unwinking eyes gleamed distortedly at him, as the beast dipped and rose in the schooner's swell. 'Is that it?' His voice was excited in spite of himself.

Fraser had gone from sight, and the girl stood watching him.

'Beautiful lines.' Blair watched the dorsal fin momentarily break the surface. 'Powerful, and completely independent.'

'You two should get together,' Gillian remarked dryly.

Fraser reappeared, a rifle in his hands. 'I'll just show you how these jokers work,' he said flatly. 'Yalla! Just heave some of that bait overboard!'

The diver swung a gutted fish over the rail, and flashed his teeth as Fraser raised the rifle to his cheek.

As the fish hit the surface the shark sprang forward, and for an instant its whole body seemed about to collide with the hull. At that moment the rifle cracked, and the tiger shark swung completely over on to its back.

Gillian gasped as she saw the huge, crescent-shaped jaws, and the rows of cockscomb-like teeth bared in pain or rage, while the shark snapped savagely at the air.

The sea, which had been empty, was suddenly alive in a thrashing torment of grey shapes, as from nowhere the sharks fell upon their bleeding comrade. The water frothed pink, and then scarlet, and the watchers on the deck saw a crazy, fearful ballet of slashing jaws and crashing, plunging bodies.

Occasionally Fraser would say evenly, 'That's a whaler,' or 'Watch him, that's another tiger,' like a commentator at a football match.

The schooner surged on and the group by her taffrail watched in stunned silence as the snapping mass of sharks faded astern.

Gillian swayed, and felt her throat. 'Did you have to do that?' She felt sick.

Blair's face was hard. 'I think I understand what he was trying to do, Miss Bligh. He was trying to show us what we're up against.'

Fraser jerked open the bolt and sent the cartridge-case spinning over the rail.

'Not "we", Major. Them!' He pointed towards the two divers who had returned to their work. 'D'you still want to go on with it?'

Myers, who had silently joined them, mopped his face with a fierce determination. 'Well, I for one will be wearin' a suit!' He still glared at the frothing water, and added quietly: 'I only 'ope them blighters don't like the taste of it!' He smiled anxiously at his feeble joke, but nobody else seemed to hear him.

Gillian stared from one to the other, not trusting herself to speak. Each of the men seemed to be vying with the others to prove something. Was it because of her? she wondered. Would it have been any different had she taken Grainger's advice and stayed ashore?

Fraser tucked the rifle under his arm and started to relight his pipe. Round the stem he said slowly, 'Still, maybe we'll be lucky, eh?'

Blair watched the girl's shoulders droop, and wondered what had ever prompted a girl like her to become a globe-trotting journalist. She looked done in, and for an instant he wanted to comfort her, but something in her wide eyes prevented the right words from coming. Instead, he said, 'Let's hope we don't see any more of them.'

A subdued Watute placed chairs round the table on the poop, and announced that breakfast was ready, and Fraser, after glancing at the compass, waved gravely towards them. 'Breakfast, folks, if you feel like it?'

Blair met the girl's eyes. 'Come and sit down. You'll feel better after you've eaten.'

As he reached to steady her arm she drew back, and he felt the old pain begin to throb in his foot. Her movement reminded him of Marcia.

Gillian had to grip her hands together to control her taut emotions, and the tone of Blair's voice had almost made her lose control. But as she had automatically withdrawn her arm from his reach she had seen the shutter drop behind his eyes, and she had known that she was alone again.

Blair drew up his canvas chair to the table and sniffed the coffee. 'You're doing us very well, Captain.' He consumed the thinly sliced paw-paw, apparently engrossed, but his eyes moved slowly round the small group, and his mind was alive and busy.

The trip had started badly, and he thought it was probably his own fault. All that must be remedied at once. He watched the girl as she toyed with her food, her eyes hidden by her glasses. She seemed just about all-in, and it

28

was somehow out of character. He looked aloft at the high, tall mainsail.

'I suppose you will condense all this into a few well-chosen lines, Miss Bligh?' He spoke evenly, but his blue eyes were serious and friendly. 'I rather think the Captain here would make a more interesting story than mine.'

She played nervously with her fork, the black lenses of her glasses fixed on his face.

'I'm not sorry I came, Major Blair.' Her voice was again steady, and she appeared to be giving his words a great deal of thought. 'In spite of everything, I think I can understand how you feel about finding the wreck, although I can't think what you hope to use in your discovery.'

Blair relaxed slightly. Myers was watching the girl with renewed interest, and knowing him as he did, Blair knew that the man was already thinking of something other than the sharks. Fraser, too, was smiling and at ease, one eye on the sails and the ship.

Watute cleared the table, and Fraser watched the boy curiously, noticing the sullen frown on his face.

Blair pulled the chart from beneath his chair, and spread it where they could all see. He placed his cigarette-case within their reach and leaned forward over the chart.

'You see where I've put the mark? That's more or less the exact spot where the ship struck the reef. The airline pilot got a fairly good bearing at the time.'

Fraser's mocking smile vanished as he craned his head to get a better glimpse at the position. They could hear his heavy breathing as he considered what he saw.

'Well?' Blair watched his reactions through narrowed eyes. 'What's the verdict?' He saw the quickening professional interest in the big Australian's face, and felt satisfied. If Fraser for once felt that his knowledge was being challenged, he might well avoid finding the wreck at all. Even the promised bonus money might not sway such a man.

'They couldn't have hit a worse spot,' he said at length.

Blair concealed his impatience. 'Can you anchor there, or nearby?'

Fraser nodded slowly. 'Near enough. It's the eastern end of the reef. There is an extinct volcano at that end of the island which will help to fix our position very well.' He nodded again, as if satisfied.

The girl leaned her elbows on the chart, and Blair found himself looking down the front of her blouse. She lifted her head slightly and he quickly looked away.

'Are we calling anywhere first?' she asked.

Blair glanced at Fraser. 'I'm leaving that to the Skipper. He knows what I want, and he'll know the best places to get information.'

'Sure, sure!' Fraser grinned, and looked like a pirate. 'There are only two jokers stupid enough to live on the island. One is the trader, a chap called Jim Hogan.' He indicated a tiny bay at the western end of the island. 'Resolution Bay. They say Cap'n Cook landed there once. Can't think why. He's a useful bloke, and can give us pretty up-to-date information about the local tribes.' He shot a quick glance at the girl. 'They're all right, but I like to know what they're doin', see? Then there's the mad missionary.' He grinned at their expressions of surprise. 'Yep, there really is. He runs what he calls a mission school here.' He pointed to a spot at the southern tip of the island where the reef started its journey across the wide southern approaches. 'His name is Ivor Spencer. Completely mad, of course, and he spends most of his time teachin' hymns to the native kids and bewailin' the state of the world.'

Blair's voice was quiet. 'But that must surely mean that

the natives can't be too fierce? I mean, Fraser, if they send their kids to school?'

Fraser sighed. 'They're only a few of the local boongs. There are a few coastal villages, which are more or less harmless.' He tapped the chart again. 'But you see this strip which crosses the whole of Hog Island from north to south? Well, that's the Motă country. They don't leave it much, 'cause they don't need to. I guess they just ignore old Spencer. He's been there a few years' on an' off.'

'What about during the war?' The girl asked the question, and Blair glanced at her in surprise. He had been about to put the same question.

'*And* during the war. Although he altered his camp quite a lot, I believe. He's a queer cuss an' no mistake. But it might pay us to question him,' Fraser conceded.

Blair stared at the glittering water. During the war he had been on the island. He might even have seen the *Sigli*. 'How far is his mission from the position of the wreck?' His voice was calmer than he felt.

Fraser shook his head slowly. 'Near eighty miles, accordin' to this. Unlikely that he saw anythin'.'

'Unless the boat passed in front of the point before the wreck.'

Gillian plucked at her blouse as the sun crossed over the rim of the mainsail.

'Could be.' Fraser rubbed his chin. 'We'll ask him, anyway, but let me do the talking, eh?'

Blair controlled his smile. 'Surely. But we mustn't overlook anything.'

Fraser glanced quickly around the deck. 'While we're together like this,' he began, and Blair saw that he was uncomfortable, 'I just want to tell you about my mate, Michel. He's a bit different from you, an' I'd appreciate it if you didn't fill his head with too many yarns about the outside world. It might make him unsettled,' he added awkwardly.

'I hadn't thought about it much.' Blair relaxed again. He had thought that Fraser was about to raise a fresh problem. 'But I shall try not to raise his hopes about mankind!'

Gillian sat, tight-shouldered, in her chair, her body seemingly taut with sudden irritation. 'What is he, then? A poor animal or something?'

Fraser smiled soothingly. 'It's not that, miss, but he's happy here, and I don't want him hurt.'

Myers wiped his palms on his trousers. ''E's all right. Bit full of 'imself, but then all Wogs are a bit like that, ain't they? I remember when I was in Alex durin' the war—'

Fraser planted a fist on the table and cut him short. 'He's no Wog, see? He's a good bloke, but a bit simple, an' I don't want him upset!'

Myers grinned, showing his small teeth. 'Suits me, mate. I don't care what 'e is.'

Blair winced. Practically my own words. He stood up, and walked to the rail where the girl had hurried as soon as Fraser had interrupted. He stood easily to the motion of the deck, and caught a brief touch of her perfume. She seemed to be trembling.

'I'm sorry you get so upset about this sort of thing,' he began. She didn't answer, and he hurried on: 'But you can't change people all the time.'

She spoke without turning her head. 'Another lecture, Major? Don't you give me any credit for knowing anything?'

'It's not that. I really didn't want you to come on this ship at all, you know.'

'That was obvious,' she said curtly.

He continued evenly: 'But now that you're here, I want you to relax. I think I understand why you are here now. I

32

think you're trying to forget your normal existence for a while, and yet your work and life in the past just keep cropping up to spoil things for you. Am I right?'

He waited for an outburst, and when she failed to speak he felt vaguely uneasy. But he knew he had spoken the truth. Normally, he would have felt pleased, even superior, but as he stared at the stiffly held head beside him he was merely troubled.

Marcia had been right about one thing at least, he pondered. 'You just don't begin to understand women,' she had said on numerous occasions. 'You're too full of your stupid ideas about traditions and honour!' That part hadn't made any sense to him, but Marcia had become rather less and less reasonable with him as the years had passed, and he no longer looked for sense in her words.

There was a soft step on the planking, and Michel Tarrou touched his gleaming cap in greeting.

'Sorry to be so late.' He smiled, his eyes on the girl's face. 'But it is my duty to attend to the engine every morning.'

Gillian turned to face Blair, a lick of fair hair drifting across her cheek in the humid breeze.

'Perhaps Michel will show me over the boat, eh?' Her mouth shone invitingly against the tan of her skin.

Tarrou bobbed. 'Delightful! A great honour!'

'I hope you didn't misunderstand my remarks.' Blair cursed inwardly. It was hopeless to say what he wanted with that great grinning fool standing there. 'I meant well.'

'Save it, Major. I'll do the story for my magazine, because I've been told to. There's nothing in my contract to say I have to be patronized by you!'

She swung her body round, and Blair's throat constricted with something like pain. That was the sort of girl he had wanted. Perhaps Marcia had been like that, and had changed. He cursed again. He was the one who had changed, and now with his plan beginning to take shape he had started acting like a tongue-tied young idiot. He turned away from the others as he heard Tarrou say grandly, 'We shall start by examining the forward part of the vessel.'

Tarrou led the way forward, beyond the spiralling foremast and up on to the raised forecastle deck, where the long pointing bowsprit dipped and soared towards the inviting water.

He polished his sun-glasses, and after setting them on his ears he surveyed the ship and pointed to the two crouched divers. 'They will dive for the wreck when we find it,' he said. It was not what he had intended to say, but now that he was alone with this beautiful girl he could not muster his thoughts in their right order. He had carefully rehearsed all this when he had been examining the engine, but with her beside him he was confused.

Gillian stared down the full length of the schooner to where Blair still leaned against the taffrail. Everything was so simple to him. He was typical of his breed, in the superior, irritatingly aloof manner in which he had condensed her whole life for her. What had he said about being glad to get away? She frowned, and was immediately aware that Tarrou had stopped speaking. She smiled quickly. 'I beg your pardon. What did you say?'

Relief flooded his face. 'I am just saying that this is what we call a fore-and-aft schooner. These two masts with the two big sails on booms make her easy to handle. The boys can manage all the sails at once without very much trouble.' He licked his lips and looked around for inspiration. 'She is one hundred and thirty tons, and one hundred and ten feet in length.' He paused as she rested her hand lightly on his sleeve.

'Tell me, Michel, what d'you think about all this? D'you think we will find this wreck?'

Tarrou stared dazedly at her hand. 'Captain Vic will find it,' he stammered.

She moved away and sat on the bulwark. The breeze explored her throat and flapped down the front of her blouse. She knew he was staring at her, and a feeling of uneasy pleasure crept over her. She had met so many of them now, and she still wanted to believe that some of them at least were different from what people like Blair imagined. She studied Tarrou's simple face and felt vaguely sorry for him. It irritated her to feel anything but companionship, but it was so often the same when dealing with men of Tarrou's upbringing and nature. The more she tried, the more confused they seemed to become. She glanced at the two divers. It would be better to be like them, she thought. Life might be plain, dangerous or even empty, but they at least seemed normal, and indifferent to the tides of prejudice. Her thoughts moved to Blair again. He was so like Andy. He, too, had been sure of himself in a super-confident manner born of a family whose success was measured against the millions of dollars it had accumulated.

She tried to remember how he had looked, but she could only picture his eyes, bright and restless, rather like Major Blair's. They had met during a hot summer in Washington, when she had first started her career of journalism. It had been at a rather listless party which broke up early, and she had found herself with Andy. He had great charm. He had also been engaged to be married, but she had not found that out until afterwards. Until after the night she let him make love to her. She shuddered when she remembered his soft, almost gentle voice. 'You're mine, Gil. For always.' It was like a line from a cheap novel. But she had believed him. She had confronted him, after a despairing, but still hopeful search, in his Long Island cottage. She had expected remorse or perhaps even a plea of forgiveness, but instead he had smiled calmly and asked her how much she had wanted. 'I hope you're not going to make trouble, Gil,' he had said lazily. 'I'd hate to have your name bandied around a little.'

She had slapped his face, but unlike the cheap novel he slapped her back and had her driven back to town by a leering chauffeur.

Meissberg had guessed half the story, and dragged the rest out of her. His advice had been to forget it, and when she spoke of her rights he had arranged her first foreign assignment. He had seen her off at the airport. 'So what d'you expect, girl? For the man to shoot himself already? You forget him. Make with the career. It pays better!'

Meissberg. Probably in Andy's pocket as well. But what could she do now? She had often really believed that becoming the good journalist she had set about to be was compensation enough. She had become instead more and more isolated from the reality she searched for.

The *Queensland Pearl* plunged over a low roller, and the rigging sighed in protest. High overhead two frigate birds idled on their scimitar-shaped wings, apparently motionless against the glaring sky.

She clasped her arms across her body and trembled in spite of the heat.

Tarrou took her silence for interest, and squatted down on the bulwark beside her. 'Tell me about America,' he faltered, 'will you, Gillian?'

She started at the sound of her name, and stared at him blankly. 'What do you want to hear?' She hardly recognized her own voice.

Fraser watching from the poop cursed loudly, and felt for his pipe.

Sitting on the taffrail, Blair, too, watched them, his face dark and thoughtful. It was like a pattern, he thought. The ship seemed to have drawn them all together for some set purpose, but he could not put a name to it.

Only Myers seemed indifferent, as he whistled softly and honed his diver's knife.

3

The dawn of the second morning showed the small schooner like a white-painted toy on a blue mirror, and although the sky was free of cloud and maintained its harsh brightness, there was an urgency in the air, which expressed itself in the thrumming breeze against the tan sails, and the occasional ripple of catspaws across the sea's smooth surface.

Fraser stood loosely behind the wheel, his cap tilted rakishly over his eyes as he squinted ahead at the shimmering green hump of the island, a shape which had risen from the sea with the sun, and had grown without effort even as he watched, so that the uncertain outline of the distant volcano could be seen distorted behind a fine haze.

The boys jabbered amongst themselves, with all their usual excitement at making a landfall, and under Buka's directions began to shorten sail. The engine had come to life, and panted patiently beneath his feet, while Tarrou waited to give him all the power he might need.

He glanced momentarily at the girl as she stood against the weather rail, one hand shading her eyes, the other holding her hair, which ruffled gently at each hot caress from the breeze. Blair stood apart and yet near her, his eyes showing nothing, but his body tense and expectant.

Fraser licked his lips and wondered. It would have been better to have carried passengers who were untroubled by strange missions or unspoken thoughts, he decided. The previous evening had passed without further event, and he had managed to break up some of the tension by telling them about the islands, and as they sat on deck in the cool of the evening, drinking cans of Ballarat beer, he had pointed with something like pride at the dim shapes of the various groups, while the schooner had threaded her way between them, and past the distant reefs and lonely, unchartered rocks, which for no reason jutted from the dark water, their fanged shapes shrouded in spray and glistening with a million rivulets, as they fought a ceaseless battle with the sea.

The schooner slowly edged her way round the snout of Hog Island, and at one point they were within a mile of the towering, sheer-sided cliffs, which looked as if they had been sliced short by a giant hand, the discarded pieces dropping to form a girdle of broken rocks at their feet. A thin, spider-like pier jutted out from the small sheltered bay which rolled back beyond the cliffs, and behind the small white beach he could see the familiar untidy cluster of shacks which represented Jim Hogan's trade store. A few palm-thatched huts were scattered along the edge of the encroaching jungle, and from the latter he saw running brown shapes, like beetles, making for the rickety pier.

Gillian turned briefly towards him. 'That pier doesn't look any too safe, Vic? What's the idea of having a thing like that?'

He laughed, a deep, friendly sound. 'Old Jim just patches it up a bit from time to time. I bring the *Pearl* here every two or three months, and apart from his own cutter,' he indicated a neat white boat moored at the far end of the pier, 'he doesn't reckon on getting many visitors.'

She shook her head slowly. 'He must get plenty lonely. What makes a man shut himself away like that?'

Fraser considered the question. What makes us all do it?

Jim Hogan was an Aussie like himself. A man in late middle age, he was a heavy drinker, who allowed life to pass him by, because, he supposed, life for him meant booze, independence and women. His trading with the local natives brought him the first two, and Fraser knew that he was never short of a lubra or two either. He had some deal with one of the local headmen, and with the result, he could always be sure of a smooth, dusky girl for his other requirements.

He looked slowly at Gillian and smiled secretly. 'Reckon he just likes the climate,' he said.

The engine drowned her next words, and he gave his concentration to conning his boat round the end of the pier, to where scores of waving hands reached out to seize the lines as they were thrown ashore.

A thick-set, heavy-jowled man, in a grubby shirt and stained duck trousers, walked heavily through the chattering natives, his brick-red face split into a grin, and his eyes screwed up to examine his visitors. With surprising lightness he vaulted over the rail and shook Fraser by the hand. With his faded eyes on the girl he guffawed noisily. 'Well, damn my eyes, Vic! You sure are a one for surprises! You ain't due here for another month yet! Or have I been dreamin'?'

He listened in silence as Fraser explained his mission, his eyes puckered in surprise.

'How long you stoppin', then?' he asked when Fraser had finished.

Blair nodded towards the headland. 'Just for tonight. I thought you might be able to help me.'

Hogan shook his grizzled head. 'Nah. Vic's got as good idea as me about this place. What he don't know don't matter much.'

'What about this Spencer fellow? Is he any use, d'you think?'

40

Hogan nudged Fraser. 'Talks like a proper Pommie, don't he?' He grinned disarmingly as he saw the other man stiffen. Don't mind me, cobber. I got no manners, d'you see? Nah, Spencer's worse since the time he used to run round the islands spoutin' the flamin' gospel at every Abo in sight. He just squats in his ruddy mission with that lot up there on the point and curses fit to bust!' He laughed as if it was some huge joke. 'Mind you, he's got plenty of guts to squat on the Motă's doorstep.' He jerked a calloused thumb towards the green wall of the jungle. 'They killed a couple of Abos from this village last week. Two youngsters wandered off doin' a bit of huntin', and were found next day done in.' He jerked off his floppy felt hat and ran his fingers through his short ginger hair.

Fraser was listening intently. 'Sure it was the Motă?'

Hogan grunted with scorn. 'Yeh. Their heads was gone, and various other parts of 'em as well, if you get my meanin'!'

Gillian spoke for the first time. 'Is that all that happens? Can't anything be done to stamp out this sort of thing?' She walked to the rail and stared at the grinning, uncomprehending faces which peered up at here. 'Why in hell's name do your governments accept these responsibilities if they can't or won't keep order and help to protect the natives?'

Hogan grinned at her with admiration. 'Hear, hear, miss! Should 'ave taken a page outa the Yanks' book! Do what they did with the Red Injuns, you know,' he winked at Fraser, 'kill all the bastards off!'

Fraser tapped his thick shoulder. 'Jim, you're a no-good lump, if ever I knew one. Now get your boys to collect your booze from the hold an' shut your gate!' Turning to the girl, he added: 'Don't be too hard on him. He's been out here so long he's washed his brains away!'

Hogan sighed. 'S'right miss. Forget it. Can't help these poor devils much. Nobody can, 'cept themselves, an' they hate the flamin' sight of each other!'

Fraser walked with him to the open hatch over the dark hold. 'What d'you make to the weather, Jim?'

'Worried?'

'I don't like bein' near that goddamned reef at this time of the year, Jim.' He shook his head. 'I'm responsible for these people aboard, an' old Grainger'll hold me to it if anythin' goes wrong.'

'D'you care? They look a bit loopy to me!'

'I've got my licence to consider. Anyway, the girl's pretty dinkum, eh?'

Hogan studied Gillian's body as she leaned over the rail with Myers. 'Too right.' He nodded emphatically. 'You can leave 'er 'ere when you go!'

Gillian leaned forward to point out something to Myers, and against the glare of the sun and water they saw the clear outline of her breast. Hogan whistled and nodded again. 'Like a rat up a pump!'

Fraser half smiled. He was used to Hogan's sort. 'You'll frighten them with all this talk of headhunting an' that. You worried, too?'

Hogan for once did not smile. 'Am a bit. Gettin' too long in the tooth for this caper. 'Nother year an' I'm quittin', gettin' out.'

Fraser puffed at his pipe, allowing the smoke to mask his brown eyes. He had not seen Hogan like that before, and it troubled him. He scoffed: 'You're like all the others! You'll never see Cairns again!'

Hogan fumbled for a cigarette. ''S'fact, Vic. I'm goin' while I can. See my cutter by the pier? She's provisioned and fuelled up. I can quit when I like. I can get to Port Vila at a pinch.'

'Get away! The boongs wouldn't touch you, Jim! They need a store here, if nothin' else!'

Hogan pointed to the open space beyond the trade store. 'See that? I've had the trees cleared away right up to the edge of the jungle. If I get trouble I want a good field of fire!' He laughed nervously. 'Even me flamin' lubras 'ave skipped of 'ome!'

Blair's shadow fell across them, and he forced a smile. 'Well, Major, I 'ope you'll come up to the store this evenin' for a noggin before you're on yer way?'

Blair met Fraser's glance, and saw the almost imperceptible nod of the head. 'Be glad to,' he said calmly. 'I'd like to stretch my legs.'

Hogan glanced at the crippled foot and whistled. 'Blimey, Major, it looks as if some joker 'as done that already!'

Gillian turned at the words, and saw the pain cross Blair's face. She waited for his retort, but he merely replied in a controlled tone, 'I'd like to come, anyway.'

Hogan grinned. 'Good on yer, Major.'

Fraser shrugged helplessly as Blair limped away. 'You're invited too, Miss Bligh.'

Gillian watched Blair's hunched shoulders disappear down the companion-way, a frown on her face. It was the first time she had seen Blair's composure broken, and the result was different from what she had expected. Or was it different from the way she had hoped it would be? Pity, mingled with resentment, only helped to confuse her thoughts. She shook herself out of it. 'Sure, I'll come along for laughs,' she answered dryly.

Hogan led his boys ashore, and Fraser stamped down to his cabin. 'Sorry to disturb you, Major. I didn't want to talk in front of the others.'

Blair sat wearily at the small table, the charts unheeded

beneath his elbows. 'Well? I guessed that Hogan had told you something.'

Fraser leaned against the doorpost. He was surprised at the dullness in Blair's voice.

'Seems he's a bit worried about the Motă playin' up. He's practically made his place into a fort.'

'It won't affect us where we're going, will it?' The blue eyes were staring at nothing.

'Can't say, Major. If we keep clear of the shore, an' hold a good look-out, we should be all right.' His brown face wrinkled into a frown. 'Don't worry about Jim. He's dinkum. Just a bit squiffed.'

Blair yawned and stretched his arms over his head. 'I've seen plenty of men acting like him before.'

Fraser smiled, but did not understand. 'How d'you mean, Major?'

'Before they were killed.' The words dropped like stones into a millpond. Blair studied Fraser's stricken face. 'But let's enjoy our night out first, eh?'

The sun dipped lower over the island and made its evening gold halo around one tall, purple-tinted hill. In the fast-fading light the breakers along the deserted beach loomed crisp and pure against the night-blue of the sea, and at the end of the makeshift pier the schooner and the small white cutter creaked against the rotting piles and shone eerily on their dark backcloth.

The trade store seemed to consist of two large rooms, with a few tiny adjoining compartments, and was surrounded by crudely constructed huts for the stores, which were impervious to ants, crabs, or light-fingered natives. In the main building, stacked from the bare floor to the corrugated iron roof, were the choicer selections of Hogan's trade. Great sagging piles of cheap cloth, their flowered prints and garish colours already faded by the sun's rays, and a disordered heap of axes, hoes, galvanized pails and long strings of beads mixed freely with the spider webs which hung from every rafter.

Hogan's room was not much tidier, but had at least some appearance of comfort. Blair eased himself into a fat armchair, the shape of which suggested that it had been dragged halfway round the world to this forgotten island, to end its days beneath Hogan's bulk, or be destroyed by insects. He glanced idly around the long room and noted the twin strips of barbed wire along the front of the open veranda, and the two heavy shotguns which stood by the blistered sideboard. There were heaps of old newspapers and magazines, but no books, and on the planked wall hung a calendar, two years out of date, adorned by a nude girl advertising a Sydney soft-drinks firm. Hogan had not stopped talking since they had trooped in, and busied himself pouring giant measures of gin and whisky into an assortment of glasses.

A tiny Chinese woman, her ancient face lined and expressionless, dressed in a man's pyjama jacket and faded blue trousers, silently filled the table with plates of tinned food and what looked to Blair like stale buns. He sipped the whisky and shuddered. It was a completely unreal atmosphere, and both Hogan and Fraser added to the impression by their solemn discussions about Australian affairs, mixed with sudden outbursts of loud laughter at some private joke or other in which the others could not join.

Gillian had changed into a cream skirt and pale-blue blouse, and he noticed that she had discarded her sunglasses. Her eyes gleamed brightly in the harsh glare of the Tilley pressure lamp, and he found himself watching her very closely and seeing her more clearly than at any time on the ship. No longer hidden by the slacks which she had been

45

wearing since her arrival in Port Vila her legs, he saw, were slim and beautifully shaped, the bare skin golden in the lamplight.

He swallowed hard, and downed the whisky with something like fear. Immediately, Hogan was across the room, the bottle poised in his red fist.

''Ave another, Major.' He was already looking the worse for wear, and it seemed likely that he had been at the bottle for some time before their arrival. 'Drop er good stuff this. The real flamin' juice!'

Gillian placed a hand across her glass as he peered down at her. 'No more just yet, thanks. I'm surprised you're not giving us some of the local brew. It seems a shame to drink Scotch out here.' She waved towards the window, and they heard the steady pounding of the surf.

Hogan filled his own glass, his forehead dripping with sweat, although the air was already noticeably cooler.

'Nah, this is the stuff for you, my love!' He reached down and patted her knee. 'Kava is the poison that the boongs fancy. Christ! It takes the bloody life out of yer legs, an' that's no good ter me!'

Gillian could feel the hot pressure of his fingers on her knee and wanted to pull herself away. She suddenly remembered when, as a child, she had seen a little boy seized by an ape at a circus. The keeper had pleaded with the child to keep quite still, and she had seen his white, terrified face, frozen with fear, but quite unmoving, as the ape casually pawed at his body. The keeper had crept up behind the animal and laid it low with an iron bar. She forced her body to remain relaxed, and met the trader's eyes squarely.

'Well, here's to you, Jim Hogan!' She held up her glass with a jerk, and she felt his hand reluctantly leave her leg to find his glass.

46

Blair breathed out slowly. God, this place is beginning to get me down. Every tension and threat was multiplied and distorted here, he thought. He had seen the girl's eyes, and watched Hogan's hand. It had not needed much imagination to guess what he was thinking. His eyes fell on Tarrou, who had sat awkwardly on the small chair behind the girl. His face seemed to have gone a shade paler, and his nostrils were flared like a nervous animal's. A feeling of disgust welled up inside him. It would have been almost worth it, he thought viciously, just to see Hogan give Tarrou a beating. He seemed to imagine that he was the girl's personal guardian, and perhaps something more. She might be sorry if she kept encouraging the damned Wog.

Fraser slopped some more whisky into his half-pint glass and drank with obvious satisfaction. He grinned at Myers, who was tipsily peeling a banana.

'What d'you think of the islands, eh? Bit different from the old country?' Fraser's grin was lopsided, and his usually steady gaze was bleary and wavering.

Myers grunted. 'Rather 'ave Southend,' he answered cheerfully.

Fraser slumped alongside Blair, his face suddenly sad. 'What about you, Major? Why don't you forget this goddamned wreck an' just enjoy yourself?' He peered into Blair's face, as if to see the answer to his question.

Blair sighed, and pulled his shirt free from his stomach. He could feel the raw whisky working in his blood like fire, and Fraser's dark face hung over him like a piece of carved wood. Over Fraser's shoulder he saw Tarrou whispering to the girl, who had dropped her head to listen, her lips gleaming scarlet against Tarrou's white shirt. He saw, too, the wild, almost insane light in the half-caste's eyes as he stared intently at her neck, hair and bare arms.

Blair shook his head and tried to concentrate. 'What's

47

the matter, then? Can't you find the wreck for me?' His voice was unnaturally loud, and he saw the girl's clear grey eyes watching him. In some strange way that seemed to please him, and he repeated his question.

Hogan, who was sitting on a pile of old newspapers, hiccuped, and laughed loudly. ''E couldn't find a hearse in a bleedin' thimble!' He belched again, and continued to stare at the girl's legs.

Fraser chuckled. 'To hell with you, mate.' Turning again to Blair, he added in a conspiratorial tone: 'He's cheesed because his little lubra's done a bunk on him.'

He shambled across the room to continue with his argument, and Blair lay back limply in the sagging chair. He saw the little Chinese woman flit past him to fill his glass, and he smiled up at her. 'Thank you,' he said carefully.

Her lined face split into what he supposed was a smile, showing her black lacquered teeth, then she was gone. He peered at his watch.

Hogan seemed to sense that the party was nearing its close, and he staggered to his feet, grabbing vaguely at the various bottles to see their contents. 'Plenty of time, folks. Party's jus' gettin' warmed up!' With frantic haste he cranked on an old gramophone, and as the strains of the 'Anniversary Waltz' floated through the smoke-filled room an expression of childish pleasure crossed his shining face. 'C'mon, my love,' he grinned. 'Let's you an' me 'ave a little dance!' He grasped the girl roughly by the wrist and pulled her to her feet. Against his barrel-like body she looked tiny, and with another laugh Hogan began to push her round the littered floor in some semblance of dancing.

Myers had fallen asleep, but at the sound of the music began to sing in a high, unmelodious voice, his eyes slitted with effort.

48

Blair watched as Fraser staggered to his feet and began to dance unsteadily after the slowly revolving pair in the middle of the floor, his shaggy head bowed with concentration. Only Tarrou stayed still and tense, his face empty and filled with loss. Blair felt calm and resigned. There was bound to be a fight. This sort of evening always ended like that. He vaguely remembered watching some of his soldiers in Singapore brawling over a little Malayan dancer the night before the Jap invasion. The next day they had all been killed. He watched Hogan. He, too, was acting with the same wild desperation.

Gillian kept her eyes fixed on the thick shoulder opposite her face and tried to concentrate on the strains of the waltz. She was very conscious of Hogan's body pressed against her, and the touch of his hand moist against the small of her back. The pressure grew greater, and she could sense the wild excitement in his uneven breath. She had handled drunks before, but this situation was quite different. She had scarcely believed it possible when Fraser, Myers and even Blair had suddenly succumbed to their emotions, and ignored completely the protection which her sex had in the past afforded her. Hogan peered down at her, his lips wet.

'It does me good to see a proper sheila again, I can tell you,' he said thickly. 'You an' me are goin' to get on fine later.'

Her blouse had been pulled from the top of her skirt, and she could feel his hand exploring the skin on her spine. She saw a hand on Hogan's shoulder, and Blair's flat voice said calmly, 'My turn, I think?' The music had stopped, and she stood clear from the man's arm, as Blair eyed her dully. A flush rose to her cheek as she imagined the contempt in his voice, and with a sob she turned blindly towards the white gleam of Tarrou's shirt. 'I – I think I'll go back to the ship.'

With a great effort she steadied her voice. 'It's been quite a party, and I'm just a bit tired now.'

Fraser drowned Hogan's protests with a great bellow of mirth. 'Get me a drink, you randy bushman, an' take that stupid look off your face!'

Myers had fallen asleep on his arms again, and Blair still stood in the middle of the room, his hands raised uncertainly in the air.

She pulled down her blouse and smiled quickly towards Tarrou. 'Perhaps you will escort me back?'

He swallowed with excitement, and nodded. He was robbed of speech.

Blair stepped forward. 'I'll take you.' He spoke quietly, his eyes cold. 'I think it might be better.'

She looked quickly around the room, taking in the sprawled figures, empty bottles and upended furniture. 'No thanks, Major. I think I can take care of myself.' She momentarily regretted what she had said, as Blair stepped back from her. He looked as if he had been struck, but he suddenly shrugged and looked coldly at Tarrou, the old arrogance still clear in his troubled eyes, and she said with sudden gaiety, 'Come on, Michel, let's leave the *gentlemen* to their celebration!'

Hogan belched angrily. 'Told yer, Vic. Like a rat up a pump!' Then he lay back and closed his eyes.

Blair still stared at the open door, although the girl and Tarrou had vanished. The bitch. The bloody, self-opinionated bitch, he cursed. But as he stood in the now silent room he felt more alone than he could ever remember.

The moon cast an unbroken silver carpet along the pale beach, and where it met the fringe of palms at the edge of the clearing, painted the huts in broad stripes and distorted

50

their hunched shapes with its cool light. A breeze ruffled the fronds in the darkness, and the whole jungle seemed to be filled with rustlings and movement. Occasionally there would be a crazy uninhibited shriek from some distant animal, to be followed at once by a chorus of grunts, screams and howls from the others around it. Then the bedlam would die away as suddenly as it had started, and the rustlings would predominate once more.

Gillian shivered, and looked back towards the lighted door and window of the trade store. On the veranda she could see the red glow of a cigarette, where the Chinese servant watched and waited. Beneath her feet the sand was damp, and she could feel its coolness inside her sandals. Her breathing was still uneven, and she was aware of the fresh uneasiness in her mind. She gave a little cry as two small shapes scurried past her and immediately vanished into the sand.

Tarrou laughed nervously. 'Crabs,' he explained. 'They are very busy at night, to avoid the pelicans.'

She nodded. Everything was hunting something or somebody, and even the beauty of the island in the moonlight was like a disguise to something savage, without pity.

She could see the small huts of the village, with their unsafe-looking walls and thatched roofs, and here and there were a few flickering fires and dark, squatting shapes in the low doorways. Without thinking, she turned her back to the sea and stretched out her arms, as if to embrace the whole island. She felt strangely disturbed and elated, and was conscious of the cool breeze caressing her body. She felt, too, as if she was not really part of what she saw, and she laughed as if to cover her feeling of unreality. She had forgotten Tarrou, who reached out to touch her arm.

'What is it?' His voice was husky.

She shook her head. 'I don't know. It's all this, I suppose. Don't you sometimes feel that you're living on the edge of life here?'

He licked his lips and stared at her dumbly. She could see his dark eyes gleaming like twin fires, and realized that the hand on her arm was moist. Poor Michel, she thought, he is the only one amongst them who should be happy and contented here, and yet he was the only one who seemed to lack any sense of direction, unless it was patterned on something or somebody beyond his reach. She kicked off her shoes and wriggled her toes in the soft sand. 'Wouldn't you like to be something different, Michel?'

He could not understand this kind of conversation, and in any case, his heart was too full to care. Just the sound of her voice, and the gleam of her figure against the blackness of the sea was enough. Or was it? Was it that she was trying to tell him? Because she was so perfect and pure, was she trying to show him that she needed him, as he wanted her? A pulse throbbed painfully in his temple, and he could feel the mounting emotion pounding mercilessly at his defences. She was facing him, her eyes large in her pale face. He stooped to pick up her shoes, conscious of their warmth in his hand. He could not, must not, spoil it all with his clumsiness now.

'Let us walk back to the ship,' he said at last, afraid lest she should notice the tremble in his voice. 'It is a bad place to be at night.'

She walked slowly at his side towards the pier. At the far end she could see the gently swinging lantern over the poop, where Old Buka or one of the others kept watch.

Tarrou was full of surprises, it seemed. One minute he had so much to ask her, so much that he desperately wanted to find out, without the others hearing; yet once on his own he was as tongue-tied as a child. She frowned inwardly.

52

Why in God's name do we keep thinking of these people as children? Yet they made it so difficult.

The ship was silent, and but for the dark shape of the watch on deck there was no one to be seen. She paused at the taffrail, suddenly tired.

'Hell, I'm about done in! Either it's the climate or too much drink!'

'I am sorry you had to suffer the indignity of all that drink, Gillian.'

She stared at him, but under the lamp his face was solemn.

'They do not understand how to treat a lady!'

She squeezed his arm, and smiled. 'Sure, I can imagine. Still, men are mostly the same everywhere, I guess.' She realized that he was still unsmiling, and added: 'Except you, of course. You at least don't make an exhibition of yourself.'

He followed her down the companion ladder, his eyes mesmerized by her very movements.

'Well, thanks for the escort, Michel. It's been fun.'

He stared past her at the neat bunk and the folded pyjamas. A newly trimmed lamp swung from the deckhead, its golden light making the cabin look pleased with itself. She was still smiling at him, and he felt suddenly huge and powerful, the blood pounding in his veins like tribal drums.

He saw his own hands dark on her slim shoulders, and wondered dazedly what he could do next. 'We are happy together, Gillian?'

She felt the power of his hands pressing on her shoulders, and noticed the change which had come over him. Even his eyes looked different, their dark depths mysterious and rather wild.

'We are that, Michel.' She yawned elaborately, suddenly

53

aware of the silence in the ship. She wished that Fraser would appear noisily on deck, anything to break the spell. 'Well, I'm for bed. See you in the morning, Michel!'

He had started to tremble, and his eyes smarted with tears of remorse at his own clumsiness. She was backing away from him, and already the strip of lamplight was narrowing as she began to close the door. Like a blinding light it dawned on him, and he felt his insides turn over. Of course, a lady like Gillian could not allow herself to be bandied around like a cheap lubra. He had seen how she had rebuffed a man like Blair, who was powerful and rich, and how she had been disgusted by Hogan. She was his, but she wanted to wait for his signal, and his moment. When he was ready he would take her, and all the others would be as nothing. He forced himself to bow, so that the wildness on his face should be hidden. 'Our time will come, Gillian,' he pronounced gravely. 'All will be well.'

She closed the door and leaned against it, suddenly weary. These crazy natives took a bit of following, she pondered. She saw her face in the mirror, and wrinkled her nose with disgust. 'You!' she spoke aloud. 'Don't forget you're Gillian Bligh, the defender of the weak!'

With a sigh she kicked off her clothes, and leaned forward to study herself in the mirror. A supple, well-shaped body, she decided. And what use was it? She massaged her smooth stomach angrily and sat on the bunk. Suppose Blair walked in? What would he say? She smiled, but was unable to make the idea into a joke as she had intended. She cocked her head on one side, as she had seen him do, and said softly, 'I say, old girl, you're improperly dressed, what?' She fell back on to the bunk and kicked her legs into the air. If I dislike him so much, why in hell's name do I keep thinking about him? She reached for the light, still angry with herself. A thud sounded on deck, and she heard Myers singing 'Nellie Dean', his voice pitched too high and filled with self-pity.

These men, she swore. Can't have a drink without behaving like bloody animals. As her head touched the pillow she was asleep.

In his cabin Tarrou trembled excitedly beneath the sheets, his head hidden so that he need not speak to Myers, who was staggering around the small space with one leg caught in his trousers and the other hopping and stamping as he cannoned into everything and tried to hold his balance. He muttered and swore with thick monotony, but Tarrou ignored him.

Soon. Soon, he told himself. He would be able to take her to some quiet place, where they would be alone. He would watch and wait, and it would be their own special secret.

Myers gave an extra loud grunt and fell down on his face. His pink legs kicked once and then he began to snore.

Blair limped down the veranda steps and stood for a moment to adjust his eyes to the dark, and allow the whisky to accustom itself to the fall in temperature. He had left Fraser and Hogan sprawled on the floor, and found that he was neither tired nor drunk. He felt quite clear-headed and rather at a loss. He lit a cigarette and peered towards the crouching jungle. To him it represented a challenge and he smiled bitterly at the nodding palms. In there I would probably be some use, he thought. The campaign in Burma had taught him a few tricks of the trade, and it somehow cheered him to remember that he had only been trapped by his injury. He kicked out with his deformed foot, the old hatred welling up inside him. No wonder they treat me the way they do, he reflected moodily. Out here I'm not the one who is envied and pestered by every bloody little upstart;

I'm just the man with too much money, who is putting everyone else to a lot of inconvenience. He threw the cigarette away with disgust, and walked faster along the beach, the sea reaching up to hiss at his feet as he passed. And when I go back, how will it be then? He smiled as he thought of his partner's lined face. 'I hope the trip was satisfactory, Rupert? I have done my best to hold the fort while you've been away.' The last part would be filled with reproach. Poor old Henry. Worked hard all his life, and could never see anything with his tired eyes but bridges, bridges and more bridges. And Marcia. She would be able to tear away his delusion of peace within an hour of his return. She would soon see that the trip had been merely an escape to a past which she could never share, even if she so desired. And with him back in harness she would do her best to destroy his dream.

Then there was Gillian Bligh. Flaunting herself in front of that idiot Tarrou. He grimaced. That was unfair, and he knew it. She had probably been wanting to escape from that ghastly party, and had certainly found him little different from all the others.

He found that he was back at the pier, and he stopped to listen to the sea.

If only I could have met her some other way. He stopped that train of thought immediately. It would have made no difference, I have come to these islands for one purpose, and it is plain bloody stupid to start complicating things.

The moon gleamed serenely on the water, and the breeze sighed contentedly amongst the palms. Their combined music flung the lie back in his face.

4

Fraser lifted his old telescope and trained it across the lee rail towards the sloping headland. The schooner dipped heavily across a steep roller, and he staggered against the rail with his thigh. The motion made the anvil start up again in his head, and he had to grit his teeth to avoid cursing aloud. That damned Hogan.

When the schooner had cast off Hogan had been standing on the pier amongst his boys, his face haggard and unshaven, and openly unwilling for the ship to leave. Bloody old fool, he thought, as he studied the harsh outline of the cliffs through the glass. Perhaps it was as well that they were going to get on with the job. It was a pity it wasn't a wreck full of gold or pearls, but working would get the hangover out of his system. He grinned, and winced as a fire burned behind his eyes. He always said that, after a binge, but it made no difference.

Tarrou wandered silently across the deck, to stare with listless eyes at the shore.

'Well, nearly at the reef, Michel. I hope the weather holds.'

'Nothing wrong with the weather, is there?' His voice was flat.

'Glass droppin' a bit. But I daresay we'll live.' He paused, as a distorted memory formed in his brain. 'What in hell's name did you get up to last night? Didn't see you after you buggered off with the sheila.'

'We talked.'

Fraser grinned. 'Well, I didn't imagine you were in bed with her!'

Tarrou's eyes flickered. 'Please, Vic.' His voice was pleading. 'Don't *you* talk like that. She is a wonderful girl. She is something I have often thought about.'

Fraser snapped the glass shut and turned on him with exasperation. 'Don't talk so bloody wet, man! Sure she's a nice girl. I like her, too. But keep a sense of proportion, for Christ's sake!'

Tarrou eyed him miserably. 'How is that?'

'Well, Michel, it's hard to explain.' He waved the glass irritably. 'You know what I mean, so don't look so dumb. She's a sheila, right? But in the States she's *somebody*, she *matters*! Surely you don't think that she gives a damn what becomes of us? She don't give a cuss for the Major, so you can't imagine she bothers about a chap like you?'

Tarrou merely smiled. Inwardly he was unhappy. It was a pity that Fraser was jealous of him, he thought, but Fraser's opinion of things had ceased to be important. 'I think you are mistaken, Vic.'

Fraser grunted. 'You're as silly as a two-bob watch, Michel. Don't go an' make yourself miserable over a woman, for Christ's sake!'

Watute's shrill voice floated down from the foremast head. 'Deck! Reef him show!'

Fraser shouldered Tarrou to one side. 'I'll talk to you later!' He peered through the glass and saw the thin feathers of spray jumping along the bottom of the headland. He knew that the Phalarope Reef ran from that point and crossed the whole bay in an unbroken line. Unbroken, but for two small gaps, which his father had thought fit to show him.

'Go an' start up the old diesel,' he said curtly. 'I'll sail her in, but if the breeze drops we'll need you.'

Tarrou nodded, his eyes shining. You all need me, he thought.

The girl came on deck, a camera in her hands. 'Is that it?' She pointed at the breakers.

'Yep. That's Phalarope Reef. Many a poor trader has had his bilges trimmed by that!'

She levelled the camera. 'Fancy name?'

'H.M.S. *Phalarope* was wrecked about four miles from here. She was a frigate. Went down with all hands.'

The girl shaded her eyes. Without the sun-glasses they looked like cool grey pearls, he thought.

She smiled. 'How long ago was that?'

'Coupl'a hundred years ago now.' He grinned down at her. 'Don't worry. *I* know where it is, you'll be quite safe.' He looked quickly around the deck. 'Enjoy the party last night?'

She wrinkled her nose, and he noticed that there were freckles on her cheeks. 'Rough!'

'Yeah. Rough is the word for old Hogan. But he's all right.'

'But what a way to live. He looks like a man without hope.'

Fraser shrugged. 'Maybe. But what sort of a life is there in the world where you come from? Do they all have hope?'

She smiled, her teeth were white and even. 'I asked for that.'

'By the way, I think you're lookin' much better since you came aboard.' He grinned awkwardly. 'You know, more relaxed. I think this old tub is doin' you good.'

Gillian tossed the hair from her eyes and looked away. Blair was watching the compass over the helmsman's shoulder, his face creased in a frown. 'Here comes the boss,' she said. 'He looks worried.'

'It's *his* money. But I don't think it's that.'

59

'Well, I'm waiting for the news? Give!' She eyed him with mock anger.

Fraser watched the set of the sails and smiled crookedly. 'He's got girl-trouble!'

Gillian's smile faded. 'But he's married and everything.' Her mind raced over her notes. They were, as usual, thorough and complete. There was no mention of that side to Blair's nature. 'How do you know?' The disbelief sounded in her challenge.

Fraser cupped his hands and bellowed towards the fo'c'sle. 'Stand by the flying jib there, you awkward lot of monkeys!' The seamen grinned back whitely as they scampered forward. 'Because I know her, that's why!' He winked at her triumphantly.

Her laugh echoed along the deck, so that by his engine Tarrou smiled with pleasure. 'Now I know you're blowing your top! Well, go on, finish it. Where is she? What's her name?'

He pulled his cap over his eyes and nodded to the helmsman, before taking over the wheel. Blair glanced curiously at them as Fraser said calmly: 'She's standing in your shoes. I think you know her name!'

She felt the colour mount to her face, and she groped vaguely for her sun-glasses. She stared at Blair, but he had returned his gaze to the chart and compass.

Fraser eyed her momentarily before giving his full attention to the reef. 'S'fact. Ask him!' He grinned, knowing that Blair's ignorance of the conversation made such an idea impossible.

She clenched her fists and stared from one to the other. Then she stamped her foot and walked quickly towards the bows.

Blair picked up the telescope. 'What's the matter with her?'

Fraser shrugged, and felt the press of the wheel against the rudder. 'She's in love, I shouldn't wonder.'

Blair frowned. 'Well, that's her affair,' he answered stiffly. 'What are you doing now?' He forced the girl from his mind but he found himself watching her bare legs silhouetted against the sky as she stood up by the seamen.

'See that pinnacle of rock towards the beach? Well, that's my aiming mark. I steer straight for that an' then put her hard over. We'll have some sail off her before that, but my lads know what to do.'

Above the strumming of the canvas and the swish of water along the lee rail Blair could now hear the sullen thunder of limitless surf crashing against the hidden reef. Every so often a great force, more formidable than the others, would lift itself from the sea, and rise broken and frustrated by the barriers of rock and coral, before falling back into the tormented surf.

The schooner heeled slightly, and Blair had to grasp the rail to prevent his feet from sliding from under him.

The sharp stem lifted and bore down on the fast eddies which criss-crossed the approaches to the reef. Beyond the menace of the implacable wall beneath the surface, the water of the bay shimmered blue and inviting. He could well imagine the storm-tossed frigate, and the poor little *Sigli*, seeing the calm bay as a reprieve from their miseries.

The breeze freshened, and the canvas thundered overhead, as if in answer to the reef's challenge. Blair saw Fraser's wrists twist against the kick of the wheel, and saw his eyes flicker briefly from the sails to the swinging bowsprit, as it curtsied across the uneven water, pointing the way for him to steer. He could almost feel the undercurrent adding its power to the terrible suction which wrenched the keel from one side to the other, and made the taut rigging moan in protest. They were all committed now

61

. . . and he tore his eyes from Fraser's expressionless gaze to watch the dancing spray ahead.

Old Buka loosened a belaying pin in the stout bulwark and automatically ran his fingers through the coiled lines, making sure that no kink or snare would add to the hazards when it came time to alter course. Blair could hear him muttering in that strange mixture of pidgin and island dialect which was quite incomprehensible to him.

Gillian had planted her back against the foremast, and seemed oblivious to the spray whipping at her face and the snap and twang of ropes and braces on either side of her. She held the camera like a gun, and moved it slowly along the jutting headland and stayed for a while on the chattering seamen in the bows.

Blair clawed his way to the rail and leaned as far out as he dared. The sea no longer looked inviting and serene, but gave him the immediate impression of timeless cruelty and immeasurable depth. The surface seemed to churn in all directions at once, and where it seethed in contest with the schooner's bow-wave it appeared to be performing a savage dance, the short, steep waves reaching up to confuse the ship and drive it from its course.

Then, without warning, he saw the reef. Where there had been only empty, dark water and tormented foam he found his eyes mesmerized by a great shoulder of pale green, which, as he stared with fascinated eyes, seemed to writhe and change shape as the ship bore down on it. His mouth had gone quite dry, and he wanted to call out to Fraser and tell him of the reef's nearness.

As the keel surged between the narrow gap in the coral it heeled violently on to its side, and Blair was looking straight down on to the glittering, distorted mass which, as far as he could tell, was only a few feet beneath the surface. In that small instant of time he was conscious of its vastness and jagged strength, and also of its depth of colour and cruel beauty, as the filtered sunlight played amongst its embrasures, giving green, pink and yellow reflections, and showing the nervous, darting shapes of a million fish, which sought shelter against its walls.

He was vaguely conscious of Fraser's short, harsh shouts, and the screaming of ropes through the sheaves, as the twin thirty-foot booms swung across the slanting deck and the rudder bit against the racing water. Protesting with every block and every timber, the old schooner bucked round in a tight semi-circle, and for a moment Blair thought the crazily flapping canvas would dismast her, or drive her back into the reef. He swallowed hard, and looked along the deck at the girl. Their eyes met, and he grinned at her, the excitement within him transforming his taut face so that she too smiled and, with exaggerated relief, blew the hair out of her eyes.

The vessel had already steadied on to even keel, and as the boys shortened sail he felt the diesel begin to pound beneath his feet, and with calm dignity she cruised smoothly into the bay. With impotent fury the breakers still pounded against the reef, but within its protecting walls the bay was calm and at peace, its blue unruffled surface speared and interlaced with panels of lighter green.

Fraser laughed shortly. 'We're in! Suit you, Major?'

Blair nodded slowly, conscious of the tension in the man's tone. It had been a strain for him too then, he pondered. In some way that gave him comfort. 'Well done. It's been worth it all, just to see this.' He waved towards the distant shore, its white beach almost smoky under the heat haze, and the dark ranks of palms and manchineels seemingly unbroken from one end of the bay to the other, the fronds streaming and rippling in the south-east trades. He could see the old volcano quite clearly now, a purple triangle against the bare sky, like the shark's fin had looked as it cut through the peaceful water.

The schooner moved closer to the shore until, with a clatter, the anchor plummeted down, dragging the oiled cable after it, as if eager to delay their journey. With the engine stilled and the way off the ship, the anchor took command, and the schooner swung lazily in the current, her sides throwing up another reflection to add to the pattern.

Fraser pointed with his pipe stem. 'Reckon we'll go over to the mission an' see old Ivor Spencer. That suit you?' He did not sound very enthusiastic.

Blair watched the boys swinging out the heavy dinghy, and shaded his eyes to study the cluster of small buildings on the headland. 'It looks a bit lonely.'

'Sure. And beyond all that bush,' he indicated the inviting beach, 'between us an' that volcano, there are the meanest bunch of jokers left on this earth. I reckon they're the last of the really primitive people, untouched by our civilization,' he said soberly.

The dinghy splashed alongside, and as if in response to some signal two dorsal fins planed to the surface, to cruise with graceful menace along the sides of an invisible rectangle.

Fraser grunted. 'Two big fellas already. Couple of makos, I think.'

Blair found that he was able to watch them without horror. Fraser lived amongst these dangers every day of his life, and in the tropics everything seemed to be larger and starker than in the world outside. The reef, climate and the savage tribes who hid in the lush green of the bush, all were exaggerated, and outlined with the brush of a surrealist painter. It was somehow right that these fish, too, should be as they were. They belonged here. He did not. He watched the gleaming blue shapes move in closer to the dinghy. Their colour made them hard to distinguish, and he wondered how Fraser could tell one from the other.

Fraser seemed to read his thoughts. 'Notice the extra dorsal fin? It's very small, not like the tiger you saw. The colour, too, is a help.'

'Are they dangerous?' Blair remembered the unbelievably savage spectacle of the sharks tearing each other into bloody shreds.

'Yep. Though they'll keep clear of anything they don't trust. Trouble with sharks is their damned curiosity. They keep movin' round a diver in the water, till one of 'em moves in a bit too close and noses him over. Their skin is like flamin' glass-paper, and when they've give you a nudge you know all about it!' He shrugged. 'If they nudge you enough to draw blood . . . that's it. You've had it!'

Fraser pointed to the scarred old seaman called Kari. His bent back was criss-crossed with a pale mesh of ugly slashes, which bunched the dark skin together like a crudely mended garment.

'Sharks?' Blair looked at the native with new interest.

'He was lucky. He an' two others were divin' off Malekula some years back. He was grabbed by a tiger, but managed to wriggle clear. Stuck his thumbs in the brute's eyes, believe it or not. The other two bastards were torn to bits.' He smiled grimly. 'It ruined him for divin'. Still, he's a good hand in many ways.'

Blair lit a cigarette, and watched the drifting fins. He tried to shut out the image of his parents and his sister as the *Sigli* had careered on to the reef. If only it was over quickly for them.

The girl was standing by the rail above the bobbing dinghy. 'Who's for the shore?' She was squinting against the sun and her tanned face looked damp under its probing glare.

Fraser spoke softly. 'Do you want her to come too?'

Blair walked briskly to the rail. 'I think so. Her mind is probably better trained than mine for gleaning information. She might pick up something that I could easily miss.' He was surprised by his own answer, but when he saw Tarrou emerging from the engine hatch he smiled bitterly. It would keep him away from her for a bit.

He saw Fraser take a small key from around his neck and pass it to the half-caste, and heard him say: 'Keep an eye on the *Pearl*. No visitors aboard while we're away, see?'

He rejoined Blair without waiting for an answer, and Blair sensed that Tarrou was displeased both with his orders and with his captain.

'What was the key for?'

Fraser turned his body so that the girl should not see and gently pulled open his trouser pocket. Blair could see the heavy pistol resting snugly against his leg. 'As they say in the Pommie navy, that was the key of the *Pearl's* main armament. I always take *this* ashore, just in case.'

'Hadn't I better take it?' Blair's eyes were cold.

'Not bloody likely.' Fraser grinned calmly. 'This is a peaceful visit, not a flamin' invasion!'

Blair shrugged, and stepped down into the boat. Fraser had the easy knack of upsetting him, but at last he had the feeling that he was getting the man's measure. We shall see, he thought, as he settled himself on the warm thwart of the boat. I think that they all want to show me that out here I am the one useless person aboard.

Gillian jumped lightly down beside him, and he was painfully aware of the hot pressure of her body against his. Fraser's bulk made the boat sway precariously, and as Wabu pulled on the thick oars Blair saw the gap widen between the two craft, and when they were well clear of the schooner the two sharks fell into line behind them, to follow the dinghy towards the shore.

Blair mopped his streaming face with a sodden hand-kerchief and fought back against the impatience which always seemed to control him as soon as he was away from the ship. The boat lurched, and he felt the pressure of the girl's smooth arm against his own. It was soft and somehow comforting, but he found that he was tense on the edge of his seat, willing her to remain at his side. She twisted in her cramped space, and he saw the tiny droplets of sweat on her upper lip and the hair pressed damply against her forehead. She pointed towards the shore, unconscious of his scrutiny, and of the dark patches which with each effort of movement moulded the thin blouse against her body.

'I can see people!' she said. 'That must be your mission-ary friend, Vic!'

A tall white figure stood quite still amongst the gesticulating group of natives which had run down the steeply shelving beach from the now hidden mission to line the very edge of the sea.

Fraser snorted. 'You'll be sorry you came. He's a bloody religious maniac, if you'll pardon the expression. This sort of place is about all that he's fit for. Don't say I didn't warn you!'

Blair noticed the difference between the schooner's native seamen and those who waded happily to grasp the dinghy's gunwale. Short, and much darker than he had expected, their faces showed none of the finer lines he had seen on their counterparts in Port Vila, and he had thought them crude enough. Their black bushy hair and short, sometimes bowed, legs gave their bodies the wild appearance of true bushmen, interbred for hundreds of generations, their faces lacking any of the expressions which he could recognize and assess.

Behind the jabbering, pointing men he could see the

womenfolk of the settlement. Like the men, they were small, and but for small bark belts decorated with leaves were quite naked. Long, lustreless hair hung from their shoulders, and as they danced up and down to get a better view of the visitors their small breasts jerked in unison with their various necklaces of teeth and polished shells. Blair noted that most of them had a gap in their front teeth, where two had apparently been removed by force. Fraser had already told him that it was the sign of married status. He was immediately aware, too, of their pungent smell, but this he quickly forgot as he studied the tall white man in their midst.

Ivor Spencer was certainly tall, by any standard, but against the natives he looked like a giant. It was as if all the power in his body had gone into his height and had left the rest hollowed out and unfinished. He had no chest, so that his long narrow head was thrust forward at an unnatural angle, in a constant position of questioning belligerence, an impression completed by the deep-set grey eyes and narrow nose, which hooked over his thin mouth like a beak. The white shirt and trousers which covered him from throat to ankle looked vaguely out of date, and as Blair stepped awkwardly from the boat amongst the suddenly silent natives he saw Spencer sweep off the ancient topee to reveal a tall pointed head, its scalp bald, and strangely unmarked by the sun, encircled by a few tufts of iron-grey hair, like bushes around a weather-worn boulder.

He nodded briefly, but showed no eagerness or pleasure in his restless eyes. 'I see you have brought visitors, Captain Fraser?' He stared coldly at Blair, his voice surprisingly deep and resonant. 'What do you want here?'

'My name's Blair.' He waved Fraser's reply into silence. 'I have come from England to try to find the wreck of a boat called the *Sigli*. I know that it lies on the reef, and intend to examine it.' He added firmly: 'I wonder if you know anything of this wreck? I don't wish to interfere with your peace and quiet longer than I can help.'

Spencer smiled without humour. 'England, eh? I am afraid that I am not impressed by emissaries from that country of dishonesty and sloth. What is it this time? Pearls or gold? No doubt you are well versed in the ways of Fraser and his like!'

Blair relaxed, like a spring unwinding after a great strain. Here at last was a man he could appreciate. Spencer's unreality only helped Blair to fit him more easily into the picture where nothing was ordinary or commonplace.

'I am concerned with neither. The *Sigli* was wrecked during the war, as you may know. My family were aboard at the time. I wish to find out what happened to them.' He watched the other man digesting this information, and had the feeling that he already knew the answers.

'I know nothing of that.' He waved a thin arm over the heads of the watching natives. 'Here we all work for perfection in simple things. These people are my task on earth. I do not wish to have their minds confused and scarred by the filth of the other world. Your world!'

Blair allowed his gaze to wander along the ranks of staring faces and uncomprehending grins. He was aware that the other man was watching him like a hawk. My reaction is terribly important to him, he thought.

'You have set yourself a stiff task,' he said at length.

Spencer thrust out his long chin, his eyes gleaming. 'Whom the Lord loves He chasteneth!' he shouted triumphantly. 'Now go away! Keep your people clear of my community!'

Fraser interrupted harshly: 'We have everything we need aboard, the Major here just thought—'

'I *see* you have everything! Even to your painted harlot!'

69

He called out sharply in a strange sobbing dialect, and the natives moved back a few paces, as if Blair and his party were unclean.

He limped forward after them, his face taut with anger. 'Who the hell d'you think you're talking to?' He was conscious of the girl's quick intake of breath behind him. 'D'you have to be so bloody-minded? I merely wanted information.'

Spencer raised his sun-helmet like a silent offering. 'And all you gained was the truth! Go now, and remember, if you choose to come in anger,' he pointed quickly to the small spears and wide-bladed knives which the women were handing to their menfolk, 'you shall be met with just retribution!'

Blair faltered. There was a tense air of expectancy hanging over the natives, but they were not watching him, they were looking at Spencer, as if to determine what they might do.

Blair thought of the revolver in Fraser's pocket and eyed the brown mass of silent figures. He was suddenly furious with himself. Once more he had made a mess of things, and he could imagine the satisfaction in Fraser's eyes.

In a surprisingly flat voice he said: 'I won't bother to introduce you to the lady, Spencer. As you apparently have neither the wit nor the intelligence to appreciate anything approaching reality it would be a waste of time. I don't know what you're supposed to be teaching these poor natives, but I hope they don't stumble on the truth one day and pay you back!'

He swung on his heel and limped down the beach. His back tingled, as if expecting a blow, but he could see from Fraser's expression of angry watchfulness that for the moment all was well. Still under the watching stares he walked over to the girl, and took her hand. All his actions

70

now seemed governed by another force, and he felt a trifle light-headed.

'Here, let me help you into the boat.' Without giving her time to resist, he piloted her down to the lapping water. She opened her mouth as if to speak, her eyes across his shoulder, to where Spencer stood surrounded by his court, but Blair shook his head. 'Not now; I might have to punch that half-wit in the eye!'

Wabu dipped the oars and pulled away from the beach, his eyes on the villagers filled with contempt. He was a Torres islander, and not a simple bushman. He felt the pressure of his diver's knife against his naked stomach, and bared his teeth in a cruel smile. These bushmen, he thought, they would never be anything.

Blair was aware that his foot was throbbing like a drum, and he bent to massage it. He stopped himself with sudden irritation, but as he straightened up in his seat he saw her eyes watching him with an expression he had almost forgotten.

'Major, you're quite a guy,' she said softly. 'You actually made me *feel* like a lady. Imagine!'

Blair smiled uncomfortably. 'I'm afraid I made a bit of a mess of that. The whole expedition nearly came to a sudden end then.' He held her eyes, and she still smiled.

Fraser sighed deeply and, sliding his big hand into his pocket, replaced the safety-catch on his revolver. 'He's got worse since I saw him last,' he said, watching the dwindling figures on the beach. 'Mad as a coot. I shall tell the D.O. when I see him.' They did not answer him, and Fraser looked at the girl's wide mouth, which was still smiling. 'Told you, didn't I, Gillian?' He winked, but she met his gaze easily.

'You've got a one-track mind.'

Blair's smile faded, and he turned deliberately in his seat

to study the schooner. Blast them, he thought, the old bitterness welling up inside him, they've been having some sort of bet about my reactions. His eyes clouded over, so that the schooner's shape became distorted, and he was unaware of the sudden pain in the girl's eyes. He was conscious only of the overwhelming desire to get on and find the wreck. To be finished with this place, and all that it had come to mean to him.

Myers lay comfortably in the deck-chair on the small poop, an unlighted cigarette hanging from his lips. He could feel the sunlight pressing down on the awning over his head, and although he occasionally fanned his red face with his handkerchief, he could find no relief now that the breeze had gone, and the deck once more felt white-hot beneath his shoes.

'God, it's 'ot!' he complained. When Tarrou did not answer he turned painfully to see what he was doing. He was still leaning against the mainmast, the telescope trained rigidly on the shore. 'Like a bloody kid!' Myers muttered irritably. 'Standin' there behavin' as if 'e expected a signal from the bleedin' Admiralty!' The sudden burst of anger drained the strength from him, and he flopped back in the chair, his eyes closed against the sweat which coursed down on either side of his button nose.

Tarrou stood quite still, his world confined to his racing thoughts and the small circular picture in the telescope. The questions which surged through his aching brain would not wait to be answered, and he stared unwinkingly at the dinghy as it shoved off from the beach and began to crawl towards him. He had felt a real pain when he had seen Blair take the girl's hand. It had been so easy, so self-assured. He had taken her as if she was one of his possessions, indifferent to the staring islanders and the mad missionary.

72

What had made that happen? Why had she not resisted? He could feel the heat across his back like the breath of a fire, but it did not register as a discomfort. What could he do to show her that he, Michel Tarrou, was ready and willing to give up everything to protect and serve her? He began to tremble again, and bit his lower lip savagely to punish his inability to hold the glass steady.

The small boat drew nearer, and he held the girl's face framed in the telescope, until in his imagination she seemed to be looking straight at him. As she looked up at the ship he saw her bare throat and the moistness of her lips, and he looked quickly at Blair to see if he was going to touch her again. He hung the glass by the wheel and walked shakily across the deck to steady himself before they came aboard, a puzzled frown on his face. He had seen the anger on Blair's face and the cold hard look in his eyes. What was happening now? He stared with sudden agitation at the dozing Myers, as if he might have the answer. What was it that Fraser had said? He forced himself to think back. 'Surely you don't think she bothers about a chap like you?' That was it. He rubbed his hand across his face, like a man awaking from a bad dream. A terrible doubt was growing within him. Just suppose she was having a game with him? He allowed the thought to settle, and waited for the truth to sweep its ugliness away. Nothing happened. The thought remained. He forced himself to explore what was rapidly becoming a possibility. Suppose she and Major Blair were enjoying some joke between themselves? They did not know he had been watching them through the telescope, and they were merely acting a part to draw out the full extent of his foolishness. A great pain began to burn behind his eyes, and he shook his head from side to side in his misery. It would mean that Fraser was in it, too. Was that possible? He stared again at Myers. Him, too. All of them were trying to take away his place in their world, and were secretly baiting him like a trapped animal. He staggered against the wheel and gripped the spokes until it looked as if his knuckles were going to burst through the flesh. *You're wrong. She wouldn't do that to you. She could never be anything but perfect.* He felt a hot tear drop on to the back of his hand.

The dinghy scraped alongside and he could hear Fraser shouting his name and calling for the boys to hoist in the boat. Like a soldier about to face overwhelming odds, Tarrou straightened his back and, with his face impassive once more, stalked towards the rail. Only the redness of his eyes and a slight tic which had developed in his cheek tried to betray the turmoil which had replaced his complete happiness.

The girl swung her legs over the rail, a troubled smile about her mouth, and stood fidgeting with the camera. Blair followed, and walked straight past Tarrou to stand with obvious impatience as Fraser yelled again for the dinghy to be hoisted.

Blair forced himself to study the chart which Fraser had pinned on the flat roof of the companion-way. *Why don't you grow up! Stop acting like a Sandhurst cadet with his first date.* He was suddenly aware of her perfume and the warm nearness of her body. He looked up, and saw the disquiet in her wide grey eyes. He didn't trust himself to speak, but felt the resistance drain out of him like blood.

'Listen, Major.' Her voice was soft but insistent. 'I don't know for sure what happened out there, but thanks for looking after me.'

He pulled the gold cigarette-case from his breast pocket and shakily flipped it open. She twisted over his arm to stare at the inscription: *To Rupert, with love. Marcia.* Above the finely engraved words and the date was a regimental crest.

74

A prancing stag and crossed lances.

'Your wife will be glad to see you back, I guess.' Her voice sounded subdued.

Blair nodded vaguely, and stared through the case into the past, when Marcia had slipped it casually into his pocket. It had been when he had been given a company, and the regiment was preparing for embarkation to the South-East Asia campaign. She had looked beautiful and remote as they stood in the dockyard loading shed, with the thin drizzle falling over the trudging lines of khaki as the troops filed up the steep gangways. He had wanted to hold her, and not let go. To bury his face in her neck, and shut out the sounds of steel-shod feet on the good English waterfront. But she had patted his sleeve and reproached him like a small boy. 'Steady, Rupert. Lady Gould is looking at us. We don't want to give the wrong impression!' Lady Gould was the Colonel's wife, and as Blair stared fixedly into the past he saw another picture. That of the Colonel sitting in a rain-filled dugout, his horsy features puckered with the effort of reading a soggy letter from home. 'I say, Rupert, my old girl's taken up knitting for sailors! What d'you think of that! Never done a hand's turn before but now she's making balaclavas for the boys in blue. Bloody fantastic!' Blair had smiled dutifully, and returned to Marcia's latest letter. He re-read it a dozen times, trying to find a warmth, a comfort to ease the misery of Burma, but the letter was merely a window into a world of terrible shortages and irritating discomforts of wartime England. She had ended that letter by remarking, *'Imagine, all the decent champagne has gone on the black market, it really is too trying!'* The battalion had stood to, and the letter had been stuffed into his pocket beside the cigarette-case. As the machine-guns had started to rattle through the jungle he had suddenly laughed, and a subaltern had torn his frightened eyes from the darkness to look enquiringly at his Major. Blair had patted his arm reassuringly. 'Imagine, John,' he said, 'all the champagne has gone on the black market!'

He shook himself, and offered her the case.

She helped herself, and squinted through the glare at his face. 'You were *miles* away. What happened?'

He fumbled for his lighter. 'Voices from the past. It's over now.'

'I wonder. Does your wife know you've got a "painted harlot" with you on this trip?'

He stared at her, his eyes searching. He watched her lips quiver and break into a smile, and then he, too, began to shake with almost insane laughter. 'By God, no!' He gripped her wrist desperately, as the laughter melted away. 'I'm sorry I'm such a damned stuffed shirt, Miss Bligh. I really am sorry. But I'm extremely grateful for your being here now.' He breathed out heavily. It had been quite a confession.

'Thank you. And I don't know what you thought we were talking about in the dinghy, but I guess you were wrong about that, too!' She slipped her forefinger under the button of his shirt and pulled gently. The touch of her finger against his stomach made him feel a little weak. She grinned impishly. 'You can start by unstuffing *this* shirt! Gillian's the name. Okay?'

The clatter of the anchor cable pulled Blair back to his senses. The old capstan clanked painfully as link by link the chain jerked back through the fairlead. Fraser stood stiff-legged by the wheel, and smiled his lazy smile. Well, well, he thought. Wonders will never cease.

Only Tarrou missed the sight of the grey headland gliding astern, and the long sweep of the bay opening up before the schooner's bows. He crouched beside the thundering engine, his hands welded to a beam, his steady

76

monotonous curses drowned by the roar of the giant flywheel and the distant pounding of the propeller. Major Blair had put some spell on her. That was why he had taken her ashore with him. His eyes were pressed shut, and he rocked his body back and forth in the gloom of the tiny engine-room. I shall break the spell. I shall show her that I am the one who can treat her as she deserves!

The propeller shaft spun in its greased bed, and the bilge water shimmered and jumped to the tune of the vibration. Tarrou remained crouched as if in prayer, conscious only of his task, and the vengeance which he would wreak on anybody who tried to hold him from it.

5

The steady beat of the diesel engine faltered and died, as Fraser allowed the *Queensland Pearl* to glide effortlessly through the clear, subdued water of the bay. Overhead, the afternoon sun was at its peak, and so great was the heat that even thought became a real effort. The sun had lost its shape, and the blue of the clear sky had faded beneath its searing power to leave only a pale, shimmering haze, which transformed the sea into a glaring mirror of distorted light, and seemed to suck the very air from the vessel's deck. As the schooner had moved cautiously across the bay the beach had drawn nearer, and the invisible reef, too, had become closer, as the bay had narrowed, and the thrashing propeller had driven them towards their destination. Fraser lifted his hand and dropped it heavily to his side in a signal to the small group on the fo'c'sle. With a rumble the cable ran jerkily over the bow, and allowed the heavy anchor to plummet down once more to disturb the quiet water. Fraser stepped back from the well and wiped his hands slowly across the seat of his trousers. He nodded to Blair, who had been standing beneath the small canopy across the poop, and pointed to the haze-distorted shape of the volcano.

'Right in line. I reckon that we are as near to the wreck as we can get in safety.' He waited for an answer, but Blair was staring at the glittering water, as if he expected to see the wreck rise up to greet him. 'I see that your bloke is gettin' ready to go down already.'

Myers had appeared on deck, his thick arms filled with equipment and his long rubber frogman's suit.

Fraser grinned wearily, and dashed the sweat from his eyes. 'He insists on wearin' that suit. He reckons it's safer than goin' down in the raw!'

Blair tore his eyes from the sea and watched Myers as he laid his equipment down in a neat array on the deck. The boys crowded around him to watch, but a scowl from Myers deterred even Old Buka from touching any of the gear.

Blair smiled. 'He's very particular about how he works. A very good diver, all the same.'

Fraser grunted, and walked out into the glare. 'Come on, you jabberin' shower! Swing out the boat!'

Blair beckoned Myers across to him, his face set. 'Are you going down now?'

Myers shrugged and licked his lips. 'Might as well, sir, I might find the wreck first go, an' then I can get it marked, an' perhaps get a bit of a look before the night comes on.' He flexed his fingers. 'I 'ope you won't be disappointed, sir.'

'Disappointed?' Blair eyed the other man's sweating face, and considered the remark. What did he expect Myers to find, anyway? He patted his fat shoulder and jerked his thumb towards the two native divers who were swinging down into the dinghy. Their dark, muscular bodies gleamed like oiled mahogany, and they moved with the eager grace of wild animals. 'They'll be nearby while you're working, in case you need a hand.'

Myers' lip curled with contempt. 'Them? I only 'ope they don't get in me bleedin' way!' He glared towards the shore and its long sweep of vivid green jungle. 'Ah well, I think I'll get started. It's too 'ot up 'ere.'

Myers stripped to his shorts, and allowed Blair to help

him into his tight-fitting suit. As his fat body slowly disappeared into the shiny black skin some of his nervous irritation faded, and the familiar feel of his working dress made him lapse into silence, as he checked the air bottles and adjusted his wide belt. It was always the same for him before going down. In the Persian Gulf, or the River Thames, there was always the moment of doubt, and then the feeling of exultation once he had got started on the job.

Myers was an unimaginative man, who had become a good diver quite by accident. He had been given the chance during the war, whilst serving with the Navy, and after the armistice he had spent many months helping to salve the wrecks which littered the harbours of Germany, and had to be swept up with the other debris of human folly. A civilian firm had taken over the task from the service divers, and he had stopped on to help get them accustomed to the placing of the wrecks. Quite suddenly he had found that he was unwilling to give up the work, and the prospect of leaving the Navy to return to his former job – he had been a bus conductor in Battersea before joining up – filled him with disgust. He had gone straight to the dockside office and asked to see the salvage master.

Since then he had never looked back. He had dived in practically every sea and important river in the world, and had helped to guide the foundations of Blair's bridges, or to remove underwater obstacles of every description, and had slowly become one of the company's most reliable divers.

With his ability, and corresponding rise in salary, his social and domestic life, too, had changed. He now lived in a neat suburban house well outside London, and was looked on if not with respect by his middle-class neighbours, then certainly with envy. George Myers was seldom without cash in his wallet, and his new car was often outside the mock Tudor doors of the Royal George Hotel, where his loud Cockney voice could be heard calling for drinks for his friends, who secretly despised him. He had married a plump little widow with two children, and had felt that all was at last well for George Myers.

He had expanded with pride when his stepson, Henry, had done well at school, and had gone on to university. It just didn't seem possible that all this was happening to him. His wife had insisted on having the best of everything, because, as she put it, 'it doesn't do to let the neighbours get on their high horses!' Although she was careful not to annoy George, she soon let him know that she had rather married beneath her, and he should work all the harder because of it. She had, in fact, been the daughter of a coal merchant, who had made his money on the black market during the war, but she did not advertise that point.

George, however, was almost content. He liked his work, and was able to move about the country from job to job as it arose. But just lately he had been rather worried about the way his savings were dwindling. In his mind he could, and did quite often, list the more recent of his wife's status symbols. New car, an enormous television, as well as the constant stream of money for Henry at the university.

He shrugged his shoulders more comfortably into his suit and frowned inwardly. Suppose I find I'm too old for diving, what then? He could not somehow visualize his wife taking kindly to a severe cut in salary and all that it would mean. If only she would save a bit.

Blair eyed him gravely. 'Ready?'

He nodded, and walked heavily to the bulwark, and lowered himself carefully into the bobbing dinghy alongside.

The boys gasped with awe as he pulled the webbed flippers on to his feet and dangled them over the side of the boat.

81

Fraser followed him, and shouted up at Tarrou, who stood silently for the foremast. 'Lower the other boat, mate! This may take quite a while!'

The boat shoved off, and Blair had to shade his eyes to watch, as the oars dipped and rose slowly on the flat water.

Wabu and Yalla sat together in the bows, while Kari tugged at the oars, his scarred old back glistening with the effort.

Fraser sat high in the stern, trying to gauge the exact position to put down the red-flagged marker-buoy which nodded over the gunwale beside him.

Myers shut his mind to all else but preparing himself, and again checked his heavy knife, the waterproof packet of shark-repellent and, finally, his air bottles. What a bloody waste of time, he reflected, but the money will be handy. He scowled, and shifted from that train of thought immediately.

Once he looked back at the schooner, its white shape making a twin with its reflection on the smooth sea, and the tan sails limp against the heavy booms. He could see the other dinghy being lowered like a toy alongside, and idly noted that a figure was climbing to the foretopmast head with slow, unhurried movements.

Fraser followed his eyes, and nodded approvingly. 'That's Michel. He's goin' up on look-out.'

They both looked automatically to the rifle which was propped against a thwart, its magazine loaded with soft-nosed bullets.

'Could 'e spot a shark from up there?' Myers touched the hot metal of the gun as if to reassure himself.

'If it's a big one on the surface. But don't worry, mate, you'll be all right.'

Myers smiled without humour. 'Yeh, I bleedin' 'ope so!'

Fraser jerked his head. 'Right! Drop the hook!'

A small anchor splashed down, and after what seemed like an endless amount of line had been paid out the small boat was held steady. Occasionally, a long unruffled roller would cruise easily down from the reef and lift the boat like a cork, and they would watch it carry on towards the shore, where its spent power would end as a mere caress for the white sand.

Myers adjusted his nose-clip, and fixed his goggles into place. I'm glad we're not working on the other side of the reef, he reflected, as he felt rather than heard the sullen thunder of the surf beyond the coral barrier.

He patted Fraser's knee and, without a further glance, rolled over the gunwale and hung momentarily by one hand from the mooring rope. His face glistened with spray as he checked his mouthpiece and steadied his breathing, the well-tried movements almost automatic, while his webbed feet trod the warm water to the delight of the watching boys.

Then, with a quick thumbs-up, he was gone, and Fraser settled himself in the sternsheets to wait, his watchful eyes never still beneath the peak of his cap.

They had already been forgotten by Myers, as he planed smoothly downwards, his hands moving like pale animals against his rubber suit. Above his broad back the surface shone like a golden mirror edged with blue, and as he moved leisurely forward, and deeper, he was fascinated by the dashing and quivering armies of tiny, multi-coloured fish, which surged towards him, only to stop motionless, before tearing away in another direction, as if to be free of this weird black creature which invaded their private world.

He was pleasantly surprised by the temperature of the water, although as he neared the reef his body was moved lazily by warm and then cool currents alike. A forest of waving weed reached up at his slow-moving body, and he strained his eyes ahead, where the threatening darkness of the deep water mocked him, yet at the same time filled him with curiosity.

People often said of George Myers that he was too ungainly and heavy to be any use as a diver. If all his doubters could have seen his easy, rhythmic movements, as he moved with quiet grace amongst the sea-bed jungle, they would have been amazed, and ashamed.

He touched a sleeping fish, as he skimmed between two smooth-sided boulders, and smiled as it dashed away in a panic, and then, after squinting at his big wrist-compass, he moved more slowly towards the pale, shimmering slope of the reef.

It was like nothing he had ever experienced.

As he stared upwards at the rugged, knife-edged embrasures, he could see the countless ledges and gullies, their weed-screened shapes distorted and magnified by the filtered sunlight, and constantly changing as the green and yellow growths waved and beckoned in the powerful cross-currents. He was reminded of a sunken castle, or the wall of a forgotten city. He shuddered, and watched warily as the pressure of the water lifted him carelessly towards the menace of the coral. He took a quick glance at his depth gauge. Sixty feet. He turned his body with an effort and began to swim along the edge of the reef, keeping one eye on its outline and the other on what lay ahead.

A long grey shape moved slowly away from the reef, and began to swim parallel with him, its streamline body shining slightly as a shaft of distant sunlight played along the rough skin and lined the edge of the dorsal fin with fire. As Myers stared at the shark it vanished, and for several moments he peered anxiously in every direction, his mind suddenly ice-cold and alert. The shark did not come back, and he decided to go forward again.

He shivered, as a current of cold water swept over him, and for a few moments he felt a twinge of panic. You're getting old, chum. Scared of your own shadow! He forced himself to think more calmly, and swam a little faster, his feet moving up and down in a steady, powerful rhythm.

His movements began to get heavier, and he noticed that his breathing was more jerky. Have to go up in a moment, he decided. Been allowing myself to get soft. Must have a rest.

A white-and-black fish halted in front of his face, and stared at him with pop-eyed amazement. Myers moved aside, but the fish darted nearer, its small puckered mouth moving in time to its gills.

Myers groaned inwardly. Get away, you stupid thing! He shook his arm wearily at it, and then chilled, the fish forgotten. He had to hit out with his hands, using them like paddles, as he stared wide-eyed at the rusting wall of weed-dappled metal which soared to meet him. The ship was pointing straight at him, the battered stem buried amongst the waving green jungle, and the rest, half hidden by the thousands of sea-growths which explored every available piece of the twisted superstructure, was gripped by the bottommost teeth of the reef, which had torn open the hull and littered the sea-bed with the vessel's entrails. Even as he stared he saw the broken guard-rails, and the shattered mast, which pointed drunkenly across the slanting deck, its tangled rigging a mass of weed, the movement of which gave him a passing impression that the ship was alive and breathing. With great caution, his weariness forgotten, he slowly moved up and over the edge of the deck, his stomach knotted tight, as if to receive a blow. It was a small ship, by any standards, and what had remained through the years was picked clean by the sea, leaving only the twisted steel plates and the mocking skeleton of a wheelhouse, the front of which had fallen out, to reveal the splintered deckhead and the abandoned wheel.

Myers steadied himself against the bridge ladder, and allowed his practised eye to work for him. He never failed to be impressed by a wreck, no matter how old or how recent. It had been different in Germany, where the sunken ships had often been crammed with hideous human remains. One diver had gone mad after forcing a jammed bulkhead door in a sunken refugee ship. The wretched, faceless occupants had risen on the current and swam to greet their rescuer. But here, on the deck of this small, deserted ship, it was different. He moved on up the sloping metal, his fingers catching on the encrusted barrel of a discarded rifle, a twin to the one which Fraser had in the dinghy above. He moved it with an effort, and wondered what had happened to the wounded soldier who had owned it.

As he turned round the rear of the wheelhouse, he sensed a movement behind him. His heart seemed to stop, and with a grunt he tore the knife from its scabbard and swung to face the other way. A great hand squeezed his lungs as a figure seemed to move up through the torn guard-rails, its teeth white in the half-light. Wabu, the diver, his greased hair waving like sea-fern over his grinning face, gestured happily to Myers with his own knife, and then shot towards the surface, his naked body changing colour as it rushed to meet the sun.

Myers had to wait several seconds for his breathing to return to normal, then he, too, relinquished his grip and glided upwards. As his head broke the surface he immediately felt the sun on his face, and was glad of it. He was still shaking as the dinghy pulled over to him, and the sinker of the marker buoy went plummeting down. His plump hands rested on the warm wood of the dinghy's gunwale, and as Fraser removed his facepiece Myers worked his stiff mouth vigorously before turning to the dripping native in the bows.

'How was it, sport?' Fraser squinted down at the red face. 'I hear you found it first go?'

Myers tore his eyes from Wabu's smooth face. 'Stupid sod!' he said hoarsely. 'I might 'ave gutted 'im like a fish!'

Fraser grinned, and began to pull him into the boat. 'What was the flamin' wreck like? I guess most of the poor devils what was in her must have been killed instantly, eh?'

Myers' face was creased in a deep frown. 'It wasn't like that at all, Vic,' he answered slowly. 'The davits was empty, an' the falls 'ad bin run out.' He allowed the words to sink in, and they both looked towards the distant shore, which gleamed so invitingly beyond the schooner.

Fraser licked his lips. 'Took to the boats, did they? I wonder what Major Blair will have to say to that?'

The marker buoy bobbed above the hidden *Sigli,* as in silence they pulled back to the schooner.

There was no moon, and the stars appeared very small and far away, their glittering shapes shaded by motionless streaks of fine, vaporous cloud, which hung like steam above the little schooner, and seemed to hold the air still and lifeless. The bows lifted slightly to each roller from the reef, and the shining anchor cable would rise momentarily in protest, only to fall back into the black water, as if it, too, was exhausted by the heat of the day.

A blaze of harsh light glared from the poop, where a Tilley storm lantern hissed on a small cane table, protected from the blinded insects by the long rolls of mosquito netting which surrounded the small space of the poop like a transparent tent.

Apart from the distant sigh of surf against the beach, and

87

the occasional scream of a hunted animal, there was nothing outside the great circle of light cast by the lamp, and because of it the figures around the table seemed drawn even closer together.

Only Blair remained standing, and as he moved restlessly from one side of the deck to the other he was conscious of their eyes watching him, following him, and yet telling him nothing.

Fraser, in his battered deck-chair, sat hunched forward, a glass of beer untouched in his big hands, his face empty of expression.

Myers sat on the deck, his plump shoulders resting against the companion hatch, his fingers tracing an invisible design on his crumpled slacks. He looked resentful, almost hostile, as Blair halted, one hand smashing into the other with exasperation.

'Don't you see?' he began again, as if by keeping the subject alive he might revive their interest. 'It's all quite different now.' He saw Gillian place her glass of Pernod carefully on the table and begin to search for a cigarette. Her face looked damp in the lamplight, and Blair was again conscious of the humid air which hung over the ship. Nothing moved. Not even the slightest breeze disturbed the netting, and he could feel the sweat coursing down his spine in a steady stream. He stared at the others. Apart from Gillian, they looked as if they had given in. No longer cared. He pressed his lips into a tight line. They had never cared, of course.

Fraser glanced at the others and sighed heavily. Tarrou, perched on the arm of his chair, one foot swinging listlessly, while his eyes flickered from Blair's face to the girl's hands, as they groped for a cigarette.

Fraser held the glass up to the light. 'Well, speakin' for myself, Major, I don't see that things have changed much, for you at least.' He paused, but Blair's cold eyes were quite motionless. 'After all, if George here had reported that the boats were still aboard the wreck,' he shrugged, 'let's face it, you'd have been quite satisfied, now wouldn't you? As it is,' he gestured with his glass, 'maybe they got the boats away, and maybe they reached the beach. Maybe. But what the hell. I guess they're just as dead as if they were killed outright by the reef.' He smiled uneasily, as he saw the pain in Blair's face. 'No offence, Major, but I'm right, aren't I?'

Blair turned away, his shoulders stiff. How could he begin to explain the feeling of loss which he had experienced when Myers had returned to the ship with his findings? He thrust his hands into his pockets, and felt his fingers dig cruelly into his flesh. This was just how Marcia had said it would end. To go back now, as Fraser obviously wanted, would leave him with an even greater uncertainty than before. Marcia had known, and now all these others knew, too. He had seen the resentment in Myers' red face when he had bombarded him with questions about the wreck, and he knew that behind his back the diver would be already thinking of the trip home, and the extravagant wife he had left behind. Gillian had kept silent, and that seemed as good as a supporting vote in favour of calling off the whole adventure. He limped irritably to the table, and poured out another glass of Pernod. Fraser was speaking again, his voice directed at them all.

'An' the weather bothers me a bit, too. George has said about the hot and cold currents in the deep water, an' that only confirms what I thought earlier.' He rubbed his hand along his thigh, leaving a damp patch in its wake. 'I reckon we're in for a blow. We always get a few Willy-Willies about this time of year, an' we don't get much warning.' He faced up to Blair, his face set. 'An' I don't reckon to get caught on the reef in a flamin' tropical gale.'

The girl's voice was low and controlled, yet she had been silent for so long that its sound startled both Blair and Fraser, so that they halted in their actions to watch her.

'You men make me sick!' She shook a wing of hair free from her face, and eyed them calmly. 'You, Vic, think that the Major is just a guy with too much dough, and has a screw loose into the bargain, right?' She did not wait for an answer. 'You've lived out here all your life, and are supposed to be a professional sailor, yet all the time you bellyache about storms, savage tribes, and hell knows what—'

'Now see here—' began Fraser, his jaw thrust forward, but she slapped her hand sharply on the table, her grey eyes blazing.

'No! *You* see here, mister! You want to look at a map sometime. You'll hardly be able to find the New Hebrides on it, let alone *this* crummy little island! Why not tell the truth? All you want is to get back to that shanty-town you call Port Vila and swill away Major Blair's cash in that shack you appear to imagine is the last word in civilized elegance!' She sat back and drew on the cigarette. 'Well, for once, Captain, you've got nothing to say? I'm glad, because I didn't want to come on this shindig in the first place, but now that I'm here I want a story, and a good one, see?'

Fraser grinned sheepishly, and ran his fingers through his hair. 'That was quite a mouthful! I sure underestimated *you*!'

She smiled briefly. 'You're not the first.'

She lifted her gaze to Blair, who was watching her with quiet fascination. The lamp shone on her smooth skin, and reflected on the tiny droplets of perspiration along her upper lip. Her voice softened. 'And you, Rupert.' She cocked her head on one side. 'I don't quite know what to make of you.'

90

At any other time in his life Blair would have been livid with rage to be considered so candidly in front of others. He merely stood under the low netting, his shoulders slightly stooped, his face suddenly tired.

'I guess you've been so used to bulldozing your way across other people's ideas you've almost forgotten how to deal with a situation like this.' A tiny insect, which had managed to penetrate the defences of the net, landed on the top of the glowing lamp, and disintegrated. She watched it for a moment. 'I wasn't joking, Rupert, I do want a story, so let's consider the facts. Okay?' She glanced quickly around, from Myers' blank expression to Tarrou's intent watchful stare. She returned to Blair, who had not moved.

'Tomorrow we can go ashore, and the boys can have a search along this end of the bay. They might find something.'

Myers' mouth opened and shut. 'What, fer instance?'

'Pieces of the boats, perhaps, or some old equipment.'

'What, after twenty years?' Fraser's voice was scornful.

She was unmoved. 'Any better ideas, master-mind? I thought not!'

Blair began to pace again, and Gillian relaxed slightly in her chair. It was as if her voice had started him working once more.

He frowned, his mind busy. 'And if we find nothing?'

She smiled. 'That Hogan character. He trades with the natives. He could take us to meet one of the headmen. They would probably be able to help. Vic has already told us that nobody ever comes to this island. Even the District Officer only gives a cursory glance when he passes in his patrol boat.' She shrugged. 'So what the hell? Seems to me that twenty years or twenty days, it doesn't make very much difference out here!'

Blair bit his lip with excitement. 'How long would it take

to get to Hogan's trade store overland?' He snapped his fingers with impatience, as Fraser rasped his palm across his chin.

''Bout a day an' a half.' He grinned widely. 'She's quite a girl, eh, Major? Got us all stirred up again!'

'We needed ideas.' He studied her face with care, as if he was afraid he might miss something.

'We'll start early tomorrow,' he added more briskly. 'Fraser, you'll come with me, and you, Myers, can stay with the ship.' He allowed his eye to fall on Tarrou. 'I suppose he can handle the vessel if need be?'

Gillian glanced quickly across at Tarrou's grave face. ''Course he can,' she laughed, 'and if a storm blows up he can save all of us!'

Blair eyed Fraser. 'What d'you think about it?'

The Australian groaned. 'Hell, Major! When you move you sure move fast. But we're not supposed to bother the natives, you know.'

'We have a perfect right to visit the trade post, *and* the mission if necessary. I don't intend to allow any stupid red tape to stop me now!'

Fraser spread his hands on the table. 'Suit yourself,' he said shortly. 'It's your money, an' I'll come with you tomorrow. Michel can stay on the ship; he's done it heaps of times.' He shot the half-caste a searching glance. 'If a Willy-Willy arrives while I'm away, he can stand out to sea.' He smiled lazily, but his eyes remained hard. 'Can you find the break in the reef, Michel? In an emergency, I mean?'

Tarrou pulled down the edge of his tunic, and lifted his chin with pride. 'Yes, Vic. You have shown me the place. I can do it!' His voice was unnaturally loud, and he was aware that they were all looking at him. In his mind's eye he saw the schooner breasting the reef in a flurry of immense breakers, with himself at the wheel, and the girl clinging to his waist, her bare arms imploring him to save her. He felt the stirring sensation in his loins again, and dropped his eyes hastily. He had to stifle his excitement when he heard Blair's cold voice say: 'I'm afraid you won't be able to come along, Gillian. I don't think I would feel very happy to take the responsibility—' He faltered, waiting for her protest, but she shrugged, and smoothed the front of her blouse.

'As you say, Rupert.' She used his name with casual ease. 'I'll stay and keep an eye on the beach party.'

As Blair went over the details with Fraser she watched them from behind the cigarette smoke. She liked the way Blair's mouth curved when he smiled. She chuckled to herself. It was a pity she couldn't confide her plan with him, but he would immediately make some obstacle and close up on her. No, it was better this way. Once he was away looking for Hogan she could make a few investigations of her own. In her mind she turned over all the possibilities. There was still something of great importance which she felt had slipped her notice. She had racked her brains, but whatever it was it still eluded her. The one certain factor which she arrived at over and over again was the missionary Ivor Spencer's part in the puzzle. She was convinced that in him she would find the key.

The watch on deck padded across the foredeck, his bare feet making no sound as he checked the cable and scanned the black water. He twisted his head to listen as Fraser's laugh echoed along the deck.

'I dunno what old Jim Hogan'll say when we burst in on him. Probably tell us to go to hell!'

The girl stood up and stretched her arms above her head. 'I'm for bed.' She yawned elaborately. 'I have a feeling that tomorrow is going to be hard on all you little men!'

The four men watched her body as she stepped over the coaming and began to descend to her cabin. As her face was level with the deck, Blair stepped quickly forward. He smiled. 'And thanks for getting us sorted out. You were a great help.' He held her eyes.

'It was nothing, Rupert! You just needed organizing a bit!'

As she closed her cabin door she leaned her back against it and closed her eyes. Her body felt suddenly cold and clammy, and she was trembling. Watch it, my girl. Don't make a fool of yourself again.

Her mouth drooped, and wearily she began to undress. She suddenly hated her cameras, and the worn luggage which was scattered across the cabin floor. She stared at her reflection in the mirror and tried to see herself as Blair would see her.

She swore, and stuck out her tongue. 'Where the hell have you been all this time, Gillian Bligh?' she said with despair.

As the first dinghy grounded, bows on to the beach, Fraser vaulted lightly over the gunwale, and with Wabu on the opposite side guided the sturdy little boat clear of the breakers until its keel gripped the white sand, so that when the water receded it lay like a small abandoned fish. He helped Gillian to step ashore, and then shaded his eyes to peer quickly up the steeply sloping beach to the encroaching green wall of the jungle. Myers heaved himself over the gunwale, and paused to look across the inviting water at the motionless schooner. It was barely seven in the morning, yet already he was beginning to sweat, and the prospect of poking about along the edge of the beach did not improve his temper. He watched the other dinghy dipping and swooping towards the beach, Yalla, his dark head turned to judge the distance and gauge the moment to rest on his oars, grinned obligingly as Gillian ran up the beach, her camera trained on the approaching boat. Blair waited for the keel to grind on the sand, and then he limped across to join Fraser and Myers.

'Damned quiet, isn't it?' he said, after a quick look round. 'No wonder they call this a "bad place".'

'Yeh. Not a damned footprint or anythin'!' Fraser squinted again at the green wall.

'Hold it, you explorers!' They looked up to where Gillian's slim shape was outlined against an overhanging thicket of sea-grapes. She swung the camera expertly to include the whole group, with the schooner in the background, and then turned to face the trees. It was rather disturbing, she thought. No noise, no movement, but for the nodding of the palm leaves as they shivered in a breeze which she could not feel. It was as if the island was holding its breath. With a quick glance at the others she stepped carefully over the tangled thicket nearest her, and stood quite still. She was immediately aware of the complete change which her movement had made. She was in another world, and as she peered through the mass of fallen palms, cactus and manchineels, she realized how far away her own world had become. She watched Blair pointing up the beach with a piece of smooth driftwood, and saw Wabu and Yalla scamper off to begin a search at the far end of the bay, while Watute and the scarred seaman, Kari, began to work along the opposite way. She smiled as Blair waved his stick impatiently and shouted something to the boys. The moment he had stepped ashore he had automatically taken command of the operation, and even the unruffled Fraser looked clumsy and humble by comparison. She noticed, too, that Fraser had a rifle slung loosely over his shoulder, and Blair carried another.

She turned her back on the sea, and contemplated the tangled mass of the jungle which confronted her. After the first few yards the overlapping branches and fronds overhead reduced the visibility to nothing, and from the dark, humid shadows she caught the thick sickly smell of rotting vegetation. It was a frightening place, she decided, and quite unlike anything she had experienced. It lacked the grandeur of Africa, or the blazing vastness of the Australian bush. It was somehow evil, and at the same time she had the very real impression that she was being watched from several directions at once. With sudden anxiety which she could not explain, she stepped over the thicket and stood again on the beach, conscious of the growing warmth and the sudden pounding of her heart.

Blair walked stiffly towards her. The gold case snapped open, and for a while they smoked in silence.

Fraser and Myers were working along the edge of the jungle, scrambling and cursing over the fallen palms, as they peered and poked into every available space. Farther away, their bodies shining like oiled wood, Wabu and Yalla disappeared, their machetes swinging lustily, only to reappear in another place and signal to the watchful Fraser that they had found nothing.

Blair ground his cigarette underfoot and shifted the rifle-sling on his shoulder. 'I suppose you think I'm wasting everybody's time? I'm beginning to think so myself.' He sounded weary.

Gillian shook her head. 'Keep clam, Rupert. Something may turn up.' She studied the firm line of his chin and the restless blue eyes. 'After all, we're not exactly equipped for this sort of thing, are we?'

He smiled thinly. 'No. I was offered the use of a company salvage tug, and God knows what else, but I thought that this way would be better.' He groped for words. 'More private, if you understand?'

'I think so.' She thought, You're a funny guy, Major. Full of surprises today.

'Anyway,' he fiddled with the rifle-sling, as if trying to come to a decision, 'I'm not sorry it's turned out like this. It's given me time to think about things, and about the way I've frittered away my life.' He broke off anxiously, and peered at her dark glasses. 'I hope that didn't sound too pompous?'

She showed her teeth in a wide grin. 'Not *too* pompous, Rupert.'

'Out here one can get a better sense of perspective. It's like looking at life from the outside.'

She nodded, remembering the feeling of isolation as she had watched from the jungle's screen.

Blair continued, his voice calmer: 'This is something I just had to do. Had I been older when I lost my family it might have been different. Or had I been somewhere else when they disappeared from life.' He shook his head. 'I just don't know. What I do know is that I have always had the strangest feeling that I was wanted in some way, even before I knew where the wreck had taken place. Does that sound odd to you?'

'I don't think so. But I hope you feel better when it's all over.'

Impulsively he gripped her wrist. 'I shall. The real reason I'm glad about all this is that I met you, Gillian.' His voice faltered, and she felt the grip on her wrist slacken.

She stood quite still. She knew that Blair would say that, and yet at the same time she had been sure he would not. As he stood so open and strangely defenceless facing her, she wanted to pull him close, and by so doing exclude the past, as well as the future.

Instead, she laid her hand on top of his and said in a small voice, 'Thanks, Rupert.'

He laughed. 'I thought you'd walk away from me when I said that!' He opened his case again. 'I'm just bloody useless when it comes to this sort of thing.'

She massaged the back of his hand, and was conscious of the feeling of weakness, and then of power, which moved hungrily through her body.

A shout echoed along the beach. Yalla waved the machete like a sword. 'Here fella land 'em boat!'

Blair and Gillian stared at each other for one long full moment, and then he grinned nervously. 'Well, we'd better go and see, eh?'

She ran her tongue along the edge of her lip. 'I guess so.'

They still did not move, and Fraser shambled up the slope towards them, his face contorted against the sun. 'Here, folks! Did you hear that? Yalla's found a wrecked boat!' His brown eyes wandered from their faces to the girl's hand on Blair's wrist. 'Or don't you care at the moment?'

They walked past him without answering, and he paused before following them along the beach.

'Well, can you beat that?' he muttered. 'He tears the arse out of all of us to get a flamin' move on, then calm as you please starts behavin' like a bloke on a summer cruise!' He scratched his head absently, and then with a glance towards his ship hurried after the others.

Blair stood in silence as the two divers slashed away the creeper and cactus with their machetes, whilst Watute, using his hands like spades, clawed away the rotting leaves and purple fungus which filled the tiny cleft in the jungle like a hideous carpet. Apart from the iron keel and a few rotting timbers, there was little to show for their efforts. But as the blades cleared away the foliage, Blair could see that the remains of the boat could be nothing else but those of one of the *Sigli's* lifeboats. He pushed his way through the creepers, regardless of their clawing embraces around his legs, and stared at the wreckage. A rusting ballast tank, the head of a boat-hook and two steel helmets completed the finds, the rest having been eaten, buried, or rotted by the power of nature.

He looked across the boys' stooped backs, and stared hard at the mocking face of the jungle. It was strange, after all these years, he thought, that he still felt at home in its green menace. His hand moved across the polished wood of the rifle-butt, and for a brief moment he could hear the rattle of automatic weapons, the stealthy fumblings of friend and enemy alike, and above all, the maniacal cries of the hidden Japs: 'Come out, Tommy! Surrender, Tommy! We give you safe treatment!' The flat, bland expressions of the Burmese villagers who had betrayed him, and even the smell of the village, seemed to come back to him.

Fraser turned over a plank with his foot. 'That's it all right.' He studied Blair moodily. 'What next?'

Blair still stared into the shadows. 'We'll get Hogan.'

The girl looked up from between the two divers, her eyes searching, but Blair did not notice. 'We'll start at once. Tell the boys to get our gear from the boat.'

Fraser opened his mouth, and thought better of it. He shrugged. 'Right. We'll get Jim, an' we should be back here the day after tomorrow at the latest. We're bound to be able to get hold of one of the village headmen.' As he walked away he added: 'Then we can get under way again. This goddamned place gives me the gip!'

Watute gingerly picked up one of the helmets and put it on his frizzy head. Yalla laughed, and sliced the top off a fat cactus.

'What is it, Rupert?' Gillian's voice was apprehensive.

Perhaps Blair had changed back again, and had forgotten his words to her earlier.

Blair took a deep breath, and met her eyes with a sad smile. 'Sorry. Just remembering a few things.'

His eye fell on Watute, and the boy held up the helmet like an offering. Blair took it, and turned its rusted and dented shape in his hands. 'One of my men,' he said, half to himself. 'What a place to die!'

They walked away from the clearing, and stood side by side on the sand.

Her eyes behind the glass were anxious. 'Look after yourself, won't you?'

He studied her face intently. 'It's just that I want you to know,' he began, but she raised her hand.

'I understand,' she said.

Fraser walked slowly up the beach, his face resigned. 'Come on then, Major. Let's get goin'. I never like to be away from the *Pearl* too long.' He stared along the graceful sweep of the deserted bay. 'We'll branch off and take the way over that line of hills. It's quicker, and we shall be able to dodge most of the forest. Suit you?'

Blair gave a forced smile. 'Let's go. I think we're near the end of the search.'

Fraser took another look at the moored schooner. 'Yeh. I hope so.'

Blair slipped his arm through the strap of a small pack and lit a cigarette. 'Keep an eye on things, Myers. Stay in the ship, or close to it at least.'

'Don't worry, sir. I'm not keen on this dump!'

'And we'll have another talk when I get back, Gillian.' He faltered, aware that they were all watching him. 'I'm not too good at speaking my thoughts, but I hope you understand?' he ended lamely.

'Sure. Now get going before I change my mind and

come with you.' She smiled, but her eyes were misty.

She stood in Myers' shadow and watched the two lines of footprints in the sand lengthen between her and the backs of the two men. Once, when they had reached the rising slope of bare rocky ground, which jutted into the jungle and reached practically down to the sea, they both halted and looked back. Blair waved to her, but Fraser's face was grim, and he looked only at the ship. Then they turned inland, up the slope, and vanished.

She made the pretence of adjusting the camera, hoping that they would reappear, and Myers mopped his face uncomfortably.

'Let's get back then, miss. I reckon it'll be a bit cooler on board.'

Her hand shook as she put a cigarette in her mouth, and groped for her lighter. Myers waited, his face impassive. 'Lost it, miss?'

She nodded. 'Hold on a second, I'll see if I dropped it.'

She stumbled up the slope to where she had intruded on the jungle. She scanned the beach, but her mind was elsewhere. You damned little fool, she reflected, what are you trying to do? Do you think he'll give a cuss about you when he's back in the world of money and big business? You'll just be a nice little incident to be talked about with the boys. She stopped, hating her thoughts, and herself. The lighter lay half buried in the sand, and she stooped to pick it up.

Her mouth was suddenly dry and bitter with nausea, and she froze in the same stooped position, her eyes wide with terror. Behind the jagged edges of a fallen palm she saw the distinct shape of a dark shoulder, and a hand curled around what might have been a spear.

Her fingers trembled on the lighter, and with a sob she forced herself to pocket it and step backwards into the harsh

101

sunlight. Hardly breathing, she walked down to the dinghy.

Myers waved his hand, and first one then the other dinghy shoved off from the beach, and only then did she feel the uncontrollable shaking in her limbs.

Myers squinted at her anxiously. 'Feelin' a bit under the weather?'

She turned towards him, her face pale beneath the tan, and laid a hand on his arm. Lowering her voice she said in a flat tone, 'There was a man watching me, George!' She shuddered. 'I could have touched him.'

Myers shifted uncomfortably on the thwart, and glanced back at the unruffled shore. 'You sure, miss?'

Her fingers dug into his sleeve. 'I take back what I said about this place. It *is* evil! I wish to God I hadn't chided Vic about it!' Her face seemed to collapse, and she took off her glasses to peer across the widening strip of water at the bald, rocky slope. To herself she added: 'Please, Rupert, take care!'

Myers watched the tall black masts of the schooner, and sighed. She had probably imagined it, but he, for one, would not take any chances. He saw Tarrou's enquiring face peering down from the high bows, and cursed inwardly. Bloody Wogs, he thought, angrily, everywhere you go!

Gillian hardly noticed Tarrou's strange expression, and walked quickly to the canopy on the poop.

She shaded her eyes to study the rising green slab of the headland, and tried to think about Spencer and the mission. Tomorrow I must go over there, she decided. She lay back in the deck-chair and closed her eyes. Getting past it. Where's the calm and collected journalist who laughed at superstition and danger? She sighed. Had there ever been such a person? she wondered.

102

6

Jim Hogan stood uncertainly in the middle of the store and stared with unseeing eyes at the piles of shoddy cloth. Automatically he reached up and touched the unlined corrugated iron roof with a spatulate finger and winced. The metal was like the top of a stove, and although his action was pure habit he never failed to be impressed by the power of the sun, and the discomfort which went with it. Normally, he would at this time of the afternoon sit just inside the double doors which separated the store from his living-room, so as to gain the maximum advantage from any stray breeze which might choose to fan up from the beach, and then he would ponder over his unlikely future in distant Australia, or perhaps just ruminate on the past. Occasionally one or two of the villagers would loiter at the foot of the veranda and stare fixedly at some of his wares, or perhaps one of the elders or headmen might step suspiciously into the shade of the store itself to wrangle over a small deal. Today it was different, and he darted a glance back at the littered table and at the green bottle of Gordon's Gin which stood half empty by his glass. He moved slowly round the untidy room, touching the familiar articles, and trying to analyse his uneasiness. Perhaps it was the quiet, or maybe the fact that the glass had started to fall, and he had always worried about the very real possibility of a Willy-Willy blowing up and sweeping his ramshackle pier into the sea. That would mean a lot of extra work, and just lately the local headmen had been getting more cunning and avaricious about payments for jobs of that nature. It might mean a nasty cut in his profit, and thereby put back his possible date of retirement.

He looked again at the bottle, as if he half expected it to have vanished. With a deep sigh he shambled across to the padded chair and dropped his bulk on its protesting springs. He filled the glass, and sadly examined the level of the gin remaining in the bottle.

Although only in his late forties, Hogan was an old man, and at last even he was beginning to realize he was losing his taste for this, the only life he knew. For twenty-five years of his life he had traded around the islands, not very efficiently, because when he had started that type of mind was not required. There was plenty for everyone with guts enough to go out and get it. The war had changed all that, and instead of prosperity, he had watched competition from the richer traders – who never left their distant offices – smash down one small man after another.

He gulped down the neat spirit and belched, as he glared apprehensively around his room. 'Twenty-five years for all this!' He spoke aloud, another habit born of loneliness.

He stared at the bare and flaking wall, and the cracked wash-basin in the corner. The smell of the old planks and beams, of rot and termites, all were as familiar to him as the out-of-date calendar with its seductive girl posed on its stained cover. He licked his lips, and thought again about the American girl, Gillian Bligh. Some sheila. Better than all the little black bitches, he reflected savagely. It had been different when he had managed to keep a few lubras round him. Sleek little girls of around sixteen, they had made all the difference to this damned place. But the Yank, he felt shakily for the bottle, she was something else. And what was all this cock-and-bull yarn about looking for the wreck of the *Sigli*? He watched the empty bottle, trying to make up his mind. It might be another month before the schooner called again, but what the hell, a binge would soon put him right. He unlocked the black metal box, and stared lovingly at the neat ranks of gin bottles. He selected one, and relocked the chest. He started to hum to himself, his big red face set in concentration, as he ripped off the metal foil and reached for the glass.

That bloke Blair, too, was a bit queer, he decided. Vic Fraser had often told him about the stuck-up Pommie bastards he had met during the war, and Blair might well be one of them. He fell back into the chair and pulled open his stained shirt, to feel the sweat beading the thick folds of flesh.

Have to get the boys to rig me up a shower. He grinned foolishly at the thought which he had had on and off for twenty-five years. Too late now, Jim, he supposed, and then hurriedly poured another gin, as if to stem the tide of self-pity which seemed dangerously near today.

His red-rimmed eye fell on the dusty gramophone. It had been given to him by a Japanese pearling skipper before the war, in exchange for a pert little lubra from the village. He sighed again. Those were the days. Might as well have a bit of music to cheer myself up. He banged his fist on the rickety table, closing his eyes with the effort of shouting.

''Ere, boy! Chop, chop, an' fix the flamin' music box!'

He sighed, and lay back waiting. Since the collapse of his radio set during a particularly boisterous orgy, he had depended on the gramophone for that one essential link which all of his kind needed, if they were to preserve their sanity.

Wonder how Vic's getting on with the mad missionary? he pondered. His body shook to a silent laugh. 'I'd like to see 'is face when that lot burst in on 'im!'

105

He frowned, and craned his head to listen. Nothing stirred, and the frown deepened into a scowl. 'Bloody Abos, got their flamin' 'eads down again!' He struggled to his feet, and wandered out on to the veranda, being careful not to show his head to the sun which hovered directly above the little bay.

He gripped the rail, and peered blankly towards the huts of the village, and at his own outbuildings. ''Ere, boy!' he roared. 'Where the bloody hell are you?'

Some small birds took fright at his voice and scattered amongst the trees. Otherwise nothing had changed. He waited, his mouth hanging open. What the devil was happening? he wondered. There was a soft step behind him, and he spun round to face the wrinkled little Chinese woman who, since her original function had been replaced by a tropic-aged apathy, had become his cook and guardian.

He peered at her lined face. 'Where is everybody?' He shook his glass querulously. 'What the 'ell's goin' on I want to know?'

She pattered to his side, her features expressionless. 'Gone,' she said softly. 'All gone, 'cept Jo-Jo.'

Hogan blinked with disbelief. Jo-Jo was a young, half-witted native who could be trusted not to steal and worked around the sheds doing odd jobs. He had to be honest with Hogan, for his own people would have turned him out. They had little time for the mentally afflicted.

'What d'you mean, gone?'

She studied him quietly. 'Gone to bush. Run away. I have come from village.' She gestured briefly. 'The cooking-fires are cold.'

The silence bore in on them like a storm, and Hogan stepped quickly back into the room, his drink-reddened face showing his sudden uneasiness. He shook his head to clear his brain, but the woman's words seemed to

106

mesmerize him. 'All gone,' he muttered. 'It looks bad, bloody bad!'

He dropped his glass unheeded on the floor, and strode to the wall where his two huge shotguns stood propped and gleaming in their covering of oil. He snapped open the breech of one, aware that she was still watching his back.

Pulling open the drawer of the old desk, he tore open a packet of red cartridges and slipped two into the breech. He repeated the process with the other, before he trusted himself to speak again.

'Get Jo-Jo. Tell 'im to climb up on to the water-tank an' keep 'is eyes peeled!' He peered across the pathetic strips of barbed wire, and swung the muzzle of the gun towards the jungle. He realized that he was desperately afraid of this silence. 'After you've told 'im that, get down to the cutter an' check the provisions.'

'We are leaving?' There was not a tremor in her lisping voice.

He faced her with sudden affection, remembering her as she had once been when a schooner had dropped her on the island. A tiny, slant-eyed girl in a tattered cheong-sam. He stared at the wizened little creature who was watching him so meekly, and forced a grin.

'Yeh, gettin' out. Soon as I'm sure that we're doin' the right thing, we're goin' to shove off. Fer good!'

He watched her go, and then squatted down on the edge of his tin trunk and stared fixedly at the jungle.

There had been trouble before, but this was quite different, he pondered. It would be impossible to estimate what life in the islands might have been if the authorities had acted earlier and introduced more 'whites' into the trade stores and the lonely outposts. Nobody had shown much interest in this island, partly because of the hostile natives, and partly because of the lack of decent

107

anchorages. The reef ruined the southern approaches, and steep cliffs deterred even the most reckless skipper from nosing near the other shores. His store, in Resolution Bay, was all there was to show for the uneasy years of a joint Anglo-French government, lack of funds and a general disinterest all round. He belched angrily, and dashed the sweat out of his watering eyes.

He still couldn't bring himself to believe that tomorrow would be any different from any other day. There had been scares before, and there had been a few minor skirmishes in the jungle. He had often heard the elders cackling about the cannibal feasts and terrible initiation ceremonies that went on within the secrecy of those green walls, but by and large he had managed to remain aloof from the warring tribes, and, at best, had been able to do business with both sides.

He heard the sullen boom of surf on the steep beach, and tried to gauge its strength. It usually told him better than the glass what the weather was going to do. He shivered as a humid gust of air moved restlessly around the room and scattered some papers from the open desk. Seconds later he saw the breeze disturb the fronds on the edge of the clearing and make them glisten like live things.

He heard the patter of the woman's feet behind him, and saw her place his huge mug of coffee at his side.

He tried to see into her thoughts. 'Well?'

'All quiet,' she answered.

He sipped noisily, and peered over the edge of the mug towards the trees. 'Keep yer eye over there. I'm goin' to take a look around.'

He picked up one of the guns and stuffed some cartridges into his trouser pockets.

His pace quickened, and with it his uneasiness. He had never really believed such an emergency would ever occur, and now, without the attendant noises and comforting movements of the villagers, he was beginning to realize just how dangerous the position had become. Doors had been left open, and the loose-frame structure of the building, with its wide windows and flimsy defences, seemed to mock him at every turn. He thought of the approaching night, and shivered. He must make a decision, and pretty quick, he thought anxiously. But suppose the villagers came creeping back? He stopped in his tracks and frowned. All his stores would be there for the taking, and he could well imagine what would happen. He stepped out on to the dry earth behind the store and squinted up at the water tank, which was supported by the main beams of the roof.

Jo-Jo peered down at him and shrugged vaguely. He was a handsome specimen, but for the looseness of his mouth, which drooped open in a permanent grin.

'No fella come, boss!' he called.

Hogan grunted. 'Maybe. But bang on the roof if you see anythin'!'

As if in answer there was a sudden dull booming from the direction of the jungle. It started with a series of thuds, disjointed, and then slowly speeded up into a quick, insistent tempo of sound.

Hogan ground his teeth, and swung his glances from one end of the clearing to the other. Log-drums. He had heard them before, but never so close, and never before with such savage intensity. He suddenly felt exposed and helpless and, with a quick nod to Jo-Jo, almost ran back to the veranda.

All the afternoon the drums spoke and answered, questioned and threatened. And all the time Hogan sat waiting, the gun on his knees. He watched the sun move like a fiery ball across the sky and seem to touch the tips of the trees, and in its wake the shadows grew longer, so that it appeared as if the trees themselves were reaching out across the clearing, with great claws.

He had stared so hard, and for so long, that his eyes played him tricks. In the past he had been content to run his store and only take sufficient interest in the outside world as was required to pursue his living, and this sudden strain was beginning to tell on his fevered mind.

His head lolled, and he braced himself angrily, shaking his head like an old dog. For an instant he could not find his breath, and he gripped the shotgun until his knuckles shone white in his red hands.

Along the edge of the clearing stood a long line of silent brown figures. At that very moment the drums ceased.

Hogan's mouth moved silently, and he heard Jo-Jo's foot beating frantically on the iron roof.

Half to himself he muttered: 'So there you are! Christ, it must be the whole of the Motă.' He tried to count the silent figures, but his wretched mind rebelled, and he could only stare and strain his eyes, as the sun glinted on a spear, or hovered on a painted face.

She was at his side again, and he could sense her frail body trembling. 'What the hell are they waitin' for?' he said from between clenched teeth.

The minutes dragged by, and Hogan moved carefully off his box and crawled laboriously on his knees across the room, so that he could cover the whole of the clearing. Without turning he said fiercely, 'Get all that ammo from the desk, an' drag it over 'ere!'

The breeze grew stronger, and its hot breath moved insistently through the store, and chilled the sweat on his shirt and bent legs. His nostrils twitched, and for a second his eyes left the clearing. 'Smoke? Is that smoke?'

He listened with despairing impatience as she ran from the room, and tried to concentrate on the motionless figures.

Were they really still? Had the one by the old sawmill moved slightly? He licked his parched lips and moved the gun slightly.

She ran back to his side, her eyes looking past him.

'Well? What is it?'

She began to sob uncontrollably, something that she had never done before. 'The boat! It is on fire!'

Hogan jerked to his feet, his eyes popping. 'The bastards!' His voice trembled. 'They knew I'd be watchin' 'em! Somebody sneaked round the beach and fired the boat while I was bein' a bloody fool an' . . . an' . . .' He choked, and stared round the room, filled with a rising and consuming fury. ''Ere, watch the window!' He ran to the back of the store, and looked stonily at the black pall of smoke which poured from the listing cutter. The breeze gathered up the smoke and pushed it towards the watchers on the edge of the clearing. As it passed over their heads they seemed to melt into the bush and vanish.

Jo-Jo called down this information to Hogan, but he did not even look back. He knew that the attack would come later. It was now inevitable. His eye flickered to the end of the beach, and he saw a figure rise dripping from the surf and run naked for the cover of the bush. He blinked, and then, with a bellow, ran out into the clearing. The thundering reports of the shotgun echoed and rolled around the bay, and he staggered to a halt, his shoulder aching from the double recoil. The brown figure skidded in the sand, recovered, and staggered into the trees.

Hogan fumbled with the cartridges, and backed into the store. 'Come on down, Jo-Jo. You won't do any more good up there.'

He dragged his feet across the littered floor, and squatted on the box, his face sagging. The cutter had always been

111

there. It was his escape route, and now, like a fool, he had bungled even that.

He drew his fat knees up to his chin, and began to sob noisily. She crept to his side, and he felt her worn hands stroking his neck. Jo-Jo stared from one to the other, and then with a vague grin began to crank the gramophone.

The sun crept guiltily away, and as the pale stars began to glitter, and the strengthening breeze beat the surf into a savage frenzy around the charred cutter, the strains of the 'Anniversary Waltz' floated across the empty clearing.

When the attack came, it was like a great wave of sound. A long-drawn-out scream echoed along the bay, and in that instant Hogan heard the slap of feet across the packed earth of the yard. He still could not see anything, but, panting like an exhausted runner, he fired both barrels across the veranda, and then ran with the other gun to the far window and fired again, while the woman reloaded with quick, deft movements.

A spear thudded into the floor, and he heard the swish and moan of short arrows as they flitted through the side windows. Jo-Jo screamed and fell back on the floor, his throat transfixed with a thin black dart, his eyes rolling whitely as he tried to tear it free.

A naked leg swung over the veranda, heedless of the barbed wire, and Hogan's terrified eyes saw the thin bangled arm and the crude axe swinging towards him. The gun roared again, and the man's face seemed to blossom into a great scarlet flower. He heard another scream, and turned to see the woman pinioned by a writhing brown body, whilst on the other side of the living-room he saw a shadowy figure sliding rapidly along the wall.

God, God, they're inside! They're all round me! Hogan sobbed frantically, and fired at the shape by the wall. It curtsied towards him, and he saw the bared teeth, like those

112

of an animal, and the hideous paint mingling with the blood on his chest.

Hogan drove the butt of his rifle into the other savage's head, but when the body rolled aside the woman did not rise to join him. Her black eyes stared up at him with sorrow and reproach, as her blood seeped across the old calendar, which had been torn from the wall.

Hogan swung from her, the gun ready to fire again, its barrels hot under his grip. He was again alone, but for the bodies which cast unreal shadows in the fading light.

Hogan staggered against the doorpost, his head reeling. 'Come on then, you bastards!' His voice cracked into a whimper of defiance. 'Come an' finish me off!'

He swung the gun, and moved out on to the veranda. One of the shapes by the steps moved slightly, and groaned. With savage dedication Hogan ground the butt down on to the clay-decorated head until all movement ceased. He could feel warm blood running down his arm, but he hardly noticed it. He lifted his head and listened, like a hound catching a scent. There it was again. A shot. Not far off either.

Muttering and growling to himself, he ran back to the room and, heedless of the sickly smell of death, he unlocked the chest, and with his teeth tore open a bottle and threw back his head. The gin flooded his throat so that he vomited, and leaned weakly on the edge of the box. I'm alive, he thought vaguely, and felt his limbs quivering uncontrollably, so that the gun shook in his hand. A footstep grated on the clearing, and he moved crabwise to the window, his eyes like small slits.

The two pale figures moved cautiously towards him, and Hogan could only kneel and stare.

He heard Fraser call out, his voice harsh, even desperate. 'You about, Jim?'

113

Hogan still knelt, but he managed to wave his gun in a feeble gesture. He still couldn't speak, as the two men ran across to his side. He was grateful just to be allowed time to think.

Fraser finished tying the rough bandage on Hogan's thick arm, and sat back on his haunches, breathing heavily. 'That felt better?'

He saw Hogan's shoulders move in what might have been assent, or even vacant disinterest. He was merely a grey, shapeless blob outlined against the dark oblong of the veranda, and now that Fraser's eyes were becoming better accustomed to the darkness he could see well enough what had changed Hogan so cruelly. He swallowed hard, and tried not to notice the sweet sickly smell which pervaded the store, and the two white eyeballs which stared up from the corner of the disordered room. He could hear Blair moving restlessly about the other room, and the impatient boom of distant surf.

His heart was still pounding like a drum, but slowly he was beginning to gather his scattered thoughts, and tried to fathom out what was happening. A sharp bang echoed hollowly through the store, and Hogan groaned.

'Jo-Jo?' His voice was a mere croak. 'Was that Jo-Jo?' Then, as the awful memory flooded back, he struggled painfully to his feet and peered down at Fraser. 'I was forgettin',' he added abstractedly.

The bang came again, and Fraser reached out to grip the other man's wrist. 'What is it?'

'The roof.' He pointed vaguely. 'The wind's gettin' up.'

Fraser bared his teeth, as if he was tasting the air. 'That's *all* we need!' He swore savagely. 'And you say your boat's had it?'

The thick shoulders sagged even more. 'Yeh. Gone, like everythin' else.'

Fraser softened his voice. 'You've got some cash in the bank, haven't you?'

Hogan wandered across the room and stumbled over the twisted body by the wall. 'Cash? What good is that now?' He kicked suddenly at the body, and it stirred as if still alive. 'The bastards!'

'Look, Jim, I must talk.' Fraser's voice was urgent. 'We've not much time.'

'I know.'

'The weather's gettin' worse, Jim. We've got to get back to the ship. Now!'

In his mind's eye he saw the *Queensland Pearl* already rolling towards the reef. He closed his eyes with despair. He had been a madman to allow Blair to talk him into this. Tarrou would never be able to rise to any real crisis without him on board.

A strange cry echoed around the darkness, followed by silence, and Hogan grabbed up his shotgun. Fraser listened to him jamming the fat cartridges into the breech.

'Can you guide us back, Jim?' He tried to speak calmly, but the urgency of the situation made his voice harsh. 'We have to get away!'

Hogan wandered around the room, and Fraser's heart sank. The shock of all this had been too much for him, he thought. I'm stuck with two of them now, he reflected bitterly.

But after a while Hogan answered, his voice devoid of emotion. 'We can't go back over the ridge. Too many of 'em out there. We must follow the beach to the end of the bay, an' then start climbin' from there. It might work,' he ended wearily.

'Yes, that's it, Jim.' He dropped his voice. 'Listen,

115

cobber, I know things are bad, but they might be worse.' He peered at the shapeless figure before him. 'Right now we've got to think of ourselves, see?'

Hogan pondered. 'What about 'im?' He gestured to the other room.

Fraser swore obscenely. 'It's all his fault! Right now I could kill him with my bare hands!'

Hogan bent over the Chinese woman, and shuddered. He stood up again without touching her, and shook himself. 'Nah, they attacked before you come 'ere.' He shook the gun in his hands. 'What made 'em do it, Vic?'

Fraser watched as Blair's figure moved stealthily across the veranda. His fault, he repeated to himself. It was as if his presence on the island had sparked everything off at once. It was almost uncanny.

Blair stood over them. 'Is he all right now?'

Hogan sighed. 'Yeh. Let's get on with it.'

Fraser stood up and crossed the room, so that his body was almost against Blair's.

'An' this time, Major, let *me* handle things. Just don't start anything else, see?' His voice trembled with fury, but Blair seemed to be indifferent.

'Don't be a bigger fool than you can help, Fraser! Try to keep a sense of proportion!' He could feel Fraser's breath on his face.

'Don't you tempt me, Major! I'm a simple enough character perhaps, but there's somethin' about you that's all wrong!' His arm moved slightly. 'The boongs know it! We *all* know it!'

Hogan shifted his feet. 'Lay off, Vic. 'E's done nothin'!'

'An' he's not going to do any more either!' Fraser's voice was filled with menace.

Blair shrugged. 'Let's stop arguing. It's too late now,

116

anyway.' He picked up his rifle and walked to the rear door, apparently dismissing them from his mind.

The breeze dropped, and as its sigh died away there were in its place a series of short hard raps on the iron roof, and the dust on the darkened veranda was kicked up into little spurts, as the first of the rain began to fall. Then, in an instant, the downpour came in an ever-mounting roar, deafening, blinding, as if to cleanse the earth of its evil.

Fraser made up his mind. 'Now, Jim!' He shook his arm. 'Before the bastards creep up again!'

Hogan still hung back. His senses deadened by the storm, he stared round with sudden desperation at all that was left of his life. 'I can't leave 'er like that. I'll put a match to the place.'

Fraser's voice hardened. 'What good would that do? The flames would give us away and, in any case, the bloody rain'd put the fire out before it did any good! Leave her, man. She's past your help now.'

Blair spoke quietly, so that his voice was all but lost in the tropical downpour. 'Do as he says, Hogan. Can't you see he's got the wind up?'

Fraser stood quivering like a mad dog. What was Blair trying to do? It was almost as if he was trying to goad Fraser to keep his threat. 'I'm warning you . . .' he began, but Blair turned away.

Over his shoulder he said: 'Use your brains, if you've got any. There's more in this than just a local whim!'

Hogan blundered past them and walked heavily across the veranda. 'Come on, then.'

'Aren't you taking anything with you?' Fraser looked round quickly, furious with himself and with Hogan for making him sound so callous.

'I got me guns, and me wallet. What more could a joker want?' Without another glance he tugged on his old hat, and bowed his shoulders against the rain, which struck the flesh like iron pellets.

The hard earth, parched and split, was already puddled and unfamiliar beneath their feet, and Fraser hung back momentarily as the two figures preceded him down to the beach. The rain might last for hours, or it might not. Then the wind would come back. He glared fixedly at the thundering surf, and felt its taste in the rain. If the island was going mad, anything could happen. And if the schooner broke her moorings before he could get to her . . . He clamped his jaws tight and stared at Blair's back, his big hands closing over the rifle. I'll kill the bastard, that's for sure, he thought brokenly.

7

High on the schooner's mainmast a block clattered with sudden urgency, and the carelessly sheeted piece of a sail filled and flapped with a dull boom, as without warning the breeze spread out across the reef and explored the more sheltered region of the bay. The water, which up to then had been undulating and sighing gently around the schooner's high stem, lost its oily surface and was whipped into a series of steep, dancing catspaws. The vessel seemed to awake from her dream, and as she rolled heavily at her cable the torrid air moaned threateningly through the shrouds, to tease the wire stays and loose rigging alike.

Gillian stopped listening to the muffled insistence of the distant drums and stared round with sudden irritation at the deserted decks. Blair and Fraser had only been gone for about an hour, and the glare of the sun was only a promise of the heat which was to follow. Yet the sudden inactivity and sense of frustration which their departure had brought, as well as the heavy apathy of the bay, made her frown, and pace nervously from one side of the swinging poop to the other.

Dinkila, the fat Malay cook, his shapeless body half hidden by the coaming around the hold, looked up with interest from his efforts to scour a cooking-pot to watch the slim figure pacing the deck. He saw her wince as she stepped into the sun, and when she reached the safety of the billowing canopy her hair seemed to change colour, and she would run her fingers through it, as if to free herself from the clinging heat. Eventually, his land eyes tired, and the pot dropped in his lap. Soon his gentle snore floated upwards to join the noises of the spiralling masts.

Gillian threw her cigarette over the rail and plucked broodingly at her damp blouse. With narrowed eyes she stared across at the blue-tinted headland, where the haze hung like smoke, and the steep sides of the cliffs were still dark in shadow and not yet reached by the sun.

Why wait until tomorrow? she reflected. The dinghies bobbed and squeaked alongside, and she had already noted that the smaller of the two was rigged for sailing. The hot breeze played invitingly around her waist and moved across the bare skin beneath the loose blouse. She was suddenly tempted to strip off these ridiculous clothes and dive into the inviting water. She sighed, as after a brief search she found the ever-present triangle of dark fin, as it moved with infinite patience around the haltered ship.

A hatch banged open, and Watute clambered into view. He tossed some rubbish over the lee rail and stood looking at the green shore, his black eyes devoid of interest or understanding.

Gillian loosened the belt of her coral slacks, her mouth determined. 'Say, how far d'you reckon we are from the headland there?'

Watute followed her finger blankly, and then grinned. 'Long way.' He beamed unhelpfully.

She tried again. 'Can you sail that thing?'

He shifted his eyes from the headland to the dinghy. 'Sure thing, missy! Cap'n Fraser show me many times!'

She smiled. 'Good. That's settled, then. Can we sail to that place and back today?'

He gave it a great deal of thought, although Gillian had the impression that he was putting on an act for her benefit.

'We make good trip, missy,' he said with sudden gravity. 'We back 'fore night.'

She sighed with relief. 'Good. You can take me, then. I'll just get my camera.'

'I ask if we can go,' added Watute stubbornly. 'Captain say not go unless say so.'

She blew a loose hair from her eyes. 'For Pete's sake! Captain's not here, so what are we waiting for?'

He stood his ground. 'Must ask.'

She laughed to clear the annoyance from her mind. After all, he was doing his duty, she supposed. 'Okay, Watute! You get in the boat, I'll make all the arrangements.'

He flashed her a huge grin and scampered over the rail, his toes already reaching for the dinghy's gunwale. Now that the weight of his responsibility had been removed he was thinking only of proving his prowess to the gold-haired woman, who belonged neither to the Captain nor the rich Englishman with the sharp tongue.

Gillian climbed quickly into the semi-darkness of the cabin-flat, and noticed that Myers was sitting in a canvas chair, naked but for a grubby towel, his fat face set in grim concentration as he polished his diver's facepiece.

Gillian's glance took in the garish confusion of Tarrou's cabin, and settled on the coloured print of General de Gaulle over the bunks. Her heart softened, as it usually did when she was considering Tarrou. Perhaps Fraser was right. Tarrou had his dreams, and it seemed a pity to unsettle him.

'I'm just going out for a sail with the kid,' she said. 'I'll be back before nightfall, or so he says!'

Myers looked up with a jerk, and blushed crimson. He grabbed with frantic haste for his shirt, only half aware of what she was saying.

'Take it easy, buster! I'm just going!' Her warm laugh

floated along the passage, and Myers heard her light step overhead before he could recover from his embarrassment.

'Gawd, what a woman!' He stared at the empty doorway for some moments, a vacant smile slowly growing on his round face.

The dinghy had a bright red mainsail, and as Watute tugged impatiently at the sheets it flapped against the stubby mast, making a cheerful splash of colour, which clashed with the misty blue of the horizon.

Gillian settled herself comfortably in the boat, and pulled a floppy white sun-hat down over her neck. 'Right, Sindbad! Let her roll!'

He grinned and bobbed his frizzy head. He did not understand what she said half of the time, but from her tone he knew that she, too, was glad to be away from the dullness of the schooner.

He untied the painter, and shoved off from the white hull with his foot. He ducked beneath the swinging boom, and with his foot now on the tiller and his hands busy with the rebellious sail he sent the small boat skimming away from the rolling schooner and towards the headland.

Gillian laughed as the blunt bows bit into the first of the tiny wavelets, and she felt the kiss of spray across her mouth. Already the *Queensland Pearl* looked smaller, like that day she had sat with Grainger in the launch. This was more like it, she decided, and even if her visit to the mission on the headland proved to be a waste of time, and Ivor Spencer retained a stony silence, or called down the wrath of heaven upon her, the sea trip was doing her good. The boisterous and lively motion of the dinghy jerked away the weariness and fretting apathy she had felt, and when Tarrou's dark face appeared over the schooner's fo'c'sle she merely waved with gay abandon, and did not even try to hear what he was shouting. Already he seemed to be just like a strange onlooker, with neither features nor meaning.

She frowned at the thought. Suppose she was making a fool of herself where Blair was concerned? She turned her back on the ship, and adjusted her glasses. It was all in her mind, anyway, she thought, but there was still time for something to happen. She closed her mind and tried not to think about Blair as a person. It was so very difficult to get a clear picture of any sort of future, let alone one with such momentous implications that would entail Blair carelessly giving up his wife and suddenly seeing Gillian Bligh as the only way to happiness. The ridiculous suggestion did not have the result she had intended. Instead, she was conscious that the ache was still there, and somehow she knew just how desperately important it was to change her own way of life, before it was too late.

'They follow!' Watute pointed excitedly towards the sharks, which had left the schooner and followed respectfully behind the dinghy.

'Yeah. Well, they can wait a bit longer for their dinner!' She saw the simple pleasure on his small face. 'I hope you're a good sailor, Sindbad!'

He puffed out his skinny chest, and tapped the short knife which poked dangerously from his belt. 'You safe with me, missy!'

In an hour the schooner's outlines were hazy and uncertain, and in two she was only a tiny white blob against the green of the opposite end of the bay.

The island looked untouched and devoid of any life and, she imagined, just as the first intrepid seamen had found it. The white beaches, both wide and narrow, looked shaded and cool beneath the nodding palms, and the lush green of the silent jungle shone invitingly. Two more lies of nature, she thought.

She tried to recognize the beach where they had first met

Spencer, but against the dark-hued cliff every rock and tree looked different.

Watute showed no such uncertainty, however. With unerring ease he piloted the boat past one tall, isolated rock, which jutted from the clear water like an old tooth, its jagged edges alive with weed and tiny fish, and swung the tiller hard over, so that it skimmed into even clearer water, where the pale green sand moved up through the spray to meet them, and where the hiss and grumble of the surf echoed back from the cliffs, and made the land seem watchful and alive.

As before, a small knot of figures ran excitedly into the surf to catch the boat and guide it up the shallow beach. The keel grated, freed itself, and then came to rest as the water receded. There was a sudden silence, and Gillian stepped on to the glistening sand. Watute busied himself with the sail, his eyes watchful.

'You wait here, Watute. I'll go and see if the old guy's at home for visitors.'

A tiny woman, her skin criss-crossed with dark markings, grinned up at her and plucked uncertainly at Gillian's slacks. A murmur came from the others as a grim-faced man, his teeth bared with concentration, reached out to touch the camera case.

She looked round for a path from the beach, and saw Spencer. He was standing stockstill, his eyes fixed on the little group by the water's edge. He lifted his arm, but before he could call out Gillian walked briskly up the beach towards him.

'So you came back. I thought I made myself plain!' He was trembling with suppressed emotion, and the crowd fell silent around them.

He was even taller than she had remembered, and considerably older. His clothes were patched and badly

124

washed, and the ancient topee had been carefully mended in a dozen places. Nevertheless, or perhaps because of his poverty, he looked commanding, even noble. His eyes peered down the beak of a nose, and seemed to strip her as naked as the silent villagers.

'You dared to come alone? That was rather foolish.'

Gillian hardened her heart. It would be better otherwise, she considered, but under the circumstances a little toughness on her part was obviously necessary. It was not difficult. She had dealt with too many odd characters in her career to be abashed by his hostility.

'Thanks for the welcome. I'm Gillian Bligh, and I represent the *American Forecast*, as you may know already. I'd like to have a little yarn with you. Okay?' She lifted her eyebrows and waited. Sort that out, my friend, she thought.

His hooded eyes flickered, but otherwise his face revealed nothing.

'I can have you put back into that boat and sent to join your friends in the schooner.' He moved his thin hands expressively. 'Or I could tell these simple people that you are unwanted here! They would be less generous than I!' The eyes gleamed balefully.

Gillian removed her sun-hat and loosened her hair slowly with her free hand. The movement seemed to unnerve Spencer, and she answered calmly:

'Yeah, I guess you could do all those things at that. But I should point out that I have a permit from the British Resident Commissioner to visit this place, and I also enjoy the protection of the United States Government. Neither of those parties would welcome any such action on your part.' She pretended to study the back of her hand, but inwardly she was trembling with excitement. 'In fact, Mr. Spencer, I guess it might be you who gets thrown off the island, eh?'

His mouth was working in quick, nervous movements,

as if unwilling to comply with its owner's will. When he spoke, his voice trembled. 'What is it you want? Why can't you leave me in peace?'

She smiled coolly. The ice was thawing. Not much, but all the signs were there.

'That's more like it, my friend! Now let's be sensible about this. All I want is to have a little talk with you; look around maybe. I'm sorry I couldn't warn you of my visit, but I didn't have much choice, did I?'

'I knew you were coming.' It was a mere whisper.

'I'll leave my escort with the boat. Will that be okay?'

He turned to lead the way up the path, and shrugged angrily. 'These people are not savages! The boat will be quite safe!'

She waved to Watute and followed his stooped shoulders up the narrow sandy track. She saw a handful of crude canoes drawn up under the palms, and a few nets drying in the branches above. Farther up the path she could see the small roofs of a cluster of huts, and the smoke from cooking-fires. The whole of the settlement seemed to have slipped over the lip of the cliff, to hang scattered amongst the vegetation which lined its crest.

She talked easily, her eyes on his back.

'We shall be leaving the island soon now, and I just wanted to tie up a few loose ends. There are so many things I want to know about this place.' The head did not turn, and she hurried on: 'About the work you are doing, for instance. People don't realize that such places exist.'

His voice was muffled, almost preoccupied. 'That is our good fortune. All we want is to be left alone. Sympathy or hypocrisy, we can do without!'

They reached the top of the rise, and Gillian could feel the ground like hot iron through the thin soles of her sandals.

Spencer halted and stood hesitatingly by a bend in the path.

'What has that man Blair found? Is he satisfied?' He asked the questions in the same haughty, offhand manner, but she was well trained enough to sense the tension behind his deep eyes.

She held out her cigarettes, but he shook his head with impatience. She studied his face carefully from behind her glasses as she lit one for herself.

'He found the wreck.'

'That was what he came for, surely?'

A short, vicious-eyed pig bounded out of the bush and glared at them with surprise, then with a grunt ran back into cover. She could hear it crashing through the undergrowth towards the village.

She smiled warmly. 'Look,' she began again, 'let's go and have this chat. You can get rid of me then. But honestly, there's nothing to get steamed up about!'

He glared at her with suspicion. 'This way.'

He loped off along the path, and soon they confronted a small whitewashed bungalow, its corrugated iron roof glinting in the broiling light. It had one wide window, and a brass bell hung from a beautifully carved bracket by the open door.

He waited by the door. Round the sides of the building she could see the dark watching faces and, here and there, a tiny naked child would run excitedly into the open to stare at the visitor, and then rush back to the safety of its parents.

'I built this house some time ago.' He touched the flaking woodwork as if for the first time. 'It is all I need.' He swept off his old topee and waved towards the shadowed interior. 'Have a good look. I am sure your readers will be excited to hear how I live.'

She ignored the biting sarcasm and stepped thankfully

into the shade. The room was small, about twelve feet by ten, the planked floor covered by intricately woven rush mats, which only added to the air of isolation. There were several benches of finely carved wood, which she supposed to be sandalwood, and on one bare wall hung a brass crucifix.

She could feel his eyes following her as she walked slowly around the room. She stopped by a small portable organ in the far corner.

'D'you play this?'

'The people enjoy it.'

He sounded nervous, she decided.

'How long have you been in the islands?'

He seemed to wrench his mind back to deal with her question. It was almost as if he was expecting a trap.

'Forty years, or thereabouts.'

She stared at the tattered, well-used books, with their smell of mildew, all neatly arranged along one wall. She frowned. It was all too tidy. Something was wrong, but she still could not place it.

Another door opened into a short passage, and she could see a tiny kitchen and two more crudely partitioned rooms.

He followed her gaze. 'Well, sit down, Miss Bligh. I will get you some coffee.'

He clapped his hands and called something to the kitchen. She saw a short native woman in a shapeless white overall hurry along the passage, and heard the clatter of cups. Perhaps he was living with a native. Then she looked at those deep unwinking eyes and dismissed the idea. It could not be that, she decided.

'Tell me why you get on so well with these people,' she asked gently. 'I was told that they were rather . . . well, difficult.'

For a moment his guard dropped. 'I can imagine! They can never understand!'

He began to pace the floor, and she imagined that he often did just that.

'These men you are with. They know nothing! That lout Fraser is like all the rest of them. He has spent all his life here, yet he knows as little of the islands and their people as . . . as you do, and probably less!' He paused, as if gathering ammunition. 'He, too, has been out here all his life, yet has never thought of understanding the people he robs so efficiently!'

His eyes followed the small native woman as she carefully set the tray down on the chest by the window. She glanced at Gillian and grinned, showing the gap in her teeth.

Spencer's hard face softened, and he spoke to her with warmth. The woman nodded and returned to the kitchen.

The coffee was good, and Gillian remarked on this fact.

'My only weakness,' he commented shortly.

'Have you made much progress here?' She watched him across the rim of the cup.

'Progress? It depends what you mean by that. If you mean can they make souvenirs for tourists, or exchange copra for traders' trash, then the answer's no!' His eyes blazed, and he had to calm himself with visible effort. 'These people are simple, untouched. Can you understand that? Over the years I have taught them to trust me.' He was staring moodily through the window. 'To them I am a friend. It has taken a long time.'

'But surely eventually they will have to fall in with the other, more civilized, islands?'

'Never!' The word was wrung from his lips.

'The authorities assured me—' she began, but he waved her to silence.

'What do they know! My people owe them nothing. They have nothing to show for the white man's influence but poverty, disease and misery!'

129

She could sense the violent passion which had burned away his body over the years. He looked like a man possessed of a terrible driving force which would eventually kill him.

'Before the turn of this century, Miss Bligh, there were over a million people in the islands. Now there are less than forty-eight thousand!' His yellow teeth showed in a bitter smile. 'The advantages of your civilization saw to that. Hookworm, yaws, tinea, venereal disease,' he spat out the list with cruel relish. 'These people were not prepared for such an invasion. Not content with that, the clever traders robbed, and still rob them of their hard-won fruits, and give them rubbish in exchange.' He shook a bony finger in front of her face. 'Copra is sold at fifty pounds a ton in Port Vila. Go and see what the natives get for it in the first place!' He fell limply on to a bench, his sunken chest heaving.

'You seem to be well informed for one so isolated?'

'I hear many things. But I protect them here from it all.'

They sat in silence, his eyes morose on her face.

'Do the authorities know you feel like this?'

He shrugged. 'Why should they care? To them I am in the same category as Hogan.' That seemed to amuse him. 'Imagine that! Any foothold in this island is better than none. But they'll get a surprise one day.'

'How so?' She hardly dared to breathe in case the spell should be broken.

'They will find that I have beaten them. A pure community, living in peace and harmony, and needing no one. I can protect them from the outside influences which I know are bad. It is an advantage that their more accessible compatriots have not been able to afford.' He made an expressive motion with his long fingers, like a potter shaping something of great beauty. 'In this mad world – your world – they will pave the way as an example

130

to all Christian mankind!' The shutters suddenly fell in front of his eyes, and he fumbled nervously with his loose sleeve.

'I think you should leave now, Miss Bligh. I have nothing which would interest you.'

'You interest me a lot,' she said calmly. 'I can appreciate your devotion to these people, and what it all means to you. Believe me, there are others like you in many parts of the world, although perhaps not in quite such unique circumstances. What I don't understand is how you got them to trust you in the first place?'

His face was watchful, and she added: 'It's almost like you had some hold over them.'

'I think you had better go. You understand nothing.'

She smiled, but her eyes were cold. 'Why did you tell Major Blair you knew nothing of the wreck?' The words dropped like pebbles in a quiet stream. It was almost as if she had struck him. 'Could it be that you saw the Motă tribesmen kill the survivors as they landed? That you kept quiet on condition that they allowed you to work in peace? It's quite an angle.'

He staggered to his feet, his face grey with fury. 'Go away! Don't bring your filthy lies here! Get out before I have you beaten like the deceiver you are!'

She stood up. 'Lay off! I don't scare that easily, as I told you. Just think over what I said, that's all.'

Spencer looked as if he was going to have a fit. 'Lies! Corrupting, filthy lies! Can I never be left in peace!'

She walked to the door. 'I'm going.' She could feel the freshening wind sighing under the floor of the bungalow. 'But something about this whole deal is crazy, and I'm not being personal!'

She walked quickly down the path between two lines of silent natives. No doubt they had heard the shouting. He'll

131

have more than that to shout about when I've finished, she thought grimly.

Watute grinned with relief as she appeared on the beach, and pointed at the sky. She noticed that it was more hazy, and the horizon shimmered in a sickly green which made the sea look like polished steel. But not in the bay, where the water surged angrily in a mass of steep white rollers.

'Hell! Can we sail in that?' She felt a little uneasy.

Watute grinned again. 'Sure thing! We keep close to shore.'

She waded to the boat. No one came to help her this time, so she kicked her dusty feet in the hissing surf and heaved on the gunwale. The boy helped her, and soon the boat was sliding into the deep water. He frowned and pointed behind her. A tiny black child, her eyes wide with terror, was standing uncertainly on the edge of the sea. She wanted to run away, and yet some other force compelled her to wait until the American girl waded through the surf to reach her.

'What is it, honey?'

The child shrank back. Then, with a sob, she flung a necklace in the sand and ran.

Watute steadied the dinghy. 'Present, missy. She make a gift for you.'

The dinghy veered away from the beach, and Watute squinted through the spray, watching for the hidden rocks. The small boat rode the swell with gay abandon, the red sail skimming with ease across the surging, noisy water.

The necklace was wet and sandy in her palm, and she smiled as she remembered the small black face. It was merely a crude string of worn coral, with a brass trinket on the end.

Her smile felt frozen on her face.

The trinket was stamped in the shape of a prancing stag, like the one on Rupert Blair's cigarette-case.

George Myers groaned and rolled over on to his side, his naked stomach gleaming with sweat. He blinked vaguely around the cabin and licked his lips, tasting the stale, humid air which covered his limbs like a cloak. Muffled by the teak planking overhead, he could hear Tarrou's voice crying angrily, and the answering calls of the seamen. He swallowed hard, the taste of the beer still in his throat. It seemed darker in the small cabin, and he peered at the waterproof watch on his plump wrist. He sat up in slow, unsteady movements, his smooth face creasing into a tight frown. It was then that he noticed the schooner was more lively than it had been at lunch-time. And as his sleep-deadened brain began to clear, the protesting shipboard noises crowded in on him. He paused with his buttocks perched on the sharp side of the bunk, his body sagging like that of a pig, his mouth hanging open.

The cabin floor tilted and he felt his body beginning to slide off the deep mattress, but as he put out his hands to steady himself the whole ship seemed to pull itself up short, in one violent shudder. He opened the cabin door and listened, his toes gripping the worn carpet as if to give him additional leverage against the schooner's uneasy motion. A gust of warm air swept over his sweating shoulders so that he shivered, and he heard the squeak and groan of timbers, mingled with the persistent thrumming of the taut rigging.

The weather was getting worse, he decided. He began to swear with steady concentration as he tugged on his trousers and groped on the untidy bunk for his shirt. As he swayed and lurched about the cabin he thought of Tarrou's face when he had burst in on him earlier in the day. It must

133

have been shortly after Gillian Bligh had left in the dinghy, although he had dropped off in a quiet snooze, only to be rudely awakened by Tarrou shaking his arm and shouting incoherently, his dark face distorted with anxiety.

'She's gone! Left ship!' he had shouted, all the time jerking at Myers' arm. 'She had no right to go without permission!' There were tears of rage in his wild eyes. 'Vic tell me to see that she stays here, with me!' He had banged at his chest, as if astounded that anyone could defy his authority.

Myers smiled bleakly as he remembered his own reply. 'She told *me* she was goin',' he had said irritably. 'Wot else d'you expect, eh?'

Tarrou had dashed back on deck without another word, but his face had been a picture. Gone was his aloof calm and unbearable assurance. He had seemed to Myers like a man possessed.

In order to avoid him at mealtimes, Myers had retreated to the cabin, with some tinned fruit and several cans of Australian beer. It was late in the afternoon according to his watch, but it was much darker than he had expected, and as he tugged open the door and stumbled into the narrow, lurching passageway he felt the growing pangs of uneasiness.

The scene which greeted him on the poop did nothing to reassure him. For a moment he stood clinging to the companion hatch, fighting for breath. The flat, unbroken surface of the bay had vanished and in its place the sea surged towards the beach in line upon line of angry, white-crested rollers. He could hear their sullen rumble on the steep sandy slopes, and realized that was what had awakened him. The wind, which ploughed across from the open sea, was steady and hit the moored ship with savage force. It was hot, and stung his face like desert sand, so that his eyes began to stream, and he held up his hands to peer anxiously at the sky, which was the greatest shock of all.

He had come to believe that it would always be blue and clear, it had seemed as permanent as the smooth sea and relentless heat, but as he gaped at the fast-moving ridges of dark clouds he saw that the whole sky was painted in lurid shades of copper, as if an artist had gone mad, or the sun had burst across the horizon.

Even as he peered round like a trapped animal the rain began to fall, slowly at first, the heavy drops cast on the dry decks with the noise of pellets, then in a steady, scalding downpour. He saw its growing strength moving across the tossing water in a grey curtain, blotting out the end of the bay, and then even the beach.

The native seamen ran hither and thither across the decks, seemingly unaware of his presence, their faces tight and preoccupied, while Tarrou, his drill jacket streaming with rain and spray, ran the length of the ship, his shrill voice plucked from his mouth and cast to the wind.

He skidded to a halt in front of Myers, his eyes red-rimmed and wild. Myers cupped his hand to shout: 'What the 'ell's 'appenin'? Is this a 'urricane or somethin'?' He gasped as the ship shuddered again and rolled heavily in the waves.

Tarrou gripped the wheel for support. 'I thought this would happen! It's a Willy-Willy, a tropical storm!' He peered along the slanting deck, his face torn with emotion. 'I think it is, anyway! We're in a bad place here. Tide's coming in, and the wind's getting up all the time!' He jumped with alarm as the small canopy over the poop cracked like a gunshot and split into a dozen pieces. Fraser's deck-chair staggered as if alive and then lifted off the deck and vanished over the rail.

'My Gawd!' Myers stared round the ship with a new

uneasiness. Here at least he had felt safe. He had almost taken the schooner's invulnerability for granted, but as she groaned and the rigging danced and whipped in the wind, he felt cheated and afraid.

'Well, what are you doin' about it, mate? You're supposed to be in charge of this bloody scow, aren't you? For Christ's sake do somethin' about it, 'stead of standin' there like a ruptured duck!'

Tarrou had not even heard his voice. He was staring around him as if he had never seen the ship before in his life. So many things were happening at once, and yet he seemed unable to move. How could he explain to Myers what he felt, even if he had the time? Before, when he had been in storms, it had been frightening enough, but with Fraser at the helm it had been quite different.

He shaded his streaming eyes to peer at the distant reef, but it was blotted out by the rain. It thundered down on the decks and surged and gurgled along the scuppers, until with a final hiss it poured from the wash ports in a steadily mounting stream. He tried to think. She was out there in all this, he thought. Unless she had stayed at the mission, of course. That fool Watute. It was all his fault. And that fat hog Myers! He bit his thick lip until he could not bear the pain. He had let her go without telling him! The deck shuddered again beneath his straddled legs. I must do something about the cable, he thought frantically. It'll pull the anchor right out of the bottom in a minute. In his mind he pictured the helpless ship being carried by those breakers and tossed on to the shore. Perhaps she was already dragging! With a gasp he ran forward, his gait like that of a drunken man as the deck canted beneath him.

Old Buka cowered by the bowsprit, his gnarled skin black under the rain. His single eye gleamed at Tarrou as if with loathing. 'What you do? You make let ship finish on

136

sand?' The hoarse voice hammered at Tarrou's tortured mind, and he realized with horror that the respect had gone from the old man's face, he had reverted to a savage again. Tarrou groped frantically for an answer, and all the time the awful eye watched him unwinkingly, like a black button floating in blood.

The bows dipped yet again, and he gripped the forestay with both hands. He was near to panic, but the contempt in Old Buka's eye filled him with something else as well. All the past tension and frustration swept through him in an uncontrollable flood, until he felt consumed by its power.

For a second he stared down at the other man, heedless of the wind which plucked the cherished cap from his head and flung it into the greedy water. 'Call the hands! Stand by to let go the other anchor!'

He watched the man slither along the deck like a black crab and then hang precariously over the bows. He could see the taut cable, dark against the white rollers which surged down either side of the stem, and as he watched he could sense the tremendous strain being exerted on its dripping links. It was bar-taut, with the full weight of the wind-ravaged ship pulling on it. He was only dimly aware of the bodies pressing around him, and Old Buka's harsh voice barking directions. The second anchor was man-handled across the fo'c'sle and shackled to its own cable.

A splintering crash grated along the ship's hull, and too late he remembered the tethered dinghy. He was just in time to see it roll on to its back before the shattered planks were torn free and the remains of the dinghy were sucked astern to vanish into the curtain of rain.

The anchor was finally catted, and hung swaying against the high stem. He noticed that the ship was rising and falling much more now, the increased swell mounting

137

every minute as the waves surged across the hidden reef to invade the once-sheltered bay.

With the tide coming in and the water being whipped into such savage frenzy, the solitary rock which Fraser used as an aiming mark for crossing the reef would soon be covered, if it was not already. The boys crouched by the anchor, watching him. He would have to decide soon whether or not he was going to leave the bay and beat out to sea. Once clear he might be able to encircle the island and ride out the storm in the lee of the high Northern coastline. That is what Fraser would have done. What he would expect *him* to do. He remembered his face as he had turned to follow Blair up the beach. 'Beat out to sea, Michel. We shall be all right, *but look after my ship*!'

He trembled with rising fury. *My* ship. No one ever gave him anything but instructions. Where were they all when he needed help? Myers hiding on the poop; the crew muttering like mutinous bushmen; and Gillian . . . He paused at the thought of the girl and groaned with self-pity. She had gone away without even a word.

Old Buka shouted angrily, 'What for wait?'

They all despised him. He ran forward to the group of shining black bodies. 'You wait till I tell you! *I'm* in command now!'

They stared at his suffused face and fell silent. Around them the ship sighed and rattled, whilst from somewhere below came the crash of breaking crockery and glass.

Old Buka stood up, his bent body swaying. 'We all die while you are like small child!' His voiced was filled with scorn.

The two divers, Wabu and Yalla, grunted in agreement, their faces hard in the copper glare from the sky.

Tarrou fell back. 'We are getting under way, now! We

138

will use the engine to get clear! We will not drop the other anchor!'

Kari, the scarred seaman, shook his grey head. 'No, no good!'

'We will not leave Cap'n Fraser.' Old Buka spoke with calm authority.

They think I am running away. They don't understand. Tarrou thrust his hand into his pocket and pulled out the heavy revolver.

His voice was near to breaking. 'Stand by to hoist that anchor!' His mind was made up. 'We cannot stay here! Do you hear me, you stupid savages!'

They stared, fascinated by the gun. Myers, who had come running forward when the dinghy had carried away, shouted with sudden desperation, 'What the 'ell are you doin'?'

Tarrou did not turn. 'Do you know how to start the engine?' His voice sounded harsh.

Myers waved his hands. 'Yeh, sure I can. Why, fer Gawd's sake?'

'Then start it. Be quick; I will stay here!'

Myers tore his eyes from Tarrou's wild face and the tense group of seamen and then ran gasping to the engine-room hatch. His ears were deafened by the rising scream of the storm, and his head sang with the onslaught of the rain.

He half fell down the hatch, and whimpered as his knee stumbled against the gleaming teeth of the giant fly-wheel.

I shall be killed. The whole damn lot of us will. What a bloody place to die! The string of obscenities which followed were drowned by the thunder of the diesel as with a cough and a roar it came to life under his groping hands.

The familiar growl of the old engine, audible even above the noise of the storm, gave a small measure of comfort to Tarrou, and he backed slowly away from the watching

139

seamen. They seemed to relax as if they, too, realized that they were now committed.

Tarrou bared his teeth, his face shining in the unearthly light. 'Now you break that cable!' He gestured with the pistol. It was like the symbol of his new power. 'I cannot waste time heaving up the anchor.'

Old Buka grunted, and spat on the deck. One look at the pressure of water building up around the bows was enough to tell him, at least, that they would never have managed to turn the capstan. His eye met those of Kari, and he nodded. It was a tiny movement but enough to show that Old Buka was not beaten. But, first they had to save the ship.

Tarrou jammed the gun into his trousers and felt the wet metal against his leg. The fools, they had no idea of his power. He would show them.

Myers was peering over the engine-room hatch, his bald head streaming with rain. He looked as if he was drowning in it.

Tarrou stamped his foot, as Fraser had done so many times, and yelled above the din, 'Put her ahead!' To the others he called, 'Let her go!'

There was a short, metallic clang as the shackle was broken, and with a scream of relief the straining cable rattled through the fairlead and disappeared into the water.

The effect was instantaneous. Caught in the savage force of the white-hooded rollers, the schooner's bows paid off, the masts groaning against the wire stays and every block and timber in the old hull making a noisy protest.

The rain was heavier, and the wind-force seemed to be mounting with each breathless second which passed. In rising alarm Tarrou peered over the wheel and tried to gauge the swing of the bowsprit, which seemed a mile away.

Too violently he slammed down the brass throttle by his

140

side, and his heart all but stopped as the old engine coughed, missed and then picked up again. The deck vibrated as the revolutions mounted, and the screw felt as if it would tear free or come crashing through the poop.

Although his body was sodden with rain and sea alike, his mouth grew dry. The wheel was hard over, yet still the bows swung round, and the angle of the deck grew more acute.

Myers stared vacantly from the hatch, his stomach a tight knot of fear. We're leaving the others behind, he thought dazedly. Then with sudden despair he shouted into the teeth of the storm: 'Damn them! Damn the lot of 'em!'

Tarrou only noticed that the ship was beginning to heel over as it rolled heavily into a deep trough. The engine seemed to be getting louder, or was it the sound of the surf on the beach? He put all his weight on the wheel, as if by his extra weight he might swing the balance in his favour.

Then all at once he saw the glow of the copper sky move with cruel majesty over the crazily pitching bowsprit.

'She's going!' His face was split into a maniac grin as he watched the schooner begin to swing about.

Myers heard him shout, and thought that the ship was going to founder. He hid his face in his hands and began to sob.

Into the very teeth of the storm the *Queensland Pearl* fought her way, while the crew cowered down to escape the rearing waves which climbed over the high bow and thundered down the full length of the ship to cascade against the poop and down the leaking hatches.

Tarrou pulled himself against the wheel and tried to peer over the rail. Once through the gap and they could go about and run before the storm.

Old Buka shouted and waved his arm out and downwards in a chopping motion. Tarrou took a deep breath and began to pull the wheel over to port. He could see nothing, but knew that the old man had found their aiming mark, and had made the signal. Along the length of the vessel both men looked at each other. Through the torrential rain and the writhing shapes of the halyards and braces they were mere human forms, but at that moment each man saw the other with sudden clarity and a new hatred.

Beyond the reef the sea was heavier, and the swell lifted roller after roller to send it thundering against the hidden barrier, and as each successive wave shattered on the coral, and rose to be shredded by the wind, the frustrated fury of the deep water seemed to increase, so that as the streaming white shape of the schooner flung itself across the small dip on the reef's battlements it turned its rage upon it instead.

One desperate thought after another crowded through Tarrou's racing mind. Must get some sail on her. Must! Must!

He groped for the whistle about his neck and blew it hard in short, sharp notes. They were puny against the wind, but the men heard his signal. He watched them tugging at the sodden lines and falling off their feet as wave after wave smashed down at them. Eventually a small brown triangle crept with painful slowness upwards from the bowsprit, and then bellied out full and hard, as if it was a solid thing. For a moment the ship rallied to its support, then as it split and vanished the bows plunged more crazily than before. Again the whistle commanded, and the flying jib followed its mate up the twanging forestay. They all held their breaths, and Tarrou watched it with fascinated eyes.

The steep waves thundered against the transom, and then they were falling astern. Now the crests were farther apart, the troughs deeper and more engulfing. Tarrou no longer cared. They were over the reef, and as he blew the whistle again, and began to ease the slippery spokes, he knew that the worst was over.

A chorus of cries came from forward as the maintopmast splintered and plunged down like a spear, to be pulled up inches from the deck by a web of tangled rigging.

Tarrou yelled and shook his fist, his voice a hoarse croak. 'Axes! Cut it away, you trash!'

The headland bowed darkly through a gap in the rain, and then was gone, and following the reeling compass he swung the labouring ship towards the shelter of the coast. Deep water and high cliffs began to have their effect, and the crazy motion of the masts seemed to ease.

The axes shone like fire in the lurid sunset as the men worked feverishly to clear away the wreckage. With a lurch the stricken topmast swung down and plunged over the rail. Tarrou winced as the splintered spar dragged alongside, striking at the schooner's round bilges in short, savage strokes. The men had stopped cutting, and were grouped round the mass of useless rope which held the menace tied alongside the plunging schooner.

Kari ran towards the wheel and, deaf to his high-pitched voice, Tarrou pushed him against the spinning spokes and ran to see the cause of the delay. To be cheated now, when they were almost free. He shook his head as if in pain and pushed his way past the silent men. A three-inch stay, its torn strands poking out like barbed wire, had fallen in one great twisted mass across the gunwale and had pinned Old Buka underneath. He lay half over the ship's side, the whole weight of the heavy topmast tearing at his bent body. Even as he watched, Tarrou could see it cutting into the knotted muscles of his stomach, as a wire will slice a cheese in two.

Crash! The spar pounded again against the hull. Tarrou knew to an inch what thickness of timber was below the waterline. It was not enough for this.

Yalla pulled with his bare hands at the wire, but the old man was held fast. His one eye shone like fire, as if trying to hold on to the setting sun. It never flickered as Tarrou seized an axe and slashed with swift blows at the wire where it was spliced into a ringbolt on the deck. There was a rumble as the wire parted, and as the tangled mass slithered towards the rail the topmast took the full strain and tugged itself free of the ship.

Like an animal caught in a monstrous web, Old Buka was dragged backwards across the gunwale, his filed teeth bared in a savage grin. With a final jerk of his thin legs he was gone, and even the heavy spar was dragged down by the weight of the wire.

The men stared at the scored wood and the smears of dark blood which were already fading in the spray.

Tarrou swayed, and threw the axe over the side.

'I *had* to do that! Don't you see?'

But they would not look at him, and moved slowly forward to the fo'c'sle. Without speaking they began to set another jibsail.

Tarrou returned to the wheel and stood behind Kari, half-watching the man's hands on the spokes and half-looking at the tumbling wastes of white water, as if he expected to see that eye mocking him even in death.

8

Blair stumbled against the upended roots of a fallen tree and fell awkwardly into the mess of churned-up soil. Around and above him the wind rose to a screaming wail, and in the near darkness he could hear the berserk thunder of the surf against the narrow beach which they had just left behind them. He was half-blinded by the torrential rain which battered down on his aching shoulders, or was flung parallel to the ground by the force of the wind. Sand, small stones and pieces of rotten wood tore and whipped at his raw face, and he could feel the rifle-sling biting into his arm like a hot wire. They seemed to have been stumbling through the storm for hours, and its force had left him almost witless as he tried to shade his eyes from the slashing force of the rain and peer after the wavering shapes of Fraser and Hogan.

As if by some silent agreement they grouped together beneath a tight clump of jerking palms, breathless, and half dead with sheer exhaustion.

Blair leaned heavily on his rifle and moved his crippled foot in slow, careful motions. It was no good. The pain was getting worse, and the last fall had all but made him scream aloud.

He peered back at the beach and saw the long pale edge of a monster wave rear up to hang momentarily against the black sea and then thunder down on the wet sand. This time it did not fall back, but with sudden rage roared towards the edge of the trees, its fading power reaching up at the madly waving fronds, to fling clouds of spray even to their feet.

Fraser groaned. 'It's no use. We'll have to press farther up the slope. The beach gives up here anyway, so the sooner we get goin' the better.' He stared hard in Blair's direction, but it was Hogan who answered in a choked voice.

'That's right, Vic. Keep on up through 'ere, an' we'll be on the side of the 'eadland. With this sea runnin', the 'ole flamin' island'll be awash around 'ere!' He staggered against a tree as a sudden gust of wind punched at his dripping body. 'I feel a bit weak, mate,' he added in a small voice.

Fraser felt the sodden bandage on the man's arm and shook his head. 'You lost quite a bit of juice, Jim. But we'll get you to the ship okay.' He glared again at Blair. 'If it's still there!'

Blair jerked his head. 'Lead on then. At least your friends the Motă seem quiet.'

Hogan fumbled for a cigarette and then threw the sodden packet away with despair. 'Nah. They don't like this sort of caper any more than we does.'

Blair took one of Hogan's guns and slung it across his back. Using his rifle like a stave, he followed the others up the steep rise, which Hogan had said led towards the northern side of the headland. The rainwater poured down the slope towards them like a mountain stream, dislodging starved bushes, and even sizeable boulders, so that they continually had to sidestep and stumble over the churned-up ground, each step being a fresh nightmare to Blair, who fell farther and farther behind.

Hogan was getting weaker, and as he halted to regain his breath he smashed his shotgun against a tree, splintering the butt to fragments. With a grunt he threw the broken weapon down in the sand, the strength drained from him.

146

'Don't want the bastards to get their 'ands on that!' he panted.

Fraser slipped his hand round the man's waist and, like two drunks, they staggered on up the crumbling slope.

Blair noticed vaguely that Hogan's face was upturned and heedless of the pounding rain. His breath was rasping as if he was choking, and his thick legs seemed to be moving automatically, almost dissociated with the rest of his body.

As they passed through a small, windswept clearing, Blair looked up and saw the thick rolls of racing cloud. It made him feel giddy. It seemed as if the island was swinging like a pendulum beneath his feet.

He tried to reassemble his bruised mind, but only obtained a few disjointed pictures. Gillian's face repeatedly appeared, and he found that he was praying that she was safe aboard the schooner. It was odd how they all looked on the ship as a refuge. Fraser was obviously thinking of nothing else. Without it he seemed lost, and away from it was like a man robbed of his strength and will to exist.

He shook the water from his plastered hair and rubbed at his eyes. They felt raw and inflamed, and he could feel the blown sand hot beneath the lids.

Not much farther, surely. Can't keep this up much longer. Must rest for a bit. He gritted his teeth and drove the rifle-butt deep into the shifting mud, the smouldering anger within him only helping to add to his feeling of loss and disillusionment. This damned island is destroying us all. And I am destroying myself. The shotgun slipped across his shoulder and fell into the mud. He bent to retrieve it, and slithered down on his face.

He retched, and spat out the filth which moved like a miniature quicksand over his outflung hands. With every muscle and fibre screaming a protest, he tried to stand up.

He could feel the rain exploring the full length of his spreadeagled body, each drop like an individual blow. His foot felt quite numb, and he could not tell which way it was pointing. With a sudden chill he tried again, his heart pounding noisily against his sore ribs.

His shirt was torn open, and he could sense the clinging sensation of the mud across his stomach and weighing down on his bush jacket. With a groan he rolled over on his side, and with slow, agonizing movements pulled himself to his feet, and hung with weary desperation to a small palm tree. He leaned his forehead against the wet bark, and was aware of the noise of the rain. It was all that he could hear. He was afraid to release his hold on the tree and face the storm again. He knew that if he fell once more he would stay down. He knew, too, that he was alone. It was the same feeling he had remembered all through the years since that day in Burma. The sudden realization that he had lost his men, that he was alone in a hostile land, had been the same as this.

He pressed his head closer. Was this what he had come to do? To sacrifice himself completely for something which was not his fault, and yet had held him in its grip through everything which had passed? He heard the snapping of twigs, and expected to hear Fraser call, but it was only a rotting branch, flying in the wind like a misshaped spear.

A tall-sided slab of rock jutted from some bushes like a giant gravestone, and with dedicated effort he began to pull himself towards it. Heedless of the filth, he lowered his body down into the tiny piece of shelter afforded by the leaning rock, and allowed his shoulders to sag against it. He stared at his legs, which jutted out into the darkness, and felt the rain beating them like whips. There was no feeling at all in his foot.

The meaning of his predicament moved across him like

a chill wind, and he pulled the rifle out of the mud and almost without thinking began to empty the magazine with listless movements of the bolt. As he cleaned the mud from each bullet, drawing the smooth cool shapes across his tattered jacket, and refilled the magazine, he tried to imagine what the others would do when they found he was missing. The fact that Fraser had not come back for him seemed like an answer. The full realization of the man's hatred was laid stark and terrible with the force and directness of a blow.

He thought again of Gillian. She has got her story, he half smiled with bitter despair. That was, after all, what she had come for. He closed his eyes. Perhaps I shall be better off dead. He clamped his teeth together with sudden anger. What's got into you? What the hell did you expect to prove by coming to this damned island? He was suddenly aware of a new quiet around him. Apart from the slow heavy drops falling from the trees, and the gentle gurgle of water down the slope, there was silence. And as he looked up he saw the needle points of distant stars between the formless shapes of the clouds. Without the wind and the savage rain it seemed as if the island was also brooding. As if it was waiting for him.

The thunder of surf and the gale-whipped frenzy of the waves still persisted in Gillian's ears, although the effect was more muffled, like the echoes in a giant conch shell, and, as it faded, the pain in her head came back, so that a red mist hovered in front of her tightly closed eyes. As her consciousness returned she was aware, too, that the crazy motion of the dinghy was no longer there and, as her hands moved weakly at her sides, she could sense the coarse touch of blankets against her skin.

Very slowly she opened her eyes, the splitting pain in her

head making her feel faint and hover again on the edge of insensibility. She stared at the low, beamed roof above her head, and for a moment was near to panic. Then, as strength ebbed back to her, the uneven jumble of memories crowded in on her aching mind, so that she could see with sudden clarity the small boat, with its ripped sail, as the great waves picked it up and flung it towards the shore. She saw Watute, too, his mouth wide with soundless cries, and his dark scrabbling hands trying to steady her body against the shock of impact. There had been one sickening, grinding crash, and the very instant that the boat had struck she had seen the giant wave towering high overhead. Then her world had turned upside down, and she could remember nothing more.

She tried to move, but the pain burst on her brain like fire, and her throat filled with bile. She moved her head gingerly to one side, and stared at the familiar outline of the small room. She was lying on a narrow couch, a coarse blanket pulled up to her chin, and she noticed that on the opposite wall a crucifix gleamed dully in the light of a pressure lamp.

Her hearing, which had been deadened by the cruel pounding of the waves, came back with unexpected suddenness, and the whole building was filled immediately with the high, plaintive notes of an organ, rising and falling, their intensity magnified and distorted by the iron roof overhead.

She winced, and tried to relax her taut body. So she was back at Ivor Spencer's mission. Watute must have run to get help after dragging her from the sea. She tried to fit the pieces together, but it was no good. Her bruises, and the deafening insistence of the organ, defied all her efforts.

With a final boom the music stopped, and a tall shadow passed haltingly in front of the light. Ivor Spencer stood, his

150

thin face in darkness, staring down at her, his arms folded across his chest.

Her voice sounded small, and seemed to come from a long way off. 'Hello there. How long have I been here?'

She could hear his unsteady breathing, and could sense the scrutiny his shadowed eyes were giving her.

He nodded slowly. '"Nearer My God To Thee". A beautiful piece of music, my child.' His voice was low, almost caressing. 'When I play it at night on the veranda it seems to defy the jungle and keep it at bay.' He gave a strange chuckle. 'You would call that symbolic, no doubt?'

Gillian tried to struggle up on her elbows, but in a stride he crossed the space between them and pressed her head back on the pillow. His hand felt dry and hot.

'It is better if you stay as you are. I'm afraid you have no clothes as yet.' He stood back, as if to study her reaction.

She lay quite still, immediately aware of the touch of the blankets against her body.

'My servants took care of you, so your modesty is in no danger.' His tone was completely flat, and almost matter-of-fact. 'They found you just in time, it seems.'

She swallowed hard. 'I suppose I should thank you,' she faltered. 'But what about the boy who was with me?'

Spencer strode to the window, and played vaguely with his shirt buttons. 'I fear the Almighty has taken him. It was His wish.'

She closed her eyes. Poor Watute. He had been so happy, so confident that he could protect her. Her thoughts seemed to magnify themselves. She felt the beginnings of fear in the back of her mind, but in a tight voice she said, 'Have you told my friends I am here?'

He did not answer for a while. 'Friends? I regret they have gone.' He turned swiftly to watch her face and startled eyes. 'The ship has departed. It seems that they think you were drowned!' His whole personality seemed to change, as his long face split into a wide grin. 'It was His will that you should be spared to help me.'

She could hear her own heart beating, and was conscious of the great silence which enshrouded the house. It was as if the pressure lamp was the only thing which held all the evil of the unknown at bay.

She tried to speak sharply. 'Now hold on, Mr. Spencer, there's no need to try and scare me. I've had about as much as I can take for one day!'

The grin vanished, and his eyes were compressed into tiny slits of bright light as he fought to bring his emotions under control. 'Silence! You cannot blame me for this! I warned you not to come here!'

She lay still in shocked silence, her eyes following his gaunt shape as he began to pace the floor. Back and forth her frightened stare followed the long shadow as it bent and twisted across the bare white walls. Her stomach felt like liquid, and she could feel her fingers gripping at the mattress as if to keep control of herself. All the time he paced his voice ebbed and flowed like the notes of the organ. Sometimes it was so low she could only guess what he was saying, and occasionally he would halt in his stride and shout in a loud exalted tone, as if addressing an audience.

'I have watched my work grow and flower over the years! Do you imagine that I can let it wither and die because of you? Do you?' It was nearly a scream. 'This is *your* chance now. Don't you see?' He stopped by the couch and passed one hand across his brow. Almost humbly he said, 'You *do* see, don't you?'

His eyes flickered momentarily like the open doors of a furnace, and when she did not answer he added heavily: '*They* think I betrayed them, you see. They must never think that, must they?'

She watched him, her voice husky. 'Please tell me what you mean. I don't understand—' She flinched as he waved his long hands in the air.

'I told you not to pry into their affairs. They thought you had come to rebuke them for their sins.' He frowned. 'And that is *my* privilege alone. I am God's instrument, and they understand that now.'

He stepped back with such violence that he nearly overturned the lamp. The hollow cheeks were working with suffused rage. 'Don't try to deceive me! Your soft words are a temptation! But you do not have any effect here!' He gave a crafty smile. 'I saw it all, you know. I was here on the island when that boat was lost.' The words poured out in a steady flood, as if he could no longer bear to hold the secret. 'I saw those stupid creatures blundering up the beach with their guns, and their bleatings!'

Gillian felt the perspiration cold on her face, but she could not drag her eyes from him. She felt mesmerized, even stricken by this terrifying figure.

The voice droned on. 'The Motă came out of the jungle and attacked them. They had started killing them before I understood what was happening, you see. The wounded officer, the father of the ignoramus in charge of your little venture, died trying to defend his child.' He stared hard at the girl's trembling mouth. 'That is when I acted! She was my bargaining point.' His fingers interlaced in a tight, uneasy grip. 'For years I had tried to make the Motă come to me like the other villagers here. But they had defied me. They were the main burden I had to bear. But I took the child and asked to be allowed to keep her for myself. Their chief knew me, and he thought that he had the better of the agreement. He knew that if I kept the child and said nothing to our useless authorities they were safe. That child was my

153

first real link with them. They began to trust me. Until . . .' his voice quivered with emotion, 'until you came here.'

'What happened to that child?' Her voice was a mere whisper.

'She was blind. She must have been injured during the fight on the beach.' His voice was very soft. 'She died ten years ago.'

There was a long pause, and Gillian thought she was going to faint.

'She was a challenge to me. But I made her into the perfect child. She knew only love, and happiness, and every living creature was her brother.'

'You don't know what you're saying!' She stared at him with horror. 'You kept that child in this place just for the sake—' She cried out as he slapped her violently across the cheek.

'Silence! How could you possibly understand the meaning of perfection? To you it is money, or lust! You personify all the things I protected her from!' He dropped his eyes. 'She was taken by fever. Quite suddenly. I buried her on the slope, where she used to sit and pray with me. But the Motă never knew of this. They thought I kept her in here with me. So all the time they left me in peace to do my work.' The hooded eyes flickered towards the couch. 'After the schooner had sailed I knew what would happen. The Motă will have to be appeased. They will want a further reassurance from me. A sign of good faith.' He folded his arms. 'Do you not agree that my work to build a place of simplicity and righteousness is all-important? Surely even you can see that?' When she did not answer he nodded slowly, the lamplight gleaming on his pointed scalp. 'Quite so. They will come for the child.'

'But the child is dead!'

The long fingers seized the blanket and pulled it down to

her breast. Around her neck hung the necklace, with the brass ornament.

'You will be that child,' he answered gravely.

Fraser heaved himself on to his knees and, with his head cocked on one side, listened carefully, and at the same time strained his aching eyes into the black shadows of the trees. He was aware that Hogan's untidy shape had taken on a sharper outline, and he peered anxiously towards the open sea, looking for a gap in the low clouds, which moved rank after rank towards the island and beyond. His hands rasped across the stubble of his chin, and beneath his groping fingers he could feel, too, the dirt and blown sand which matted his thick hair into a tangled wig. He cursed as Hogan began to twitch again and mutter incoherently through the protection of his exhausted slumber. Fraser had sat in this same position for most of the night, fingering his rifle, and sweating at every sound which whispered through the thickly wooded slopes of the hidden headland. When the downpour had stopped, he had forced the pace even more, half-dragging and half-carrying the delirious Hogan, until he had reached the security of the steep cliff which ran sharply down to a small cove, the proximity of which had made further movement in the darkness impossible.

He groped for Hogan's shoulder and shook it roughly. 'Come on, Jim. Time we were movin'.' He frowned as Hogan rolled over on to his back and stared vacantly at the clouds. He could see his eyes shining like oyster shells, and shuddered as he remembered the carnage in the trade store. God, was that only yesterday? He shook the man again, his voice harsh. 'Think you can stand up? We'd better try to find the ship 'fore some joker finds us!'

Hogan released a long groan and pushed his body into a sitting position. To Fraser he seemed unwilling to accept the misery of their position. It was as if he had hoped to awake from just another nightmare. The nightmare remained, however, and his fat fingers moved cautiously to the bandage on his arm. 'Gawd, where are we, fer Christ's sake?'

'You're supposed to know the island, aren't you?' Fraser's voice was unfeeling. 'The sea's down there, an' I guess the headland is reachin' over that way.' He waited with mounting impatience. 'Well? What are you starin' at me like that for? You look as if you're the only bloke in trouble!'

Hogan licked his dry lips. 'Where is he?'

Fraser gritted his teeth. 'Who are you talkin' about? Where's who?'

Hogan's face moved closer, so that he could feel the unsteady breath on his throat. 'The Major. What 'appened to 'im?' He passed a hand over his face, like a man removing cobwebs. 'I'm tryin' to remember,' he added vaguely.

Fraser forced himself to breathe more calmly. All through the night he had tried to rekindle his anger against Blair, to exclude him completely as if he was already dead. When he had discovered that Blair had fallen behind he had nearly given in. Hogan's great weight, the fury of the storm, and the agony in his mind as he tried to imagine what was happening to the schooner, had all taken a great toll of his limited reserve. When he looked back for Blair, a curse already forming on his lips, he had stared with stricken eyes at the unmoving wall of the jungle, unable to accept that he had vanished. All the hoarded fury and frustration had burst from him at that instant, and with sudden strength he had dashed blindly up the slope, moving only by instinct and deaf to everything, even Hogan's persistent ramblings and groanings.

It was different now. A faint glimmer parted the sea from

the sky, and the threat of the dawn seemed only to add to his overwhelming sense of guilt and shame.

'Look,' he began sharply, 'I told you what happened durin' the night. We lost him. Back there somewheres.' He gestured over his shoulder. 'Anyway, he's gone, an' that's that.' His shoulders sagged, and he felt desperately tired.

Hogan shifted uncomfortably. 'Can't remember a thing. Poor bastard, 'e must 'ave fell down one of them gullies.' He peered uncertainly at the kneeling man. 'Oughtn't we to go back, Vic? I mean, 'e might be injured, an' that.'

He jumped as Fraser sprang to his feet. 'That's it, damn you! Make up a flamin' song about it! Whose fault is it but his own?' He bunched his great fists and shook them in the air. 'If it wasn't for him we'd be on our way back to bloody Vila, safe and sound, see? You're all the same,' he added bitterly. 'You can't see what the man'd done to us all. To him it's just a game. Hire a bloody boat, an' go pokin' about lookin' for wrecks, and Christ knows what else! Never mind who you step on to get what you want!'

Hogan stirred uneasily. 'Well, he ain't gettin' 'is own way *now*, is he?'

'That's his fault. How in hell's name could we find him, anyway?' He pointed at Hogan's shoulder. 'An' a fat lot of good you'd be. Look at you, you're bloody well helpless!'

Hogan looked down at his fat body, which in the growing light only added to his discomfort. Thick with mud and filth, his shirt in rags, he hung his head at Fraser's harsh words.

'Okay, Vic, I'm sorry. I know I owe me life to you.'

Fraser peered round, his cramped legs trembling. 'Here, give us yer hand, cobber. We'll get on now.'

Keeping as close as they dared to the edge of the crumbling cliffs, they began to move round the top of the cove towards the dark bulge of the headland. Each painful

157

second which passed brought more light in the sky and growing warmth in the humid air.

Fraser sniffed and shook his head. He had hoped that with the dawn would come that fresh, cool breath of wind which usually followed a storm, and heralded the return of the sun. There was no wind, and as the first light glinted across the heaving water below them he could see the unbroken oily surface, grey and threatening. It must have been the edge of a Willy-Willy, he thought. It may come back again, and, in any case, there's more bad weather to come.

Hogan leaned against a tree and fought for breath.

'Must rest. Beat up, I am!' He gulped air like a drowning man, while Fraser stared past him at the sea with smouldering eyes.

A thin gold spear of watery sunlight lanced amongst the trees and touched their faces. The fronds and interlaced roots still dripped with rain, and there was a sickly smell of sodden vegetation and rotting wood.

Fraser sniffed again, as if to draw the sea up to where they stood. He slipped his arm round the other man's waist. 'Here we go then. Just watch where you put your great hoofs!'

Their faces warmed in the pale glow, and they were made doubly conscious of their rags, which hung wet against their scratched bodies.

A frigate bird rose like a grey spectre from the cliff, and with creaking wings beat angrily away from the two invaders. It dived towards the sea, so that its reflection rushed upwards to meet it on the uneasy water.

Every step was agony for Hogan. Years of tropical life had weakened his resistance to any sort of sudden physical strain, and, coupled with his loss of blood from the wound, which he could not even remember, he was still suffering from shock. Try as he might, he could not recall all the incidents at the trade store in their right order. And Blair kept moving in on his aching mind to confuse him further.

He peered sideways at Fraser's set jaw and hard, searching eyes. Fancy Vic behaving like that, he thought worriedly. It was wrong of him to leave the bloke like that. He shuddered as he remembered the painted faces screaming at him over the veranda. He almost fell as Fraser jerked him roughly over a scattered pile of small boulders.

'Look!' Fraser pointed wildly. 'There she is! Look, Jim, damn your eyes!'

Hogan squinted his red-rimmed eyes against the growing glare on the sea's face. Just round the lip of the next cliff he saw the nodding white stern of the schooner. She looked very small, and yet very close to the shore.

Fraser licked his lips and felt a smarting behind his eyes. 'Th' good old *Pearl*! So she's come through all right!' He stared at the white fragment with disbelief. 'They got her through the reef!'

'Yeh. She's there.' Hogan, too, was unable to take it in. As Fraser chattered with sudden excitement he felt a growing surge of resentment. All he cared about was his bloody ship. I've lost everything, and I'm too old to start up again. And all he cares about is his . . . His thoughts were scattered by Fraser pulling his arm again.

'Let's get down.' Fraser peered round the cliff, searching for a track.

Hogan sighed. The throbbing in his arm increased, but obediently he pushed himself away from the tree and followed Fraser over the boulders. As more of the ship became visible Fraser began to curse.

'Topmast's gone,' he muttered. 'An' there don't see to be any boats left.'

Quite suddenly the trees thinned out, and they came to a

159

steeply shelving ridge which seemed to run right down towards the sea. Fraser's rubber-soled shoes slipped and skidded on the waterlogged ground, but he never faltered as with a guiding hand out for Hogan, he led the way down the slope.

Hogan tugged at his hand, and he turned with impatience on his face 'Come on, mate. Not much farther.' He broke off as he saw the numb expression on his fat face.

Hogan fought for breath. 'Over there! Two of 'em tryin' to 'ead us off!'

'What? Where?' Disbelief tinged with sudden caution hardened his voice.

'By them stones.' He added with despairing bitterness: 'You should've kept yer eyes open, Vic.'

Fraser stepped clear of the other man, his eyes slitted with concentration. 'Shut up, will you! Perhaps you imagined it.'

He swung round as a movement flickered between the thin trees. A bent brown shape ran across a patch of sunlight and vanished into a thicket farther down the slope. He felt the cold fingers again around his heart. Hogan was right. He had been too preoccupied to be careful. Blair would have known what to do.

Hogan hissed excitedly: 'There's one right behind you, Vic. Don't move till I tell you.'

Fraser stood quite still, his eyes on the other man's protruding eyes. There was a terrible ache between his shoulder-blades, and he wanted to swing round and fire, and keep firing, until the magazine was empty. Nothing happened. He watched the sweat pouring down Hogan's face, and could feel the nausea rising in his stomach.

Seconds lengthened into minutes. The rifle grew heavier, and the wood of the stock became slippery with his sweat.

Hogan's lips moved. 'Make a run for it, Vic. Leave me,

160

will yer! I'll only 'old you up.' His eyes blinked with the strain. 'Just put a bullet in me first. I don't want them bastards to get their 'ands on me!'

Something snapped inside Fraser. 'Shut up, fer God's sake! Nobody's stoppin' us, see!' With a sob he swung on his heel, and squeezed the trigger. He had worked the bolt and fired again before he realized that nothing moved. Only the echoes of the shots and the shrill cries of disturbed birds greeted his straining ears. He made up his mind. 'Come on, man! Make for the water! Just keep goin', an' I'll cover you!'

Blinking away the sweat, he crouched watchfully amongst the silent trees, the rifle moving from side to side. Behind him he heard Hogan's shuffling steps and the crash of his body through the clutching bushes. He could hardly find breath, and although he wanted to swallow he was afraid even to moisten his lips.

Come on then. Where the hell are you? The green wall danced and quivered before his fixed gaze.

A strangled shout made him turn. Hogan had fallen across a bent root, his eyes on the tall figure which seemed to rise right out of the ground.

With the sea at his back, the figure was more of a silhouette than a living creature, the feeble sunlight casting a halo of light around the weird wig of red clay and hovering on the curved edge of the broad-bladed spear which, even as Fraser flung up the rifle to his shoulder and fired, moved with almost casual ease towards the whimpering man on the ground.

The two figures lay entwined and unmoving as Fraser ran heavily down the slope. With a horrified glance at the savage's bared teeth, he kicked him free of Hogan's back, and with shaking hands pulled the spear from between the great folds of flesh on the trader's shoulders. Hogan's eyes stared dazedly at the trees, his mouth opening and shutting soundlessly, while Fraser knelt at his side, heedless of the movements on the slope and the ship which lay so close to the shore.

Blair had known that Hogan was going to die. He had said so. And as Fraser stared down at the round, suddenly unlined face, he imagined that he was looking at himself.

'Never see Cairns again, Vic.' The voice was surprisingly level. 'Used ter think about takin' a little farm just outside the old place.' He shuddered, and Fraser knew that time was running out for both of them. 'Dinkum little spot. Remember it well. Red-gums borderin' the river, an' nothin' to do all day but . . . ' His voice trailed away, and for a second Fraser thought he had gone. One fat hand moved. 'Waste of time runnin' away. Should've stayed with 'er back there. Too late now. Too late for anythin'.' His small eyes flickered with sudden alarm. 'Don't leave me 'ere, Vic, will yer?'

He shook his head. 'No, Jim. I'll see you through, cobber.'

Hogan sighed. 'Pity about the Major. Good bloke.' He sighed again, and died.

Fraser heaved the body across his shoulders, and carrying the rifle in his free hand like a pistol, walked slowly down the slope. Nothing stirred, and he was aware of the birds singing high above his head.

He felt the sand beneath his shoes, and saw the schooner lying directly opposite him, barely a hundred yards offshore.

As he waded into the sea he could see several heads staring from the ship's side, and when he struck out across the tepid water he caught a glimpse of his two divers, Wabu and Yalla, diving over the rail and making towards him.

His mind was completely numbed, and the effort of

keeping Hogan's body and the heavy rifle afloat was almost
too much for him. He did not speak as the two divers
relieved him of his burden, but paused for a while to tread
water and stare back at the deserted shore. It was as if no
one had ever landed there, and nothing lived beyond the
implacable green barrier.

He was hauled bodily up the schooner's worn side, and
sat in silence on the bulwark staring at the pool of water at
his feet. With slow deliberation he turned his back on the
shore, and felt the gradual penetrating warmth of the sun
through his tattered shirt. They all watched his face. Wabu
and Yalla, the water drying on their sleek bodies and in
their black hair, stood like carved statues, their faces calm
and grave. Kari crouched by the side of Hogan's waterlogged corpse, his lined old features filled with sadness, his
gnarled hands moving nervously across the warm deck.
Dinkila the cook, his foolish face immobile with shock, was
near to hysteria, and even Myers, inarticulate with the
whisky he had been consuming since the storm, was
sobered by Fraser's expression.

He looked slowly at Tarrou who, unlike the others, gave
the impression of movement, of nervous agitation.

'Well?' The question dropped like a stone. 'What have
you got to say?' Fraser ran his gaze wearily over the assembled group. 'And where's the precious Miss Bligh? I
should've thought she'd have had her camera ready for all
this!'

Tarrou's voice was trembling. 'There was a storm. I
brought the ship here. It was safe here I thought. They were
stupid and did not understand your wishes, Vic.' He gestured
towards the others, and Wabu dropped a slim hand on to his
diver's knife. 'It has been terrible.' He swallowed hard.
'Where are the others? I thought . . .' His voice trailed away.

Through the mist of shock and exhaustion Fraser was

163

aware for the first time that there was something more still to be endured. He lifted an arm that felt of immeasurable weight, and pointed to Hogan's shape. 'There's Jim. Blair's missin'. I guess you already realized that. What else has gone wrong, and where is the Bligh woman?'

Tarrou twisted his jacket wretchedly between his dark hands. 'It was not my fault! She left the ship without my permission. Watute went with her, and then the storm, I—'

He staggered back as Fraser bounded from the rail and seized him by the throat. 'She *what*? Say that again, you frog-eatin' bastard!'

Tarrou squirmed, his eyes staring madly. 'Don't blame me!' he screamed, aware of the dull eyes watching him. 'I could not stop her. She was going to the mission I think!'

'That's not all, Cap'n.' Wabu's voice was filled with contempt. 'He ran us on sand-bar. Engine all made bad!'

Fraser shook Tarrou's body very slowly, as if to emphasize his words. 'Why did you bring the *Pearl* so close inshore? I suppose *that* was someone else's fault, too?' He threw back his head to stifle the urge to kill the wretched man in his grip, as he had killed the Motă tribesman. 'Jesus Christ! Do you know what you've done?'

Tarrou's face ran freely with sweat, and his eyes were black with fear and hurt. For Vic to do this in front of the others, after all that he had gone through, was more than the final blow. Something had snapped in his brain, and although he was still dazed by Fraser's return the Australian's harsh voice no longer had any effect. It was only a distant rumble which threatened to interfere with his growing fury against the girl. She had mocked him, and destroyed him. She and Blair had brought down his world, and nothing was left for him, but revenge.

Fraser turned his head. 'Any other damage? Get Old

Buka here. He'll know.'

Yalla dropped his eyes. 'Him dead. He cause him to die.'

Tarrou felt the fingers loosen their hold, and he stepped back to the rail. 'It's not true! They're all against me! I saved the ship for you, Vic, and they resent it, don't you see?' There were little flecks of foam on his thick lip.

Kari tapped his skull. 'Him go longlong!'

The voice rose to an even higher pitch. 'I'll show you all! I shall get the engine going again, and then you will see.'

They were not listening to him, but watching Fraser again.

He sat down on the bulwark, his stubbled face expressionless. 'She drowned, you reckon?' It was a question at large.

Myers spoke from the hatch, his voice slurred. 'We saw 'er set off to come back, then the storm got up. Wabu swam ashore and asked one of the villagers from the mission if there was any news. That Spencer bloke said that the boat capsized.' He shrugged weakly. 'So that's that.'

Fraser sighed. 'Right. Now listen to me all of you. We're in a bad spot here if the storm comes back. We're on a lee shore, and the engine's kaput! So we've got to work like hell to get under way, savvy?'

They nodded gravely.

'And as for you *Mister* Tarrou, clean that engine, pump, or whatever it is, and don't let me see your face till it *is* ready!'

He turned away towards Myers. 'You can help the divers have a look for underwater damage. When that's done, lend a hand to Kari. I want some new sails bent on, just in case.'

Myers shrugged. 'You're the boss.'

Yalla still stood before Fraser, his narrow eyes glinting. 'We not take orders from mate any more!' The words

165

halted Tarrou as he went towards the engine-room.

'Suits me.' Fraser spread his hands on the warm rail. 'I was evidently wrong about him, that's all.'

For an instant Tarrou quivered like a man with fever, then he lifted up his head and gave an unearthly scream. As they watched him with stricken eyes, he sprang to the rail, his face contorted with a consuming madness. Then he was gone, and they watched him swimming strongly towards the beach. Without speaking they stared after him, while he ran jerkily through the surf and vanished into the trees.

Fraser again turned his back. Nothing could shock him any more, he thought.

'Okay, Myers,' he said calmly, 'you can see to the engine.'

He watched the water surging round the headland, yellow in the dawn sunlight. 'We're going home,' he added slowly as his gaze fell on Hogan's body. 'Or what's left of us.'

166

9

Tarrou could not remember how long he had been running, but as the slope beneath his pounding feet became steeper, and the glistening shrubs and roots thicker and more treacherous, he staggered breathlessly to a halt, his head hanging down to his heaving chest and his tongue lolling across parched lips. Although his body cried out for rest, and he could feel his heart pounding wildly against his ribs, he was still in the grip of that same overpowering madness which had flung him over the schooner's side and sent him careering through the bush, heedless of all possible danger, and of the noise his haphazard course was making.

Slowly he lifted his head and peered blindly through his sweat, aware for the first time of the island's great silence. Where the torpid heat had begun to penetrate the dripping trees the steam rose in a thick, undulating vapour, tinged green and purple by the backcloth of the bush, and giving the whole silent jungle an appearance of nightmarish unreality. A bird called querulously overhead, but it, too, sounded muffled, as if part of another existence. He rested his aching back against a tree, and tried to control the savage emotions which coursed through him, and which threatened to drive him forward again into the darkness of the bush. A warm trickle of blood ran wetly down his cheek, where he had collided with a groping branch. He watched a small red droplet fall on to his caked jacket, and shuddered. He had always tried to keep himself smart and clean, and even in his present agony it pained him to see the state of his clothing.

When he had waded through the surf and staggered up the small beach, he had half expected to be cut down by a spear before he could reach the first line of trees. That would have made Fraser ashamed. That would have shown all of them what they had done to him.

The thought of the schooner sailing without him made him peer momentarily backwards, as if he might still see her white shape through the trees. Not even the slightest gleam of water showed, however, and he began to wonder how far he had come.

Fraser would be sorry when he got back to Vila, he thought. His dark eyes clouded as he visualized the scene on the jetty. The grim faces, and Fraser turning from one to the other, his explanations falling on deaf ears. He clutched wildly at his throat as a new convulsion of rage and frustration ran through him like fire. Suddenly he realized that he was trying to deceive himself yet again. Of course it would not be like that at all. Nobody would care about Michel Tarrou. The American girl's death would be enough for them. Even that drunken beast Hogan was worth more than he. His whole body shook, and two small tears of self-pity ran unheeded down his cheeks to mix with the blood on his jacket.

Some of the old traders might even laugh. He closed his eyes tight, as if to shut out the picture he had created. Fraser drinking in the club, surrounded by those fat red faces. 'Sure,' he would drawl, 'I lost the stupid bugger in the bush!' And they would all laugh, and down their drinks. Then one of them would add, 'Just like a bloody boong!'

And how had all this happened? He rocked back and forth on the balls of his feet, frowning with concentration. Blair had been responsible right from the start. He had resented his friendship with the girl, and her attraction to him. He had hated the fact that he, Michel Tarrou, was strong and whole, while he was crippled and useless.

Now the girl had died, and his position in the schooner was finished. He could never look anyone in the face again without somebody saying, 'Aren't you the man who ran the schooner aground?' Or, 'Did you really believe that a white girl could fall for a joker like you?'

Remorselessly he tore down one pretence after the other, so that even the small beliefs upon which he alone had depended became less of a comfort, and joined instead the great jeering, screaming chorus in his brain.

He noticed that he had started to move again, and with bright eyes he watched his own feet marching onward up the slope. He felt strong once more, and his sense of self-pity gave way as he walked to one of overwhelming cunning and intelligence.

I shall find Blair, he decided. And if he is still alive I shall kill him. The possibility that he might already be dead, or that he might be too well hidden in the bush, filled him with dismay, and he quickened his pace, his eyes slanting from side to side, looking for any clue which might guide him to Blair's hiding-place.

Some inner sense seemed to tell him that he was alone, and he did not feel that he was being watched. It was as if all the living beings had been drawn out of the jungle by some superior power. To leave it free for him to find Blair.

Everything about and around him was sodden and still, and through the small gaps overhead he could see a leaden sky which looked heavy and threatening. He started to remember the schooner, and the screaming force of the gale which had driven her along like a mad thing. That had surely been his greatest moment. Until they had lurched across that sand-bar, and two of the sails had been blown to shreds. Those boys in the crew had done that to him. He halted in his tracks, his staring eyes slowly focussing on a strip of cloth which hung limply from a jagged branch. He circled the place, his anxious glance taking in the heavy footmarks which crossed through a trough of drying mud and disappeared down the slope. Two sets of prints. He stared ahead, trying to visualize the jungle in total darkness, with Fraser and Hogan stumbling through the torrential rain. Somewhere farther back was Blair. Why had Fraser left him behind? He creased his brow in two deep furrows as he tried to reason it out. Perhaps Fraser had been afraid to go back? He toyed momentarily with the idea and discarded it with reluctance. Something else must have happened. More cautiously he began to move through the wet undergrowth, and as the trees thickened around him he drew the heavy revolver from his pocket and carried it awkwardly in his hand. He wondered vaguely what effect the sea-water would have had on the bullets, and whether Blair would be armed.

His clothes felt dry and stiff on his skin, and he was aware of the trapped and mounting heat within the jungle. He had often heard the schooner skippers say that the 'eye of the storm' was often broken by contact with an island, but that the fury of it would return from a different angle.

He bared his teeth at the thought of Fraser battling against a new storm, with a damaged ship and a depleted crew for company. Let him see how he likes it, he thought savagely.

Once he stopped to rest, but his legs quivered so much with fatigue that he pressed forward almost at once, driving his wiry body without mercy.

The hours passed, and his tongue seemed to have doubled in size as it moved restlessly behind his bared teeth in search of moisture to cure his thirst.

One of his shoes had gone, and a leg of his drill trousers

was slit from thigh to ankle, so that it caught and flapped over each small obstacle. Must be halfway to the trade store by now, he thought. Suppose I have lost my way? He glanced round wildly, the sweat suddenly cold on his heaving chest. Through the green curtain ahead he could make out the shape of a giant boulder. Perhaps if he climbed to the top of it he could get a better idea of his position. After all, he told himself with mounting anxiety, the sea could not be far away.

A pulse throbbed with sudden pounding strokes against the inside of his skull, and he had difficulty in breathing. He did not dare move his cramped feet for fear that he should miss the sound if it came again. He jumped. That was it. Like the rustle of something moving over the ground. It seemed to be coming from the boulder.

Then there was another sound. It was like a long, low groan. With every nerve straining, he began to crawl on his knees towards a clump of sea grapes, his face feeling like a leather mask. Very slowly he raised himself on his hands and peered through a tiny gap, his tiredness completely forgotten.

He saw Blair's feet moving listlessly in the dried mud, the torn shoes jerking in short, ineffectual attempts to gain a purchase in the yellow filth which had run down around the tall rock, and which hid the rest of his body from Tarrou's sight.

He was alive. Tarrou slowly wiped the sweat from his eyes and began to wriggle round the side of the great boulder. He stopped to listen, as Blair said with sudden clarity:

'Too bloody quiet!' Then he groaned again, as the disembodied feet began to slide in the mud. 'That's right! Let me down again, damn you!' He sounded as if he was speaking through his teeth.

Tarrou began to shiver with excitement, and his hand

171

holding the revolver shook so much that he almost dropped it. He inched his way carefully round the last of the obstruction, and found himself staring straight at Blair.

He was amazed at the difference which had changed the man from a brisk, superior being to this grey-faced, ragged creature which now confronted him. His clothes were in rags, and his stained face was flung upwards towards the racing clouds, the mouth moving painfully as he tried to manoeuvre his legs. Tarrou's eye fell on the rifle. It was by the other man's side, and still within his reach.

He raised the heavy pistol so that Blair's mouth was cut in two by its thick foresight. This would finish all the humiliation and misery once and for all. He would have no time to get the rifle, he would not even know what had happened.

His finger tightened, and he felt the trigger begin to move. It was not right that Blair should die without knowing who had beaten him, he reflected wildly. Without a second thought he lowered the gun and stood up, his shadow covering Blair's sprawled body like a canopy.

Blair opened his eyes and stared up at him.

Tarrou fought to control his quivering limbs, his shadowed face devoid of expression. He wanted to scream: 'What have you to say now, Major Blair? Do you want to say your prayers?' But he could only stare, and feel the weight of the gun in his grip.

Blair gave a weak smile. 'Well, thank God someone had the guts to come back!' He coughed, and laughed strangely. 'You certainly take the biscuit, I must say!'

He closed his eyes again, and Tarrou took another step forward. 'Major Blair,' he began, his tone thick and unsteady, 'I have come—'

One hand lifted in a tired salute. 'You're a good chap, Tarrou. I am afraid I couldn't have lasted much longer. My leg's twisted, and that damned foot . . .' His voice trailed away.

Tarrou found that he was unable to find the right words. He was completely unnerved by Blair's greeting, yet unwilling to admit that he was afraid of the defenceless creature at his feet.

Blair was speaking again. 'You alone? How is Gillian?' He said her name again, more slowly. 'Gillian?'

Tarrou had difficulty in breathing. 'She is dead. Drowned.'

Blair's head fell back against the rock, and his face seemed to shrink under the caked mud. 'Oh God,' he said in a small, broken voice. 'Not her, too!'

Tarrou was shaking uncontrollably. 'It was your fault! It was all your fault!'

Blair nodded heavily. 'Yes. You are so right, my friend. And I thought . . .' He did not finish but lay back as if in surrender to the fever which showed itself in the brightness of his eyes.

Tarrou stared round the tiny clearing in desperation. 'She went up to the mission. She was drowned. It was not my fault! You were to blame!'

Blair sighed. 'That damned mission.' His voice seemed to come from far away. 'She must have been going to see Spencer.' He groaned, and allowed his legs to slip lower. 'And now she's dead. Just when I thought . . .' Tarrou noticed that he was biting his lower lip and the feverish eyes were blurred. 'And now you're here, Tarrou. Well, you can damned well go back to the ship and tell them you could not find me, see?'

Tarrou ran his fingers through his greased hair. This was all wrong. Everything was getting out of control again. He heard himself ask in a strange voice, 'Were you really fond of her?'

173

Blair's tight mouth quivered. 'Fond of her? Yes, that would be it. I suppose you think that's strange?' Tarrou did not answer, and he continued: 'She was the best thing that ever happened to me.' His eye fell on the revolver. 'What were you going to do with that? Shoot me or something?' His chest heaved weakly as he laughed without humour. 'Not a bad idea at that!'

Tarrou self-consciously thrust the gun into his pocket. 'You must not mock me! I have been through so much!' He knew he could not shoot him now. If only Blair had cursed him, or sneered at him. It would have been easy then.

Blair's voice was very low. 'The mission, you say? I wonder what Spencer knows?' Another pause. 'I let you down, Gillian. Just like all the others.'

Tarrou shifted uneasily. 'What others?'

'Family. My sister had hair like Gillian. Fair as . . .' His tired mind seemed to grope for the right word, but instead he merely sighed. 'But now she's gone, too.'

Tarrou nodded gravely. 'Her hair was like nothing I have ever seen. All the boys on board said it was like the sun.' He stopped, aware that Blair had struggled up into a sitting position and was gripping the ragged edge of his trousers.

'By God, that's it! I *knew* there was something!' He coughed, and struggled even harder. 'Don't you see, man?'

Tarrou stared at him worriedly. He was delirious, or mad. He was not sure what to do about it, and merely shook his head.

Blair's fist beat weakly on the mud. 'Why didn't I notice that! When we first landed at the mission,' his eyes shone with sudden desperation, 'none of the villagers took any notice of her hair! Yet everywhere else around here, and on the schooner, the natives were all gaping at it!' He shook Tarrou's leg to emphasize his strangled words. 'Because those people at the mission had seen hair like that before!'

Tarrou's mouth hung slack. 'Your sister?'

Blair was already struggling to his feet, climbing up Tarrou's body like a monkey up a tree. 'Must get there. You'll have to help me!'

Tarrou slipped his arm round Blair's waist and together they stood swaying in the small clearing, while Blair studied the other man's face with fixed intentness. 'You *will* help me, won't you?'

Tarrou swallowed and licked his dry lips. He was completely lost now, but he was conscious of the great feeling of new strength which Blair's own weakness seemed to have given him. 'I will help.' He hesitated. 'But what do you hope to find?'

Blair shook his head. 'I don't know yet. I don't know.'

They moved off together, Blair hopping awkwardly on his good foot and leaning on Tarrou for support.

As they started to push through the bush Blair said suddenly, 'I'm glad you didn't shoot me back there.'

Tarrou trembled, but could not answer.

'I saw you watching me, and I wondered if you could do it in cold blood!'

Tarrou hung his head, but Blair added softly: 'It took more guts to do what you did, and don't you ever forget it.'

Tarrou sighed. What sort of a man was this? He had known all the time that he was there, and yet . . . He shivered. A man who could play with life like that was a man indeed. He lifted his chin and followed Blair without hesitation into the thickening trees.

For some while Blair had been lying full-length on the stony ground, his chest supported on the edge of a small rock cavity, as he stared unseeingly at his reflection in the tiny pool of trapped rain-water. The dark, motionless water showed him his tangled hair and the thin, tight line of his mouth. Painfully he reached out with his hands and erased the picture, trying at the same time to gain some satisfaction from the tepid pool and the feel of his dripping palms across his face. Without looking round he knew that Tarrou was still standing woodenly by his feet, holding the guns and staring apprehensively at the quiet trees. Occasionally the silence would be broken with sharp brevity by a bird's call, or by the gentle rustle of a breeze amongst the leaves. Blair felt as if they were the last two people alive.

He had almost laughed aloud as, between slitted eyelids, he had watched Tarrou's clumsy approach through the bush, and seen the torment in his eyes as he had levelled the revolver across the top of the clearing which had served Blair as a hiding-place.

He frowned, and watched the rain-water settle in its small rock bowl, the wild eyes slowly shimmering into perspective to stare up at him. Why had he not called out? Suppose Tarrou had pulled the trigger? He felt the pressure of the stones against his chest, but was unable to drag himself away from the little pool. He knew that he had not cared whether Tarrou would fire or not. He groaned, and instantly felt Tarrou move closer. And now Gillian was dead. He moved his head slowly from side to side, his eyes still fixed on the reflection. She had known about Spencer, and had gone to get the complete story. Of course Spencer had known all about the wreck. He dashed some more water across his burning cheeks and pushed his hair back from his eyes.

'What are we going to do, Major?' Tarrou's voice sounded far away.

Blair tried to think clearly. It was ridiculous being addressed in such a fashion, and he wanted to tell the man so. Instead, he said: 'God knows. I expect we're lost.'

There was another silence. 'I think the schooner will go without us.'

With a terrific effort Blair rolled over on to his back and stared fixedly at the low clouds. 'Of course it'll go! What did you expect, man?' He looked at Tarrou's smooth face with sudden irritation. 'Stop thinking about it! We must find that damned mission, then we can wait there for a bit!'

Tarrou's eyes clouded as he tried to find some comfort in the words.

Blair slowly climbed to his feet, and then peered down at them with amazement. The crippled, throbbing foot was hidden beneath a neat, soothing bandage. 'How the hell did that get there?'

'I fix it just now.'

Blair whistled softly. He had not felt a thing. 'I must have been asleep,' he lied.

'You got a fever.' Tarrou sounded more subdued than ever. 'You need treatment, Major.'

Blair shrugged and thrust his hands into his torn pocket. He could feel them trembling violently, and tried not to look at the other man. Fever. That's all I need. Better get on now before anything else happens.

'Right,' he said calmly. 'Let's follow this ridge, eh? Might lead us round the worst of the bush.' Without waiting for a reply he walked unsteadily away from the pool. If I said let's fly to the ruddy moon, he'd follow me, he thought absently.

There's going to be another storm, he decided, as a break in the trees showed him a fast-moving mass of cloud. I hope that schooner is right in the path of it. He heard a sharp, unexpected sound, and checked himself with sudden anxiety. It was the sound of his own voice. The sweat broke out over his face, blinding him, but he walked more rapidly, as if to disguise his rising fever.

Tarrou kept talking. His voice seemed to drone on with perpetual sameness, like the hushed tone of a schoolboy talking in class. Blair had no idea what he was saying, it was only the tone he heard. Eager, frightened, trusting and confidential, with a 'Major' thrown in every few words for good measure.

Blair staggered against a tree and brushed away the dark hand which darted out to steady him. He thought of the other jungle he had known. There had been the same green impression of for ever. He glanced quickly to one side, as if he expected to see the lumpy shape of Sergeant Robbins and the other figures in faded jungle green, as like ghosts they moved and floated through the tangled trees. Poor Robbins, with his endless stories about Blackpool. And then there was little Eldergill, who, when his Bren jammed for the last time, had jumped from the slit-trench with doubled fists like a boxer to meet the charging, merciless bayonets.

He stopped with a jerk, his chest heaving. I am back in that same jungle, he thought wildly. He reached out with sudden strength, and grabbed Tarrou's arm.

'Get down, man!' He punched the man's shoulder. 'And for Christ's sake keep quiet!'

Together they lay amongst some rotting, evil-scented branches, and stared at the wall of trees. Blair blinked away the sweat, and made another effort to think clearly. Had he imagined that, too? Was he perhaps already in the grip of a real fever, and Tarrou had not the wit to realize it? He stared hard at the trees, so that the satin-smooth trunks danced lazily through the haze of his concentration. He suppressed the desire to laugh and keep laughing. In a second, he thought with sudden gravity, a Japanese patrol will come towards us, and then I shall know I'm going mad. He glanced sideways at Tarrou, who watched with wide, uncomprehending eyes, his mouth hanging open, as Blair pulled the rifle from beneath his leg and thrust it across the rotting wood. He licked his lips and dusted some sand carefully away from the backsight. Then they heard it. The dull, measured boom of a drum, at first muffled by the trees, then with slow, heavy persistence, gaining strength and power with each nerve-racking minute.

Tarrou began to shake, his knee vibrating against Blair's leg. Blair could smell the fear from the other man, and wondered briefly what power had forced him to leave the schooner at all.

Blair's voice was quite level. 'Keep your eyes peeled to the left.'

Tarrou nodded, and stared helplessly in the direction indicated. 'What is happening, Major?' There was almost a sob in his whisper, and for a second Blair eyed him with pity.

'I imagine we're going to have company.' He reached out to grip the thin brown wrist. 'I had a sort of feeling.' He shook his head vaguely. 'I knew that something or somebody was coming. I don't really understand it myself.' He broke off, his fingers releasing Tarrou, as something flashed dully beyond the trees.

The drum grew louder; hollow, dull, yet with such penetrating force that it seemed to keep time with their hearts.

Blair shifted slightly, as in twos and threes the short dark figures moved across the clearing, their feet swishing quietly through the shrubs, their wide-bladed spears carried with casual ease, and glinting in the occasional rays of watery sunlight, which filtered down as in the nave of a great cathedral.

A muscle jumped in Blair's neck as he allowed his body to sink lower, and with sudden calm he pulled the rifle to his shoulder. They're not like men at all, he thought, as he watched the bobbing red-wigged heads and the crudely made weapons, which added to the impression of

179

untouched savagery. He counted slowly. There seemed to be about a hundred of them, and they walked with the watchful confidence of conquerors. The much-famed Motă, no doubt. No wonder that fool Grainger had said they were better left alone.

They were completely naked, but for narrow belts of bark in which they appeared to be carrying knives or short bundles of arrows. A small group of older warriors kept together, and Blair could see that their emaciated bodies were more heavily disfigured with painted clay, and their necks and arms well laden with crude ornaments of teeth and cowrie shells. Here and there the light touched on an ancient rifle and he saw one man carrying a Winchester which must have been over fifty years old. The drum was now deafening and, as they watched, two small boys emerged from the bush carrying a long, thin, log drum, which quivered to the slow, regular blows of a carved club, wielded by a thickset savage whose body gleamed with sweat and shook with each powerful stroke.

Gently Blair eased off the safety-catch. He had noticed that the men on the end of the line would pass very close to their scanty hiding-place if they kept on the same track.

The Motă were so close now that he could study them as individuals, and see each savagely formed face, with its thick lips and deep-set black eyes. Some had their broad noses pierced by long quills, or what looked like sharks' teeth, while others carried great tribal scars across their chests and stomachs. They walked in a steady, loping gait, heedless of the scrub which groped at their naked bodies, their eyes fixed ahead as if in a trance.

Blair pressed himself down against the rotting mould, and was conscious of the insects ticking beneath his chin. A world within a world, he thought calmly. The Motă, like the insects, were no doubt convinced that theirs was the only way to live, whilst I . . . he halted his feverish thoughts and moved the rifle very slightly.

He could feel the steady tattoo of feet on the underbrush, tramping in time to the drum. The nearest savage was barely ten yards away, and Blair could see the rivulets of sweat running across his flat, muscular stomach and down the dust-spattered legs. On his right shin was a long, glistening sore, open, and apparently unheeded, and Blair watched it with fascinated eyes, as with each boom of the drum its owner grew taller and nearer. Come on, my beauty, just walk this way a bit more! He wanted to wipe his eyes, but knew that even the slightest movement would be fatal. The black stomach quivered across the hard V of the backsight, and Blair held his breath as his finger took the first pressure.

What a commotion there would be, he reflected bitterly, the sudden whiplash crack of the rifle, and then the battle which would follow. Ten rounds in the rifle and two in my pocket. Not a very long battle. Poor Tarrou. It was worse for him. It was quite likely that he might break at any second now, and either start blundering through the bush, or begin blazing away with that useless pistol. Wish I'd hung on to the shotgun, he thought, just the job for a party like this. Two extra bangs on the log-drum and, with the precision of the Guards, the whole party of warriors wheeled away from the rifle and started up the long green ridge beyond the clearing.

Blair stared unwaveringly after the purposeful figures, until his vision had misted over completely and he had to blink to clear away the sweat. When he looked again there was nothing to see but the nodding palms, and nothing to remind him of the silent warriors but the distant thud of the drum.

He turned and looked at Tarrou. The man lay on his side,

his eyes tightly closed, and both hands dug deeply into the soft ground. He nudged him, and the dark hands shuddered.

'Up!' he snapped. 'Don't want to hang around here!'

Tarrou blinked, and watched Blair's shadow grow as he stood up, and with a brief glance at the still recumbent figure beside him, begin to limp towards the ridge.

Tarrou scrambled after him, his mouth slack and wet. 'Where to? Where to?' He repeated the question again and again, but Blair did not answer. He swayed on, his teeth gritted against the pain in his foot and the mounting nausea in his brain.

As if to silence Tarrou's voice he said harshly: 'So that was the Motă, eh? Why doesn't the government do something about them?'

'The chiefs were there, too.' There was awe in the statement. 'The ones with the guns.'

'Guns! Museum-pieces, you mean! I suppose they murdered some poor wretches for those!'

A spark of the old defiance flickered in Tarrou's answer. 'The white men give them to the Motă years ago. In exchange for slaves!' The spark died just as suddenly as Blair halted and turned his cold blue eyes on him.

'*White* men, eh? Changed sides again, have you?' He laughed bitterly and plunged on again.

'Please, I did not mean —' Tarrou was half running to keep up with the stooped, limping figure.

'I don't give a damn what you believe!' Blair's voice dropped to a mutter. 'But if I had a few good men I'd show them how to behave!'

'We can do nothing, Major Blair! Let us make for the beach, perhaps they will send help for us!'

'Help? I don't want anyone's help!' He waved vaguely towards the high ridge. 'Somewhere over there is that mission.' He laughed again. 'Mission! I like that! I'm going

182

to find it if I have to tear down every damned tree on this bloody island! And when I do, I'm going to ask Mr. Spencer a few questions, oh yes!' The bandaged foot thumped on the ground in time with the distant drum. 'Too much has happened now to turn back.' He paused wearily, his face grey. 'You go where you like, Tarrou, but I'm going on!'

The clouds had thickened to such an extent that the jungle was like night, so that when they stumbled over the ridge and smelt the sea they had to stop and stare with something like disbelief. It was all there. The sloping headland, purple now under the racing clouds, the empty sea no longer blue, but a heaving grey expanse of rough pewter. The tide was high as they stared down at the rumbling surf, and the narrow beach where they had first landed to meet Spencer was all but hidden. On the extreme edge of the narrow sand-strip Blair could see a wrecked canoe bobbing in the creamy breakers like a gutted beetle. In the far distance he could see the top of a small hut, where the tiny mission village perched above the sea. Nothing moved, and the timeless thunder of the breakers beneath them added to the sense of threat and fear which surrounded the place.

'No schooner!' said Tarrou in a broken voice. 'He left without me!' Even as he stared at the empty sea he could still not believe what he saw.

The mission looked even whiter against the sky, and in the cruel light some of its magic had departed and left in its place the more obvious ravages of the tropics. The rusty iron roof, mildewed planking and the thick cobwebs, which hung like wire from every beam. The empty door looked like a mouth gaping in a silent cry, and Blair ran his eye quickly over the surrounding bush before returning his gaze to the house.

'The natives seem to have left,' he said quietly. 'No smoke from the village, and no one to welcome us.'

Tarrou's eyes protruded with fresh alarm. 'Bad! Bad!' He crouched on his knees, his fingers again digging into the ground.

Blair shook his head to clear away the dullness in his brain. 'You stay here, Tarrou.' He waved the protests to silence. 'I'm going to take a look-see inside.' He tore his eyes from the house to peer at the shaking half-caste. 'Look,' he continued gently, 'if anything goes wrong you skedaddle into the bush and wait until help comes. There's bound to be a police investigation into all this and you'll be a hero!' The black eyes still stared at him. Without will or hope.

Blair stood up and handed him the rifle. Taking the revolver from the nerveless hand he crept quickly towards the side of the house, his eyes flickering across the stamped compound.

He climbed softly on to the end of the veranda, and winced as a plank creaked beneath his feet. He was conscious of the heavy heat, which threatened to stifle him, and of the sweet smell of copra. Abstractedly he remembered his cool office, and the leather-topped desk which always seemed to be empty. Miss Cousins, his secretary, would no doubt be wondering how he was getting on, and whether he had found a wreck filled with treasure. He froze into stillness as something rustled within the gaping door.

He swallowed hard and stepped slowly to the side of the entrance, expecting at any second to hear a chorus of shouts, or feel some terrible blow from behind. The silence was much worse. In two quick strides he entered the doorway and pressed his back against the rough wall, his eyes sweeping across the dim interior of Spencer's mission.

Ivor Spencer lay spreadeagled on the planked floor, his arms outstretched in a mockery of the brass crucifix which hung from the wall. Two metal spikes had been hammered

184

into his hands, pinioning him to the floor, and, even as he watched, his mouth dry with horror, he saw the long fingers moving like small trapped animals.

The tufted grey halo of hair was streaked with bright scarlet, and as the head moved slightly towards him he saw fresh blood glisten across Spencer's cheek, from the two sightless holes where his eyes should have been.

Blair swayed, and retched helplessly. When he saw the tangled and bloody mess between the thin twitching legs he wondered how this writhing thing had managed to stay alive.

The broken mouth moved grotesquely. Gone was the resonant tone. The voice was weak, like a child's. 'Who is that?'

Blair knelt at his side, staring over the tortured body at the crucifix. He remembered the naval officer at Singapore. 'I'm afraid He's forgotten all about us.'

'It's me. Rupert Blair.' He turned his eyes to the other room. 'Is there anyone else alive?'

'Dead. All dead.' The lips bubbled. 'All but her—'

Blair's eyes moved momentarily downwards. 'Her? Who d'you mean?'

'American girl.' The sockets gleamed, so that Blair felt he was trying to see his face. 'They took her away.' The voice grew fainter. 'I thought they would see reason . . .'

Blair swayed back on his haunches. Gillian alive, only to be taken by the Motă. He clenched his teeth. 'Tell me quickly. What about the other girl? There was one, wasn't there?'

Spencer's head sagged. 'Your sister, I believe?' An awful rattle began deep in his throat. 'She died many years ago. Motă thought that woman was she . . .' The voice trailed away, but Blair gripped the bony shoulder with sudden desperation.

185

'Where have they gone?'

'Little cove . . . two miles from here . . . they call it House of Spirits . . . heathen sacrifices . . .' Some of the strength filtered back into his voice. 'But for you I would have converted all of them. I . . .'

Blair stood up and stared through the window at the shimmering jungle. He retched again, the faintness making him stagger against those twitching fingers. He felt the gun in his hand, and swallowed the rising bile as he felt a growing agony of despair and urgency. It was almost unimportant now to realize that his sister had lived and died here. Perhaps later, if there was time to think, but now . . . He turned, the gun steady in his hand. He could not leave the man like this. But it was not necessary, and already the fat blue flies were exploring the mutilated remains of Ivor Spencer.

Without even a glance in the other room he staggered out into the light and the heat. Tarrou ran to meet him, the relief dying on his face as he saw Blair's stricken expression. He flinched as Blair's hard hands gripped his shoulders, and unwillingly he managed to meet the blue stare.

'Do you know of a small cove near here? Two miles away?' The urgency made his voice harsh.

Tarrou shook his head. 'No, no! I know nothing! Please, what was in the mission?'

Blair shook him savagely. 'Think, man! Try to remember the chart! Where is that cove from here?' He was shouting now and heedless of the noise.

When Tarrou only whimpered, he added: 'You were fond of Miss Bligh, weren't you? Well, she's alive, and they've taken her to this place! *Now* can you remember?'

Tarrou's hand lifted feebly and pointed across two humpbacked hills. The old volcano gleamed implacably and with sudden clarity in the far distance.

186

'There! That way!' He rolled his eyes back to the house. 'Mr. Spencer?'

Blair shook his head, and added as if to himself: 'Convert them, he said! Like a mouse squeaking at the jungle!' Then, his eyes shining with feverish brightness, he dragged Tarrou across the compound. The end of the journey was getting near.

He remembered the quiet brass crucifix. Please God, let us be in time, just this once.

10

Vic Fraser lay full length on his bunk and stared unblinkingly at the low deckhead. Thirty feet farther along the hull the two divers completed their inspection and temporary repairs by nailing a crude tingle, well-laced with grease, below the waterline, where a seam had been forced open by the shock of the schooner lurching across the sandbar. Each muffled blow on the ancient timbers made Fraser's inert hands twitch, and he seemed to be using his utmost strength to restrain himself from tearing on deck and ordering them to get a move on.

The heat in the tiny cabin was so tremendous and suffocating that it pained him to make the effort to breathe, but he was so sick with the agony of waiting and listening that he hardly noticed it. He was still wearing his tattered shirt and slacks, which hung in a tight, sweaty shroud about his limbs, and still retained the stink of the jungle and of his fear.

Unwillingly he turned his massive head and looked again at the scattered clothing and expensive leather cases which seemed to fill the cabin with Blair's memory and presence. He squeezed his eyes shut, trying to wipe out the picture of Blair's dragging foot, and his wild, remorseless eyes.

With a groan he rolled heavily over the side of the bunk, and tore open his shirt, baring his chest as if to strip off the tormenting memories. His eye fell on the barometer, and he found that he was gripping his hair with his strong fingers until the pain made him stop. The glass had been falling steadily all morning, and the wind had altered both in direction and strength. Instead of the previous furnace heat, the wind which now moaned across the island, and stirred the dark water into long, uneasy rollers, was moist and clinging, like his clothes. There was no let-up in its power, and even the direction seemed to vary very little. The divers had remarked earlier that the water was full of strange currents. First a hot layer, then, within minutes, a cold breath in the sea itself, which would bring them shivering and spluttering to the surface. Fraser knew the signs of old. This was no ordinary 'blow'. This was to be the real thing.

He checked himself against leaving the cabin. What was the use? They were doing all they could, and even Dinkila the cook was busy with palm and needle repairing one of the sails. Old Kari merely bent over his work, his black eyes smoky and sullen, the shiny fingers moving with practised ease over the rough canvas.

Fraser stared at his wild reflection in the mirror. Myers had apparently recovered from his drinking, and now sat broodingly by the bulwark watching the water around the two divers for a tell-tale dorsal fin, Fraser's rifle in his red hands. Fraser almost cried out with frustration as he thought of Myer's face, rebellious and angry. Right now they should have been clawing their way clear of the island, the old diesel engine getting them a head start on the approaching storm. But Myers had shaken his head, and held up a small bright piece of metal. 'Water pump, sheared orf!' he had called from the engine compartment. 'Bloody engine's a write-orf, less you got a spare, eh?'

When Fraser had stormed at him, Myers had suddenly hardened, his round, sweating face filled with tired contempt.

''Oo th 'ell d'you think you're yellin' at? Wot can *I* do abaht it, eh?' He waved his grease-stained hands about the ship. 'Look at it, carn't yer? No bleedin' radio, so we don't know if there's goin' to be a 'urricane or a blasted snowstorm! Now that the pump's sheered orf the engin', you announces that you ain't got any spares!' He hung on the edge of the coaming, his face suddenly old. 'Christ, man, you've bitched this up proper!'

Fraser had stared down at him, filled with the sudden urge to kick him in the face, to shut his stupid whining once and for all. He had seen Kari watching them, and had dropped his voice to a harsh whisper.

'What the hell d'you mean?'

'Wot d'you think, mate? Poor bloody Major Blair left behind, Jim 'Ogan chopped and the girl drowned. That's quite apart from losin' a few of the crew 'ere an' there like!' His voice trembled. 'Wot did you expect me to say? That you was entitled to a bloody medal?'

If Myers had been ready to listen, perhaps he could have explained it all. He frowned again, so that the deep furrows around his mouth were like black lines. He could not even explain it to himself. He stared unseeingly at the smudged chart on the table. All he knew was that he had to get away from the island before the storm came. Before they were all finally wiped out, and the *Queensland Pearl* destroyed. He peered desperately around the dark cabin, but its familiar fittings no longer reassured him. The small skylight overhead was no longer blue. The rolling banks of grey clouds were laced with dirty brown, so that they looked like solid things.

Myers had been right, of course. He had always meant to install a radio, and a new engine, and lots of other refinements, but something had always come up to forestall him. The cabin rolled and squeaked in slow, uneven curtsies, and he had to brace his legs wide to retain his balance.

190

Through the skylight he caught a brief glimpse of the shortened mainmast, black against the angry sky. With the topmast missing, it gave the schooner the appearance of leaning forward, crouching under the starter's orders perhaps. She wanted to be away, too, he thought abstractedly. Or did she? Was he the only one who had failed her? He jumped as someone knocked on the door.

Kari stood framed by the doorway, the light from the companion hatch playing across his scarred shoulders.

'Well? Have you finished?' Fraser felt hoarse.

Kari nodded. 'Finish, yes.' He avoided Fraser's eyes. 'This bad trip, Cap'n. Buka daid. Watute daid. Mate go longlong!' He shook his grizzled head sharply. 'I think we lose more.'

'Don't talk like an old fool!' Fraser watched him with growing uneasiness. 'What do you want to tell me?'

Kari touched the brass plate by the cabin door, its inscription almost polished away. 'Built – Sydney – 1914'. He could not read it, but its smooth surface seemed to decide him. 'I sail with your father, Cap'n. Many years I dive for shell, an' I serve, an' I know my boss a good man.' He hung his head and shuffled his black feet on the deck. 'Now I know shame, Cap'n. 'Cause you run away!' He looked up suddenly, his old eyes blazing. 'I Torres islander, Cap'n! My fathers were chiefs! We no run away!'

Fraser took half a step forward, his fists doubled. 'Why you flamin' old bastard! Who dragged you aboard after the tigers had been at you, eh? Who's given you a job all these years?'

Kari regarded him with sadness. 'I know, Cap'n. But I think the spirits have taken your strength—' His head jerked as Fraser's open palm struck him across the mouth.

'Get on deck, damn you! Get those lazy boongs to stand by the anchor! We're pullin' out now, d'you understand

191

that?' His voice boomed in the humid cabin like the sound of that drum. He stared at the thin trickle of blood and spittle which ran down the old man's chin. 'There's nothing more I can do now. They're all dead, an' Tarrou's hopped it fer good!'

Kari backed towards the ladder. 'That drum say you lie!' His voice was a hiss. 'They no daid. You leaveum with your strength!'

Fraser lifted his arm. 'Get out, damn you! Do as I say, or I'll . . .' He saw that he was shouting at empty air, and heard Kari's hard feet padding across the planks overhead.

With a curse he snatched up his telescope and climbed heavily up the ladder and on to the deck, which now felt like the inside of a kiln. He walked to the wheel, his eye falling momentarily on the useless engine throttle. 'Hoist away! Break her out!' he yelled, and his voice murmured back at him from the silent shore and the glistening palms.

The cable began to clank link by link through the fairlead, and he saw Myers bending his back with the others, as if he no longer wished to be associated with him.

Fraser watched the great troughs in the heaving water, and tried to estimate the strength of the soaking, brain-searing wind.

Kari raised his head and shouted. He could still see the red smear on his chin, even at the length of the ship. He tore his eyes away as he felt the ship begin to slide sideways, free from her anchor.

'Break out the foresail an' outer jib!' He fretted with impatience as the figures moved listlessly to the halyards.

Queensland Pearl drew her faded sails about her bare spars, like an old lady dressing herself for the last time. The big foresail, followed by the mainsail, swung out on its great boom, whilst from the graceful bowsprit the small triangular jibsails whipped out like flags, as they climbed up with painful slowness to capture the wind. The schooner slowly came to life and beneath his hard hands Fraser felt the wheel buck, and over his shoulder heard the soft gurgle and hiss as the rudder bit into the water and brought the vessel creaming round in a wide arc, until the bowsprit swung and parried towards the horizon.

As she moved sedately along the headland the first gust of wind sighed in from the open and unprotected sea and hit the white hull with playful violence.

The sails filled and hardened, the wind booming around the worn canvas with trapped fury, whilst all around the rigging clattered and creaked in answer to the challenge. Spray rose over the high stem, and covered the fo'c'sle with dark designs, and beaded the skins of the seamen as they made fast the anchor to its bed.

Fraser concentrated on the compass and on the set of the sails, so that he should exclude the others from his thoughts. He reached up automatically to adjust the cap over his eyes, and felt another pang of guilt as he remembered that it was somewhere in the distant jungle. With the schooner alive beneath his feet he tried to regain the comfort which it usually gave him, and to reassure his mind at the same time. No one could blame him for what he had done. Grainger had told him, ordered him, in fact, not to go near the Motă, or do anything which might spark off trouble. It had all been Blair's doing right from the beginning. There would probably be a hullabaloo about the girl's death, but that could not be helped. It could have happened anywhere. His throat felt dry. She had been a fine girl. What did that old fool Kari mean about the drums? He felt another spasm of shame when he remembered striking the old man, but he lifted his chin and glared along the rising deck, his brown eyes hard. He had brought it on himself, he thought furiously. He had always thought of the boys as simple human beings, but they were all savages at heart. He allowed his mind to explore the biggest ache of all. Even Michel. He, too, had failed. He glanced over the weather-rail of the poop and stared in surprise at the green shape of Hog Island. It already looked small and insignificant again, like so many others of the group. Tiny, private worlds, which, as Gillian Bligh had pointed out, meant nothing to those on the outside.

He could feel the schooner gaining speed through the water as she gathered the wind into her sails and flung herself over a crest into a deep, glass-sided trough, so that Fraser had to lean his whole weight on the spokes to bring her evenly to meet the next unbroken roller. He sighed as the bowsprit lifted and the glistening hull flung the clutching waves on either side in proud contempt.

The foretopsail was being set now, and with eyes slitted against the glare he watched Wabu's muscles move like snakes as he sheeted home a block and stood back to get his breath. His face, too, was dark and sullen. They did not sing or laugh, and as Dinkila slithered crabwise along the lively deck towards his small galley he avoided Fraser's eye, his face heavy.

Myers steadied himself against the compass, his tight eyes expressionless. 'Where we makin' for?' he asked at length.

'West for a bit. Then I'm runnin' south. Might be able to get into shelter.' He cursed as the compass card swung lazily in its bowl, and eased the spokes over until it steadied.

Myers watched the hands on the wheel, and shuddered. In a minute, he thought desperately, I shall wake up, and the island will be just as it was before. The blue water of the bay, the shining, clear sky, and the native divers laughing as they watched him getting into his suit. He thought of

194

Gillian Bligh as she had looked when she had sauntered into his cabin. The cool grey eyes and wide, generous mouth. Just like her pictures. But it was not a dream, especially about Major Blair. In all Myers' difficulties and hard struggle upwards with the firm, Blair had been the one person who had treated him well. He trembled as he thought more deeply about it. When his wife had nagged him about the job, or the neighbours, or the hundred-and-one other things she complained about, it had been Blair who had brought back his self-respect. When he had tried to describe him to his wife he had been momentarily at a loss for words. In the end he had fallen back on the highest compliment he knew. 'Well, he's a gentleman, you see . . .' But, of course, she had only laughed at him.

He glared at Fraser's taut face, the feeling of helplessness only adding to one of despair.

The boys had gathered beneath the bulwark, and sat staring up at the protesting rigging and booming canvas. Myers and Fraser stood in swaying silence, each wrapped in his own thoughts.

'Drivin' 'er a bit, ain't you?' Myers asked after a while. 'Are we in any danger now?'

Fraser jerked his head. 'Take a look at the island.' He knew inwardly that, like himself, Myers was afraid to trust his own power of speech. 'I don't know what sort of storm it'll be, but we'll be well out of it if we let the *Pearl* run free.'

Myers shaded his eyes and looked back over the pitching rail. Hog Island lay directly astern now. It was, he thought, almost as if it stood in the direct path of something terrible. Something which had changed the sky to angry orange copper, so that the island appeared to have one huge halo of fire. The visibility had dropped away, and its shape was already indistinct, and the smaller islets which had seemed

195

so near had vanished like chalk sponged from a blackboard. The schooner was alone on a limitless ocean and, even as he watched, the island was lost in the haze of steam and spray.

Fraser's voice broke in on his thoughts. 'D'you still want me to go back? How long d'you think we could live in that?' He hurried on, never taking his eyes from the ship. 'You've got your life to live?' He took a deep breath. 'Well, so have I!'

Myers blinked as a sheet of spray stung his eyes. 'Wot's the use of talkin'? Yer mind's bin made up a long time, ain't it?'

'Yes. Made up.' He was talking to himself. 'I don't have any other life. I'm like poor old Jim Hogan down in the hold, I can't afford to start all over again.'

Myers shook his head. 'What will 'appen when you gets back?'

He shrugged. 'I suppose the authorities, British or French, will send some police up there to have a look-see. I don't know. In a couple of months perhaps everythin'll be back to normal. Nothin' ever changes here. It's only when outsiders interfere that we have any trouble!'

Myers felt cold in spite of the heat, and heard himself say, in a strange voice: 'Take me back, Vic. Just me.' The words tumbled out. He could not stop now. 'You can still get clear, an' I'll go an' look for the Major. Will you do that, Vic?'

Fraser's hands shook on the wheel. 'For God's sake leave me alone! What use would you be, eh? When you were in the last blow you took to the bottle, didn't you? Well, *didn't* you?' He shouted louder when Myers' stricken face did not change. 'Nothin' but bloody heroics! Let me tell you that heroics are for jokers who can afford them, and we can't, see?'

196

Myers moved away. 'You think you've saved yerself by slangin' me, don't you? Yer wrong, mate. You've lost everythin'!' He thrust his round face towards the other man. 'By Christ, I wish I'd 'ad the guts to leave this mornin'! But I never thought you'd be scum enough to do this!' He saw the murderous glare in Fraser's eyes and, turning his back, he staggered down the companion-way and groped his way to the tiny cabin he had shared with Tarrou.

He fell into the bunk and lay quite still, listening to his heart. You fool. You nearly did it then. Suppose he had taken you back, and left you? Then what? He was surprised to find that the thought did not frighten him any more, and with a groan he reached under the pillow for his bottle.

Alone on deck Fraser stood a prisoner of the ship and the sea. His hands were welded to the spokes which felt heavy and unbalanced. Myers' words were still echoing around his brain, and he wanted to go below and force the man to see reason. He looked around the streaming deck, but there was no one to take over the wheel.

They had left him with his ship, and his victory. He found no comfort in either.

The surf thundered against the foot of the green headland in timeless, unquenchable anger, throwing its spray like arrows on to the quivering palms, and hissing with frustration as it ran back over the hard sand and across the small gullies of rock and coral, to join the next rank of curling whitecaps.

The shape of the *Queensland Pearl* grew more indistinct and hazy as, with all sails spread she curved away from the shore and ran before the wind, her white hull glittering in the harsh light.

A lonely figure stood motionless on a ledge above the beach, his deep-set black eyes fixed on the schooner, while his thick hands rested easily on the stock of an old muzzle-loading musket.

Koata, youngest son of Naareau chief of the Motă, could feel the thin spray in the wind even on the ledge, but his sturdy, well-muscled body trembled not from its touch but from the excitement and the compelling lust which still consumed his being, but which, as son of a great chief, he had to control.

He was barely eighteen years of age, yet already his body had thickened, and his features had set into the rough, crudely formed mould of his tribe, the flat, dilated nostrils and close-set eyes being those of an older man, and his thick lips, now dry and cracked, added to his appearance of timeless and primitive savagery.

The schooner vanished into the haze, and with a soft grunt he began to climb the steep track towards the silent mission. As he walked, his short legs taking the treacherous ground without effort, his beady eyes moved restlessly and hungrily over the bush, and his fingers gripped the musket in readiness as he watched for any possible danger.

He halted on the edge of the deserted compound and surveyed the mission house with contempt. It had all been so easy, just as Tauhu had told them it would be. The hot wind moaned through the trees and ruffled the feathers which sprouted from his wig of red clay. The deep open sores beneath his armpit throbbed painfully, but he ignored them, just as he did the tight discomfort of his initiation scars, and bared his big teeth to show that nothing could alter him from what he was. There had been bad talk of late in the Motă that his father was getting old and weak. That he no longer listened to the voice of Tauhu, the servant of their god, and feared instead the threats of the priest who lived in this empty place and made strange music to the night.

He padded across the tamped earth and stamped noisily across the sagging veranda. For a long moment he stared down at the crucified man at his feet, and for a second forgot the task entrusted to him. His painted face still expressionless, he drew the bamboo knife from his belt and began to saw methodically at Spencer's thin neck. With a grunt he laid the grizzly prize on the doorstep and walked quickly into the darkened passage beyond the room. An open fire still burned in the small kitchen and, relishing the pain, Koata picked up a flaming log and carried it to the tinder-dry partition of the room. Ignoring the mutilated bodies of the two houseboys, he held it against the wood until the eager flames licked over his wrist, so that with a grimace he stood back and watched the fire spreading like a curtain over the whole wall. The smoke would be carried by the wind, but it would still be seen by the Motă, who waited beyond the House of Spirits, which had been built for just this occasion. He picked up the severed head and strode swiftly into the jungle, the excitement stirring in his loins like madness, and the taste of the kava in his throat reminding him of the feasting and ceremonies to come.

The great white ship had sailed away, and would never return. Again Tauhu had been right. The god had been displeased with them, but now that they had driven away the white strangers there was no more danger, and the girl with the hair of a sun-goddess would finally appease him. A small frown creased his ochred forehead. It had been so strange to see the white priest running to meet them, as it had been many years since any of the Motă, but for a few of the elders, had seen him. Tauhu had spoken with great understanding when he had said that the priest of the unbelievers had had no power. Why else did he allow the white girl to remain without sight?

She had screamed when they had seized hold of her, but

Tauhu had forbidden them to hurt her. He had said that she was a gift to Pato, and his alone. His thick lips trembled at the thought. It was almost dangerous just to think his name. Pato, the great god of fertility and strength, who lived in a sacred place by the pool. There the new House of Spirits had been erected, and there the Motă would make their peace with him.

He began to run, his legs bounding like a goat's, knowing that there was no danger for him in this place. The land was theirs again, and the small villages around the coast would soon know it once more.

It was a large village, and well hidden in a deep fold between two round hills. The huts, small and palm-roofed, were built close together to resist attack from without, should anyone be foolish enough to try. But years earlier, the elders had said, other warriors had come from another island, and there had been much fighting.

A great fire burned in the centre of the village, and, in spite of the midday sun, the warriors of the Motă surged around it, their feet sometimes stamping on the scattered embers as they danced with great concentration to the mingled beats of half a dozen carved log-drums. At that moment the beats were slow, and they were reliving the excitement of their attack on the mission. The wide-bladed spears stabbed at the air, and the wild-eyed men chanted, sobbed and snarled with mounting frenzy as the tempo beat with remorseless insistence and the drummers bobbed and swayed over their charges, their faces completely absorbed in the rhythm of the dance.

Tall gourds of kava were being carried round the dancers by the small womenfolk of the tribe, and occasionally one of the warriors would pause to pour the burning spirit down his throat before stamping away with renewed power.

At one end of the clearing sat Naareau. He was small and

200

shrivelled like an old nut. His parchment-dry skin hung loosely on his emaciated body, and his small, spade-like hands lay twitching in his lap. Only his watchful, bird's eyes betrayed his emotion and sense of power, and as his young son Koata ran breathlessly to his side he smiled gravely, showing his broken black teeth, and distorting the savage scars which crossed his sunken cheeks.

Naareau was immensely rich, and the land which surrounded the village was alive with his tusked pigs, his wealth, his power to bargain, or to win over enemies he could not destroy.

Now that the killing was over he could not remember why it was that he had waited so long to act against the intruders. He had watched the lowly fishermen from the other villages growing soft as they crawled to the trade store, or bowed down to the white gods, and he had waited for a sign. His waiting had been mistaken for weakness he knew, but he had had to be sure. He licked his old lips and signalled to a small girl who was carrying the kava. This would long be remembered, and his whispering enemies would be as nothing. He tasted the fire of the liquid in his stomach and belched happily. The girl watched him in awe, but quivered as his gnarled fingers explored her body. Naareau wondered secretly if he was now too old for such pleasures. Perhaps when he had appeased the great Pato all would be well again.

The drums thundered louder, and the air became even thicker with the stench of sweat and kava, mingled with the scent of half-cooked meat. In the great earth ovens, tended over by the watchful women of the tribe, the succulent meat was almost ready. The fire warmed the old chief's body from within, and he felt young like his favourite son. His father before him had taught him many things, but of late the white men from beyond the reef had forbidden those

201

teachings, and had prevented the regular ceremonial feastings of human flesh. Now the need for secrecy was past. The Motă had almost purged itself of its weakness. Soon the girl with the hair like the sun and eyes like pearls would make final amends.

Gillian Bligh sat quite motionless on the edge of a long bamboo bench, her fingers hooked like claws over the smooth bars which formed the seat, her head hanging so low that the forced pressure of her chin against her breast brought a dull, throbbing pain, which she felt was her only contact with sanity and self-control. Outside the darkened interior of the hut where she had been marched by the painted warriors of the Motă, the persistent pounding of drums and the spine-chilling screams of the prancing men around the fire repeatedly threatened to unhinge her mind, and only by sitting quite still and holding on to one desperate thought after another could she bring herself to consider her fate, and at the same time prevent herself from screaming with complete terror.

She remembered Spencer's wildly elated face as he had burst into the mission that morning. She groaned; it seemed like part of some nightmare which was refusing to be vanquished by the noise and torment about her. He had stood looking at her with something like pity in his crazed eyes.

'They are coming, my child,' he had said. 'It will soon be over. If they require a human life as payment for their sins, then they must have it. In their eyes it is just.' He had nodded with sudden gravity. 'It is my task to show them that mine is the way.'

It was then that she had broken. Dressed once more in her torn and salt-stained coral slacks and flimsy blouse, she had thrown herself at his knees, her mind blank to

202

everything but the terrible danger which sounded in the slowly approaching drum, and in the man's hooded eyes. He had stood over her like a rock, unmoved by her cries and the clinging pressure of her arms about his legs. He had waited until her fear had exhausted her, and then he signalled to two of the mission boys to pull her to her feet.

After that things had happened too quickly to have any sequence in her aching brain. Spencer had left the room, only it seemed, to return immediately, his shoulder streaming with blood. He had fallen on his knees in the middle of the floor, his long fingers clasped together, his staring eyes fixed on her as she swayed between the two natives.

'The girl was blind!' He spoke in short, desperate gasps. 'You must not let them think that you are otherwise!' Then in a loud cry: 'I have betrayed you! No. No! It is they who have betrayed my trust!'

Then the room had been filled with twisting, naked shapes, their distorted faces, painted and savage, had floated before her terrified eyes, and later she had seen over their stooped, intent shoulders the merciless torture of the man who had given her to these people. After that she could remember little else. They had dragged her excitedly through the bush for what seemed like an endless period of time. Occasionally, more men would join the triumphant procession, and they, too, would peer at her eyes, and then run their hands quickly over her body, or pluck at her hair with obvious delight.

Only the tall native, with a glistening helmet of sharks' teeth, had prevented worse treatment she knew. It was he who had brought her to the hut, and with something like gentleness had arranged for two elderly women to look after her. She shuddered, the bile clogging in her throat. He had also been the one who had supervised Spencer's crucifixion.

She stared down at her bare, scarred feet. How could see bring herself to stand up to what was to come? She rocked back and forth on the seat, the sensation of shock making the hut ice cold, and the nausea rise up again within her.

In Africa she had often been invited to watch the primitive tribal ceremonies and dances, but never without the certain knowledge that but for close watch and supervision the old customs would be brought back to mean more than just the gentle revival of some old tradition. A British District Officer in Kenya had once told her that the only progress made there was forced. 'Controls not standards improve these people!' He had laughed at her refusal to accept such a simple idea. 'Take away the controls, miss and *you'll* see!'

The noise outside the hut was louder, and through the glowing rectangle of the door she could see the stamping figures pouring with sweat, the faces devoid of any expression which she could remember. The tiny man on the dais was chief of the Motă. That she knew. She had seen him ordering some of his men to search the mission for survivors. Yet even he had been influenced by the tall man who had put her in the hut. He was some kind of priest. No doubt the one man whom Spencer had unwittingly been fighting through all his years of misguided effort.

She could feel her nails biting into the bamboo. If only I could kill myself. She stared round the bare hut like a trapped animal, but there was nothing. The two old women had left her earlier, but it was unlikely that they would be away long.

Slowly she stood up, and felt the weakness of her whole body rise against her. With a small spark of determination she walked shakily round the hut. The walls were matted with dried mud, but nevertheless extremely strong. She looked across at the bamboo bench, as if she expected to see

204

herself watching her pathetic efforts. It was no use. The only way out was through the door. And even if she succeeded in getting clear, what then? No wonder they left her so carelessly alone. The ship had gone. They had all gone. Even Hogan had probably left in his cutter at the first sign of danger, as he had said he would. In any case, she could never find the trade store in her state.

She pressed her shoulders against the rough wall. The wizened chief of the Motā was the only authority here now, and probably always had been. She was just something which had got in the way, a convenience to be used with the same determined savagery as they had employed at the mission, only this time it was to be something even more terrible.

She tried not to think of Blair. No doubt he alone might be really sorry. She cried aloud, her voice muffled by the drums. 'I wish to God I *had* been drowned!' She imagined the caressing violence of the waves and shuddered. Then she would have been safe. Who else would miss her? Her public? She laughed hysterically at the thought. No doubt the magazine would make a really fine job of her final notice.

A cold prickle of sweat ran down her spine. When it happens, whatever it is, I must have the nerve to throw myself on to a spear, or make them kill me quickly in some way. The crude unreality of her racing thoughts took away the last of her strength, so that she found herself sitting again on the bench.

The sunlight vanished momentarily, and she forced herself to stare straight in front of her quivering body as the two women returned. They were accompanied by what appeared to be three children. They were dressed in tall stiff capes of palm leaves decorated with painted cord and small shells. Their faces and bodies were completely hidden, but their arms were loaded with gourds of crude clay and a small parcel of fruit.

One of the women, a wrinkled, grey-haired creature whose emaciated breasts hung practically to her navel, paused in her directions to stroke Gillian's blonde hair with obvious wonder. Then she muttered to the waiting children, who immediately laid their burdens on the earth floor and stood back mutely against the wall. The other woman, equally old, whose thin body was deeply marked by sores, nodded like a toothless monkey, and after a muttered conversation began to jerk the tattered clothes from Gillian's body.

She protested at once, but with surprising strength they pinned her to the bench, while first one and then the other ripped away her final link with her own way of life.

Her limbs felt devoid of either will or life, and without further protest she allowed herself to be completely stripped, and without so much as a shudder watched the two engrossed women as they sponged down her limbs with what felt like thin oil from one of the gourds.

The children did not move, and she guessed that they were completely blinded by their capes, probably in order that such a sacred ceremony should remain a mystery to them.

She swayed forward and would have fallen but for the talon-like fingers on her arms. The slow oiling process went on until within the gloom of the hut her tanned body shone like a statue against the two stooped shapes of the old women.

She closed her eyes tightly. She shut out the thunder of the drums, the glare of the sun through the smoke-hazed doorway and the blank, drooling faces of the women. Even the stench of their bodies and the complete inevitability of her fate were on the outside of her. For a few seconds she hung on to her strength before the realization that Gillian Bligh no longer existed, and the persistent probing fingers across her body awakened her to terror, and only then did she fall senseless to the floor.

The sun moved across the island, and the sky grew darker, not with the night, but with the purposeful majesty of the cloud barriers which piled one upon the other, so that even the sea seemed awed. Beyond the bays, and the small cove where the House of Spirits awaited the sacrifice of its servants, and even along the reef which was never still, the sea rolled in great troughs, as if some tremendous power was lurking just beneath the surface. Waiting for some signal before unleashing itself upon the world, and anything which lay in its path.

11

Easing his cramped body slightly between two sun-warmed rocks, Blair raised himself on his sore elbows to peer once more along the small deserted cove. The contrasting shores and beaches of such a small island were surprising, and added to the popular belief that the archipelago had once been a single, fertile mass of land, until volcanic eruptions and the constant power of the sea had taken their toll over the centuries. He rubbed one hand dazedly across his eyes and felt the rasp of sand against his sun-dried skin. Unlike the other parts of the shore he had already seen, this small cove looked as if it had once been scorched by a great searing heat, so that all vegetation and moisture had been sucked from it, leaving only the hard-packed sand on the deserted beach, and the towering walls of loose rocks and great, slab-like boulders which formed the natural breakwater and hid the green jungle and hills, through which he and Tarrou had just come.

He groaned inwardly and squinted against the glare which shone remorselessly from the sea and reflected redly against the rocks. This was the cove, Tarrou had said. To Blair it looked for all the world like a mere weakening of the island's coastline, a piece of the sea's casual exploration. Perhaps Tarrou had merely led him to the first convenient place and had then run off somewhere to hide. Blair had told him to work his way round the edge of the rocks and try to find some sign that would tell him where the Motă had gone, and what was going to happen. Involuntarily he peered down at the pale ring on his wrist where his watch had once been. It seemed hours since he had lost sight of Tarrou's quick, nervous progress, his bent body readily camouflaged by the sombre background, and now that the idea of treachery had crossed his mind he began to grow more apprehensive, and was conscious of the sickening pain in his foot.

I should have left him here and gone myself. He licked his parched lips, their arid taste reminding him momentarily of his thirst and his nearness to collapse.

His eyes narrowed, and without thought he cradled his cheek against the hot stock of his rifle as a movement by the seething surf caught his attention. He cursed, regretting the wasted effort and the subsequent loss of strength to his limbs. An assorted group of seabirds moved painstakingly along the edge of the water, their eyes and bills busy with the invisible creatures left stranded by the breakers. Blair watched them without hope. It had been too long now. Nothing was left to hope for. He felt the constriction grow in his throat as he remembered Gillian as she had been on the schooner. All the small moments returned to his mind with sudden clarity, like pictures in a forgotten album. Her smile, and the casual touch of her leg against his when they had sat in the dinghy. The crackle of the comb through her hair when he had caught her unexpectedly alone on the poop, watching the first stars in the sky. She had met his stare, her candid eyes questioning, perhaps inviting. He gripped the rifle in despair. How different it should all have been. If I had not been such a stupid, self-opinionated fool.

He was suddenly alerted by the seabirds which had stopped hunting and were shuffling uneasily in the sand, their bills prodding at the air with alarm. Then he saw Tarrou, running breathlessly along the stony edge of the beach, being careful even in his haste to follow Blair's instructions about leaving no tell-tale prints.

Blair forced himself to lie still until the panting, sweat-stained half-caste flung himself down at his side, his mouth gulping in the torpid air, his eyes closed with exertion.

He waited, too, for the bad news, the announcement from Tarrou which would tell him that this was just another failure.

'I find place.' Tarrou forgot his careful grammar, forgot everything but the small, terrifying triumph of carrying out a mission alone, and one that he had imagined would only hasten his end.

Blair's hand closed like a clamp on his arm. 'Where?' There was open disbelief in the cold eyes. 'Even with this damned haze I can see the end of the cove. There doesn't seem to be anything else here?'

In slow, halting sentences, his breath still unsteady, but driven on by the anguish in Blair's face, Tarrou explained how he had scrambled around the whole of the cove twice before he had noticed a deep cleft in the rocks at the middle of the highest part of the wall, a place still sheltered from the sun, and which showed traces of damp, as if the sea had surged through the gap and had penetrated the island's defences. Very slowly he had moved his body through the crevice, his legs sinking into the bog-like sand, and rubbing against the green strands of weed which clung to both sides of the natural gully. As he passed through the towering boulders the noise of the sea had faded, and even the impatient thunder of surf against the distant reef had been stilled. He had found himself looking down on a great round, saucer-shaped depression, about a hundred yards across, and filled with wet sand, except in the deepest point about the centre, where a small pool of trapped sea-water still glistened, cool and inviting, its surface unbroken but for a small black rock which jutted a few feet above the surface, its worn crevices already dry and dull. The depression was hemmed in on all sides by jungle, until the point where it met the great mounds of rocks which formed the sea wall.

Blair listened intently. 'You mean that the pool fills up with sea-water at high tide? Is that it?'

Tarrou nodded. 'There was a building on the other side of the pool. I saw some men guarding it.' He watched Blair's eyes harden. 'It was the place we were looking for,' he finished quickly.

'Anything else?' Blair was already looking along the beach again, as if he expected to see the gap for himself.

'I think not, Major.' He closed his bloodshot eyes and remembered again the awful quiet of the place, and the damp, listless air which hung over the stagnant pool. The sea would surge through the gap at high water, and the pool would become a lake, and so cover the small rock. One day perhaps, he thought, the sea would explore further, and eventually cut the island in two. It would be a good thing. He jumped as Blair jabbed his arm.

He was pointing up at the long line of weather-smoothed rocks. 'Can we get up there, d'you reckon? And if so, could we see down into the place where the pool is?' He noticed that his arm had cast a shadow along the stones by his side and, as he watched, the shadow faded and vanished.

He glanced up at the thick clouds, their heavy shapes darkened with strange brown hues, and their bellies hanging low over the glittering water. They looked as if they would burst at any moment and drop liquid fire into the booming surf below. The noise across the reef became more insistent, and turning his head, he saw a thin black line appear momentarily across the empty sea, as in the falling tide the hidden barrier of coral rose to challenge the

211

sky, and the surf which battered at its defences. Then it was gone again, until the next heavy Pacific roller charged fruitlessly to the attack.

'We could, Major.' Tarrou sounded doubtful. 'But can you climb?'

Blair dragged himself to his feet, his teeth clenched against the pain. 'Just give me a hand, blast you? I've got to get up there!'

Once, as they moved like beetles up the smooth, heated boulders, Blair slipped, and fell several feet into a crevice, his head jerking back in agony as the hard rock broke his fall. Not daring to look at Tarrou's anxious face, he tugged himself free, and began again. When they reached the top of the wall, and fell exhausted amongst the thin layer of scrub and the stinking carpet of bird-droppings, Blair only rested for a few moments before he again pulled himself to his feet and staggered, slipping and falling over the stone teeth which topped the wall, towards the tallest point of all, where Tarrou had said the two overhanging ledges met across the rock funnel, and where the sea was admitted to the pool. Even then, but for Tarrou's restraining hand, he would have fallen over the other side, or shown his scarecrow figure to the two natives who stood like statues on the rim of the pool. Their painted faces were clearly visible against the green jungle, as was the thin, pointed hut which met its own reflection across the quiet, unruffled water.

Blair blinked away the sweat and settled himself against a tiny parched shrub. All around him the rock floor shimmered and swam, and what little air there was seemed lost to the scudding clouds. What now? He tried to think. How could Spencer have been so sure what was going to happen? It was this impossible waiting and blind searching which was beating him now, he thought bitterly. Tarrou's dust-streaked face was devoid of understanding. Perhaps, like Spencer, he was waiting for a miracle.

Tarrou watched Blair's inert body and forced himself to speak, as if to break the spell of loneliness which the burning rock seemed to inspire. He had been holding on to his nerve with every ounce of his strength, but the sight of the two silent warriors and the deceptive calm of the pool was more than he could stand.

'What you going to do, Major?' There was a quiver in his voice.

'Wait. Just wait.' His tone was flat, as if he was only half-conscious.

Tarrou wanted to keep quiet, but he could not control his voice. 'What *can* we do, Major?' He stared fixedly at Blair's sweat-stained back, his eyes misting with the sense of fear and unfairness which the man had caused. Even now, in defeat, he was still assured, even secretive, and Tarrou wanted to seize him and force him to understand. 'We will die up here!'

Blair moved his legs, and Tarrou saw the raw, inflamed flesh of the crippled foot through the bandage. 'Well, go and hide if you like.' He moved the backsight of the rifle and measured the width of the pool with his eye. 'You kept your word by bringing me here. Now hop it, if you want to!'

Tarrou hobbled on his knees like a deformed beggar. 'Why you talk like this?' The words bubbled out of him. He could not stop now. 'All the time you treat me like dirt, eh? I help you, and still you try to make me feel bad! You a big man outside.' He waved his clenched fist vaguely towards the sea. 'Here you nothing but trouble! You can't do nothing here. The Motă are bad. There is nothing you can do!'

Blair twisted his head towards him and smiled without warmth. 'Feel better? Now shut up, or clear off!'

Tarrou still sat uncomfortably on his knees, the humiliation welling into tears. 'It's not fair! You have everything you want all your life. I got nothing but my job. Now I got nothing at all.' He waited, but Blair did not move. 'See? You don't care about me!' His voice rose to a scream.

Blair hissed at him with sudden anger. 'Keep your voice down!' Then, more quietly: ' If I had my cheque-book I'd write you out a cheque for any amount you wanted. Would that help?' There was no answer. 'Now, listen to me, and I'll tell you something. I need you here with me, get that? I *need* you!' He watched the pain in the black eyes. 'If you want to go, that's your affair, but if you decide to stay you'll have to go through with it.' He eyed him searchingly. 'And I mean just that. I'm going to save that girl if it kills me and you too!' He looked up, his face haggard. 'Well, what d'you say?'

Tarrou gazed down at him with amazement. He was no longer surprised to hear himself agree to stay, he was past all surprises now. Before he had turned his fanatical stare back to the pool, Blair had tried to smile. Instead, Tarrou had seen the tears of desperation in the man's eyes.

He sat quietly behind Blair, and began to mop his face with a scrap of his shirt. It was all quite fantastic. Blair had known that he could not do anything without him, and yet he had gambled on the uncertain knowledge of Tarrou's own pride. He no longer hated Blair, or envied him either. He had only sorrow for this strange, lonely man who waited for the impossible to happen, and yet in his own simple fashion, Tarrou was glad he had decided to remain with him to the end.

Free of the shore, the schooner plunged eagerly on the port tack, her slim hull slicing through the unbroken surface of

214

white lace and shuddering to each rise and fall of the tremendous swell which gave the sea the appearance of a great moving desert. Some of the troughs were so deep that the ship seemed to be anchored in a valley, the height of the surrounding water robbing the huge sails of wind and causing the vessel to reel as if out of control, until the bow-sprit lifted and pointed the way clear, the canvas booming with triumph once more.

Fraser slithered down the last few steps of the companion-way and groped his way blindly along the narrow passage. Around and above him every spar and timber groaned and squeaked in protest, and as the stern hung momentarily over a deep trough he had to grip the handrail to prevent his body from reeling full length on the deck. Then the stern dropped, and he held his breath until he could hear the great sluicing roar of cascading water as it poured along the low gunwale and hissed over the deck above.

Wabu had at last relieved him on the wheel, and had stood stolidly, his hands resting firmly on the spokes, while Fraser gave him the course.

'Keep her west by south!' he had shouted above the moan of wind in the rigging. 'Watch her head. Don't let her pay off too much!' He had waited, hoping for the flash of impish humour in the native's eyes, but there had been nothing.

He reeled into his cabin and stared worriedly at the disordered clothes and cases which lurched unheeded across the floor. The oil-lamp swung in fantastic circles above his head, and he started as a metallic crash sounded from the other cabin.

Frowning, he stumbled across to the girl's door, and stood undecided, his head cocked as if he expected her to call out. With an oath he thrust open the door and stepped

215

quickly inside. His feet kicked against the small typewriter which had skidded from the table and burst out of its case. He picked it up, and stared morosely at the few feminine garments on the bunk, and at the well-worn travelling bags. Even her perfume seemed to triumph over the tang of salt and wet rope, and he licked his lips, suddenly unsure of himself.

'What could *I* do?' he asked the empty cabin. 'I must be goin' mad!'

He half-listened to the sounds of the labouring schooner, and was conscious of the quivering vibration of the hull as she flung her one hundred and thirty tons over the water towards safety. That fool Myers, he reflected savagely. Bloody useless in any sort of a jam, but he'll swear it was all my fault when we get back. He could imagine Grainger's grave face, and the long-drawn-out questions. The schooner heeled over and hung uncomfortably for several seconds. Poor old girl. She's near the end of her days. He banged his fist hard on the table. 'Why don't they understand?' He shouted wildly at the bulkhead, and in the small cabin along the passageway Myers stiffened in alarm. 'I'm savin' their ruddy lives, an' this is all I get!' The words echoed hollowly, and seemed to stay with him.

Wabu leaned his slim weight against the wheel, and then turned briefly to nod as Yalla joined him in silence, his hands already helping to take the strain. They stood side by side, fighting each uneven gust of wind and watching the swinging compass card with expressionless eyes.

Old Kari sat hunched under the weather-rail watching them, his head nodding to the rhythm of the ship.

There was a crash as the companion hatch banged open and Fraser heaved his body over the coaming, his eyes squinting up at the whipping masts. Three pairs of eyes watched him with sudden interest, but Fraser ignored them as he tightened his belt and pulled an old yellow sou'wester over his tousled hair. His face was flushed, and he felt the madness rising in him like another storm.

Yalla's eyes were dark as he watched Fraser take a long pull from the bottle before throwing it over the side. It was empty, and Fraser grinned at him, his teeth white against his stubbled chin.

'Well, you bloody heathen? Who the hell're you starin' at, fer Chrissake!' He swayed, and shook his head with forced solemnity. 'Stand by to go about!' He saw the expressions of disbelief in their smooth faces. 'Thought about it. It's all wrong, but,' he shrugged, suddenly glad that he was committed, 'there seems to be no other way.'

He took over the wheel and leaned loosely across it, savouring the life which flowed up from the rudder deep beneath him, and from the sails which reached out to embrace the angry sky. As if in a dream he saw the boys slithering to the braces, feet splayed on the wet planks, their eyes slitted against the needles of spray which coursed over their dark bodies. Kari and Dinkila joined them, and from somewhere Myers came hurrying, calling for the boys to show him what to do.

Fraser waited his time carefully, watching the sails and the sea with practised eye. Then as the *Queensland Pearl* answered his touch on the helm, and the canvas whipped and flapped protestingly, he felt her swing round, the twin booms tearing at the halyards, so that every block and wire screamed like a live thing.

He watched the ribbon of blue sky fade to one side, and as the ship completed her turn he found himself facing the great molten mass of storm-cloud which hung across the horizon like a forest fire. The eerie glow was reflected in his eyes as he drove his ship straight back along her old course.

He felt rather than saw the boys resetting the sails with

renewed strength, but the sudden throb of canvas overhead made his eyes smart. He gripped the spokes tighter. 'That's it, my girl! We'll show 'em!' His face split into a maniac grin, and he shouted at the darting figures ahead of him: 'See how she goes, lads? Take a look ahead, will you! It may be the last time you bastards get a chance!' He tilted his head and laughed up at the sails and the quivering masts.

Later, as he fought the sea with his hands, he wondered what had changed his mind. Perhaps it was the whisky. He chuckled mirthlessly. Maybe I'm just a damned stupid Aussie, but I just don't like bein' pushed around!

He thought of Hogan's body lashed down in the empty hold. He at least was unworried. He watched the great writhing swell of water and gritted his teeth. What would happen if they were beaten by the storm? When those rollers broke into waves, and the wind really got up, he would have little time to consider the sense of his decision. All his life he had nursed the old schooner, and had tried to ease the passing of the years by careful handling. All that was past now. He felt like a man driving an old and trusted horse until it dropped.

'Dinkila! Get me another bottle from my cabin!'

He tried to shut out the sounds of the groaning timbers, and waved the seamen away when they came to relieve him at the wheel.

He took a hasty drink from the bottle and thrust it into his belt. He did not want to share this with anyone. Anyone else but her, that is. The others had wanted to go back for Blair. Duty, stupidity, curiosity, or just plain madness, what did the reason matter any more Well, I'm goin' to take them back 'cause that's what they expect of me. He knew that they needed him. He also knew that the misery of his own guilt lessened with each thrust of the sails, even though the ship seemed to be sailing straight to her destruction. There was no longer any choice.

Compared to the still, fetid air which hung over the empty pool, the interior of the House of Spirits seemed almost cool. The tall, tent-shaped building had been hastily erected of freshly cut palms, and the floor still showed signs of many feet, where the women of the tribe had stamped down the rough sand and dragged away any loose stone boulders from its surface. There were no windows, and the end of the house opened straight on to the small slope which ran the few remaining yards to the edge of the saucer-shaped pool, and was wide enough to show the water and damp sludge around the one isolated rock, and the great shadowed sea wall, unbroken but for the narrow V cleft in its centre, and through which the watery sunlight occasionally threw a distorted reflection of the hidden sea.

The jungle seemed to encircle the rest of the building in two great green banks, and the smell of rotting trees clashed with the scent of the newly cut timbers.

Tauhu, servant of the god, Pato, was well pleased with himself. With opaque eyes he watched as his assistants reverently lowered their burden on to a wide mat of woven palm leaves, their ochred faces averted, lest they should excite the anger of Pato, who now lay with threatening stillness on the mat. With the head and body of a shark, yet crouched on the crudely fashioned arms and legs of a man, Pato waited with every appearance of terrible expectancy.

Tauhu nodded. His servants had done well. He had patiently trained them for their tasks since he had chosen them from their boyhood, and had guided them through the painful initiation ceremonies, and had finally selected them as his personal assistants. Their head-dresses of sharks' teeth marked them apart from all others, and next to Tauhu made them the most feared men on the island.

He listened with contempt to the shrill cries and wild laughter of the warriors as they danced and drank around the edge of the pool. The chief, Naareau, would be there with his favourite son but, like all the others around him, would have to wait until he, Tauhu, chose to act. A shiver of anticipation ran through him. For a while he had been almost afraid that the Motă would never be convinced of their ordained path. For years they had grown soft, and had kept alive their dreams of power by mere acts of individual cunning and bravery. Some had carried out raids against the villages, and had eaten their captured flesh in secrecy. These same warriors had hidden in the bush when the white men had called at the island, and had not been able to meet his taunts. Now it was all changed. In a short while he had shown them their manhood, and had proved beyond doubt that the white men were nothing to be feared.

He dropped on to his knees and ran his hand softly over the pointed muzzle of the silent Pato. The teeth, yellow with age, gaped lifelessly in the diamond-shaped mouth, yet still retained their appearance of ferocity and power, as they had for as long as he could remember.

Tauhu was taller than his kinsmen and, unlike them, he wore no paint on his oiled body, nor was there any ornament to disguise the length of his muscular arms, which now hung relaxed by his sides. His head and face were shaved smooth, not even his eyebrows remained, and beneath the head-dress of sharks' teeth his eyes seemed to protrude unblinkingly, like those of the inert shape on the mat.

He did not move, as one of his assistants crossed noiselessly behind him, and with a few deft movements girded him with his ceremonial belt of fibre and bark. Next, he handed him his bamboo knife, and as his fingers closed around it Tauhu permitted himself a small shiver of extreme happiness.

It was practically dark in the House, and he knew that the low threatening clouds were yet another sign that he had chosen his time to perfection.

There was a movement at the rear of the building, and he lifted his eyes with practised slowness, as he always did on such occasions, so that his dilated pupils seemed as if they were the only things that lived in his crouched body.

A flap moved aside in the crudely cut wall and the girl was carried carefully towards him. He nodded with slow approval to his two men, who had brought her by the secret path from the village. They were breathing heavily and covered with sweat, yet Tauhu knew well enough that his orders had been carried out. She would not have touched the ground all the way, nor would these two have allowed anyone to see her and live.

With great care they lowered her to the ground, but kept her arms pinioned to her sides, so that between them she looked like a tall silken reed, or an exquisitely carved figure made by the gods. She wore a short kilt of smoke-cured water-leaves, and around her neck was draped a narrow garland of painted cowrie shells, which left bare her full breasts, and which shimmered together on their plaited cord, and were the only sign of her breathing and being alive.

Tauhu rose, and with slow, unhurried steps circled the trio to stand behind them. He noted the fine lines of the girl's perfect body, and the way that her fair skin gleamed beneath its rich coat of scented oil. He reached out and touched her hair, and marvelled again at its silky lightness beneath his fingers. She stiffened under his hand, and he felt the mounting pain in his groin. He scowled, and fingered his knife. He must not think that way now. Far too much

221

was at stake to be weakened by the feel of a mere woman. He thrust out his chin and glared at his other assistants. A blind woman was dangerous. It was well known that those without sight in their eyes harboured terrible evil and had to be destroyed.

Reassured, he lifted his hand before her pale eyes, and was conscious of the admiring stares of his men. He smiled briefly and signalled towards the entrance.

Instantly there was one loud blow on the carved log-drum placed by the pool, and like magic the voices outside were stilled, so that the silence of the jungle became more oppressive than any sound. Then there was a deep sigh, as from the depths of the shadows Pato emerged on his bamboo trestles and bared his teeth at the silent onlookers.

Tauhu slowly walked down the slope and turned to face the watching tribesmen. With a steady stare he confronted the old chief and the elders, and held their eyes until they had to look away and humble themselves before Pato's servant.

A rumble of far-off thunder floated over the sea wall, and a small sighing gust of wind found its way through the V-shaped cleft to ruffle momentarily the feathered weapons and head-dresses of the assembled tribe.

The tide, which had steadily mounted against the sea wall throughout the day, thrust its first exploring finger through the cleft, and as Tauhu spread his arms as if in welcome, a thin trickle of water spread over the lip of the depression and melted into the sand. As the waves crept up against the wall the trickle of water increased, so that even as Tauhu called down the wrath of Pato on the enemies of the Motǎ, his voice high and surprisingly shrill, the limpid patch of trapped water in the centre of the basin shivered and began to widen.

There was a sudden disturbance as, squealing and

222

kicking at its captors, a fully grown pig, its tusks fantastically curved and untrimmed so that they pierced the animal's snout, was dragged down to the edge of the pool. Tauhu watched with satisfaction as his assistants waded into the wet sand and rolled the wretched animal on to its back. He permitted himself a quick glance towards the bent shape of Tabanea, the most trusted of the chief's advisers. This pig had been his cherished possession and, on the island where pigs meant wealth and status, by its size and age alone it had been the envy of all. Tauhu had long understood that the old man who watched his every action, and tried to mask the anguish in his eyes, had been the main weakness in the Motă, the one who had whispered to the chief and sown the seeds of distrust, even disbelief, of Tauhu's power. Now, as he stepped down into the rim of the depression, he heard the sudden thud of the drum and the answering moan from the warriors. They were with him now, and nothing that Tabanea or any of the others could do or say would challenge him again. They had partaken of human flesh in the ritual feast of the village. The lust to kill was still with them, and the effect of the kava showed plainly in their dilated eyes. With infinite care he drew his knife across the animal's throat, hard and deep. The squeals suddenly died and, after filling a small cup with its blood, he stood up and watched the red stain spreading into the pool, which rose hungrily with each sigh of waves against the wall of rock.

Flanked by his assistants, he strode up the slope and laid the small offering before Pato's yellow jaws. The pig's carcase rocked gently in the rising water, and then slid down the slope, making a pink cloud weave and swirl in its wake.

The drumbeats grew faster and louder and, as if to a signal, the warriors began to rock back and forth in time to

223

the persistent rhythm. Their bare feet shuffled on the rough sand in short, agitated steps, so that a cloud of fine dust rose over their heads and settled on their nodding red wigs. Their eyes were glazed, and as Tauhu watched them with his bulging, unwinking stare, he noticed that they no longer acted as individuals, but moved together, in a great pulsating mass of limbs and gleaming weapons. His chest felt tight, and only by a supreme effort could he concentrate on the timing of the ceremony, which now, before all else, must be perfect.

A great sigh rose from the packed figures, as if all the tribe felt a simultaneous pain, as the girl was led from the shadows of the House of Spirits. A mere movement of his hand, and the drummers stepped up the tempo yet again, their bent bodies shining and with foam on their slack lips. An imperceptible movement with his knife, and his assistants had twisted the girl's arms behind her so that she fell on her knees before Pato. He could see her body quivering from head to foot as his men forced her lower, so that the pale hair brushed against the upraised snout, and her breasts almost touched the sand. Again he was sorry that she was blind. It would have been more exciting to have seen her face at this moment.

Gillian stared dully at the great mass of crudely stitched skin, and down the gaping jaws which seemed as if they might snap shut over her neck. She could no longer obtain a clear picture of anything, and all thought was restricted to the great roar of noise about her, and the agonizing pain in her arms. She could see her shadow across the outstretched hands of the hideous idol, and she was vaguely conscious of the water behind her twisted body. She could no longer control her terror, but it was so great that it was mercifully numbing to her limbs, so that she hung limply in the steely grip of her guards. Like the pig, she thought. Only they'll

224

make it hurt more than that. Then she was on her feet, arms pinioned behind her, and for the first time she saw the great swaying mass of mesmerized onlookers. She tried to retch, but her throat closed tight. She wanted to faint, but her terror denied her even that. She realized that they were wading into the water, and had lifted her over their moist shoulders, so that she hung on her back, staring up at the clouds. There was a new pressure on her spine as she was lowered on to the small rock, which was already half awash. Her wrists and ankles were pulled outwards, and seemed to fit into worn grooves, where they were secured by wooden staples.

Soon, soon. Her mouth moved slowly as she spoke the words aloud. They were lost in the great sea of noise which washed back and forth across the pool, but they gave her comfort. Her head hung back over the side of the smooth rock, and she felt the ends of her loose hair moving gently in the lapping water. She could also feel it against her feet. Perhaps they will let me drown in the rising water. It was what she had wanted, anyway. Peace, sliding down into the protection of the sea.

A shadow crossed her face, and she stared up at the shining figure of the priest. His long body looked distorted, and she could see the small droplets of sweat across his stomach as he shouted across the water, his voice rising to a scream. He raised his hand into her line of vision, and her body seemed to screw itself into a tight knot. But he held no weapon, merely a small cup, which he lifted high over his head like an offering. She saw the cup tilt over, and with horrified eyes watched the thin stream of red blood pour over its lip. It was still warm, and in spite of her tensed muscles she began to writhe as it splashed slowly the length of her body. She closed her eyes, shutting out the maniac face and the panting naked limbs which stooped over her.

Like an ice-cold knife the distant memory of Fraser's words came back to her. When there was blood in the water, he had said, there would always be sharks close at hand. Even close inshore nothing was safe. The miniature sharks, or becuna fish as they were called, would flock in droves, driven mad by the scent of blood. Unlike their bigger brethren, they attacked blindly, and with savage ferocity, destroying one another to get at their prey.

Her skin tore against staples, as with sudden desperation she twisted and writhed like a pinioned animal, her naked body scraping on the rock so that the pain at last managed to transmit the message of defeat, and she felt her spreadeagled limbs begin to go limp.

She opened her eyes and stared at the misty picture of the rock barrier, with its thin cleft of daylight. Through that opening the becuna fish might already be jostling each other to gain an entry. Involuntarily she moved her fingers and toes, aware that the tepid water was over her shins and lapping behind her neck. Would it be a sudden sharp pain, or could it be slow and agonizing? She closed her mind and concentrated with every fibre in her being on the racing clouds overhead.

So it had all been a waste of time after all. How petty her hopes and ambitions had become. Now she was not even a person, not even a woman. Just an object of sacrifice, or a symbol of something only the Motă understood. A scream bubbled in her throat as something moved by her head, but she saw that the priest was still there, staring down at her.

Tauhu was aware of the great silence which had fallen when he had signalled for the drums to cease. Every eye was upon him now, as always. The swirling water had almost covered the rock, so that the white body appeared to be floating on the surface. He could not wait any longer, for he knew that it was time for the devil fish to come. He could see the expressionless faces of his assistants as they stood grouped behind the crouching Pato. This would be a lesson they would never forget.

He began to stride through the pool, conscious of the sand tugging at his feet, and the gentle power which surged around his waist.

Gillian twisted her neck and arched her body like a bow, as if to keep the water at bay. There was no sun now, and although all air seemed to have been sucked away from the pool she felt ice cold. Soon, soon. Oh God, help me. She stared back at the black cliff, and fixed her smarting eyes on the small shape which seemed to grow out of its summit. She blinked to clear her vision. The shape was moving. Not daring to breathe, she saw it move closer to the edge, and even at that distance she could see the tattered shirt and the pale blob of a face.

Then she screamed. Something hard and rough darted across her shin, and even as she cried out she saw the gentle puff of smoke from the cliff, and felt a warm breath fan across her full length. The sound of the rifle's sharp crack was half drowned by a strangled cry as Tauhu swung drunkenly in the shallow water by the side of the pool. The heavy, soft-nosed bullet smashed into his shoulder with such savage force that he fell to his knees, his terrified eyes staring down at the water which leapt up to claim him. What had gone wrong? The pool was reddening all about him, and he screamed again as he saw the swift, streamlined fish streaking towards him, their diamond-shaped mouths glinting white beneath the surface.

His body rose out of the water, already gashed and torn in several places, and then he fell on to his side, hidden by the tearing, tumbling mass of fish, which seemed to engulf him completely, and which lashed the surface of the pool into a froth of spray and red-tinted spume.

Gillian tried to cry out, but the water was lapping against her mouth. She was dimly aware that the rifle was firing again, its short whiplash barks magnified by the rock and the jungle. *Perhaps he is trying to kill me. It would be better to die like that.*

Tarrou's wet face bobbed beside her, and she felt him pulling the staples from her wrists and ankles. He looked completely terrified, his eyes white and bulging from his puckered face. She felt herself floated free of the rock, and floundered feebly in the water's warm embrace. Objects splashed into the pool nearby, and Tarrou's gasping voice implored her to hurry.

She allowed herself to be dragged, half-drowned, across the deepest part of the pool, towards the deep shadow cast by the wall. She could still hear the thrashing, plunging shapes behind her, and wondered vaguely what was happening.

Tarrou felt the rocks beneath his scrambling feet and swayed out of the water, pulling the girl behind him. For a brief instant he stared across the pool and marvelled that what Blair had promised had come true. The Motă had stopped firing their arrows into the water and had fled into the safety of the jungle, unnerved by the rifle which they could not see, and which could not possibly exist. Three dark shapes lay in abandoned attitudes of death, and Pato still stood by the House of Spirits, forgotten by the tribe he had been impotent to help.

The pool was again empty, and the rock had completely vanished. But for the sudden darting movements beneath the surface there was nothing to show what had happened.

He just managed to catch the girl as she fell against him. He felt her hair wet against his throat, and he peered over her smooth shoulder towards the deserted clearing.

Aloud he said: 'I did it! I saved her!' When Blair had

228

told him his plan he had nearly collapsed, and he still could not remember how he had made the journey down the cliff, and had waited for the shot which was to be the signal. It had been so incredibly easy, and yet . . . He tugged off the remains of his precious jacket and wrapped it round her. But now what would they do? he wondered. He was even more surprised to find that he was no longer afraid. Blair's voice, strained and harsh, floated down the cleft in the rocks.

'Is she all right? For God's sake tell me.' He sounded mad with anxiety.

'She's fine!' Tarrou fumbled for words. 'I'm bringing her up now!'

'Well, get a move on, for Christ's sake!' There was a metallic click. 'The bastards might try to work round us, but I'll give 'em something to remember us by!'

Blair forced himself to watch the green front of the jungle, although everything inside him shouted with crazy elation. He wanted to throw down the rifle and run to help that poor, shivering half-caste. Right up to the last second he had thought Tarrou was not going to make it across the pool. Blair had shouted down curses which he alone could hear as, with his sights trained on the capering savage in the water, he had waited for Tarrou to get into position. Then, when he had seen him bob up beside the girl's pinioned body, he had begun to sob with relief, the tears almost blinding him. It had been at that moment the Motǎ had rallied and had begun to shoot their little arrows at the two swimmers.

He jammed his last rounds into the magazine and ran his fingers across his eyes. She was safe. Perhaps only for another hour, but she was safe and they would be together. It was strange that they had had to suffer so much to find what they wanted.

'Lay her here by me.' He reached out to smooth the hair from her face, and immediately she opened her eyes. For a long moment they moved without expression, their grey depths still clouded with fear. Then her hand moved across to his cheek, and he felt its damp skin rasp against his stubble.

Tarrou took the rifle and squatted by the edge of the cliff. He had expected them to speak, to use some special greeting, but they only stared at each other.

He sat quite still, waiting for the trembling in his limbs to stop. Around his observation point the sky seemed to be drawn upwards in a tightly knit cone of fire. The storm when it came, he thought, would settle everything. If it did not, how could they survive, anyway? No food or water, and only a few bullets left to fight off a maddened tribe of crazy natives. His thick lip curled in contempt. It was a pity Fraser could not see him now, he reflected sadly. He would have been both proud and ashamed this time.

Behind him there was silence, like a temporary armistice with fate.

12

With the last of the feeble daylight gone, the wind mounted with steady strength, and beneath the scudding banks of clouds the sea, which had pitched and rolled all day in frightened anticipation of what was to come, broke open in a great mass of tumbling whitecaps and breakers. Unseen in the darkness, the rain sheeted down on to the writhing water, the sound of its power audible even above the roar of wind and sea.

Far out to the south-east of the islands the full brunt of the storm swung in a mad circular dance, driving one wave into another and, without giving them time to recover, swept their combined strength on to the next, so that each successive barrier of waves rose higher and more terrible, the long curving walls of black glass moving in serried ranks across the barren ocean, their white crests curling and growing with each onrushing second.

On the outer fringe of the revolving storm the old schooner parried each thrust of the mountainous water, and dug her sharp stem deeply into each successive crest, so that every plank and timber quivered as if being struck a mortal blow.

Kari had lashed his bony body to the wheel and, alongside the streaming shape of Myers, who was lending his weight to the bucking spokes, he peered steadily at the dimly lighted compass bowl, his wind-deadened ears cocked to the sounds of the protesting sails.

There was no longer any visibility outside the ship, and their world was confined to the pitching deck and the great cavern of wind and sea which surrounded and covered them.

Myers allowed his weight to shift as with a grunt Kari swung the wheel hard over, and then, as the ship laboured back on to her course, he helped him to meet the onrush of water which tried to batter the vessel round, so that she would lie open and unprotected for the next great wave.

Unsuccessfully he had endeavoured to shut his agonized mind to all this, had even tried to picture his neat little house, and remember it as he had left it so long ago. He thought of his wife, and a lump formed in his throat. After this, he told himself fervently, everything would be different. All their petty little differences seemed so unimportant, even unreal, in the face of the nightmare which now surrounded him. During the war he had seen a troopship lose her rudder in the Bay of Biscay, and drift as helpless as a child's toy yacht before the fury of a storm, which, compared to what the *Queensland Pearl* was now approaching, had been a mere gale. He gritted his teeth, his throat thick with nausea as the poop dropped beneath him, and he felt his feet bracing against the deck's new, impossible angle. He had lost all sense of time, and a few fear gripped his heart as he peered forward to look for Fraser. Suppose he had already been swept overboard and had left him and old Kari to steer the ship on for ever, or to its destruction? A surge of relief flooded through him as he saw the Australian's yellow sou'wester bobbing towards him through the curtain of rain. He saw the flash of his teeth, bared in a snarl more than a smile.

'How's she makin' out?' His voice was plucked away by the wind, and he hung to their crouched bodies, cradling them with his arms. 'I've set a few reefs on the old girl, but

232

we shall have to try an' shorten sail some more in a minute!'

Myers cupped his hand. 'Will it get worse?'

'Christ, I hope not!' He waved vaguely across the weather rail. 'Storm centre will be out that way, to the sou'east I reckon.' He made a clockwise movement with his fist. 'The eye of the storm'll be about eight miles across, an' the winds around the sides are sheer murder!' He ducked his head as a solid sheet of white spray swept over their bodies, making them choke. 'I shall heave to, on the port tack, unless I can beat it!'

Myers kept asking questions, his words lost and distorted, but Fraser no longer listened. He watched every straining movement of the stays and halyards, and listened with mounting apprehension to the thunder of the sails. She can't take much more, he thought. Must get under the shelter of the island again. If I can find it. Bloody madman, that's what I am!

A wave, more powerful than the rest, rose to challenge the schooner like a solid barrier, its presence revealed only by the curling white fingers which towered high above the bowsprit. The ship lurched, and Myers cried out as the spinning spokes grated across his ribs. The fo'c'sle vanished under the great wave, which thundered along the deck like a waterfall, cascading across the hold-coaming, and creaming around the masts, before hissing with baffled anger into the lee scuppers.

Fraser was already staggering along the deck, his hoarse voice rallying the others like a trumpet.

The thick canvas tarpaulin which had rested snugly over the deep hold had been plucked away like paper, and as Fraser scrabbled with his hands on the oak planks which covered the ten-foot opening he saw that the fastenings had been bent double by the force of the water.

Wabu and Yalla were with him, and as he passed a fresh line around the side of the coaming he saw another wave poise itself over the bows.

He felt the blow of the wave against his shoulders, and then he was buried beneath it, his fingers and feet slipping and scraping across the planking as he was borne helplessly along the deck. When he thought that his lungs would burst, he suddenly found himself marooned in the scuppers, with one leg being sucked through an open wash-port by the escaping water. Wabu still clung to the hold-coaming, and Yalla was already creeping back along the slanting deck, shaking his sleek hair like a dog.

Fraser struggled to his feet, and sobbed aloud as a shaft of agony lanced through his ribs. 'Bust!' His fingers faltered over the pain in his side. Every breath burned him like fire, but he forced himself to stagger to the hold. With something like despair he stared down at the wide gaping hole where the thick covers had once been. As he watched, he saw a white shape move lazily beneath him, and he stared back, sickened.

Hogan's body, torn loose from its lashings, floated with macabre abandon in the water which surged about the hold, and pounded noisily against the bulkheads.

Must be tons of water down there. He stared aghast at the new threat, his brain too bludgeoned by the storm to work properly. He turned to the others. 'Get on the pumps, lads! Jump to it!'

He desperately wanted to go below to consult his chart, and yet he dared not leave the deck. His depleted crew was almost beaten, and he had only to watch their sluggish movements and despairing gestures to know that they could not hold out much longer.

Myers greeted him with a forced grin. Fraser thought that it had cost him a good deal.

234

'We doin' all right, Vic? Surely we'll make the island soon?'

'Yeah. Maybe we'll sight the headland before dawn, an' then I aim to take her over the reef!' He winced as another pain explored his ribs. 'We might be able to ride it out there. If not,' he shrugged, 'we'll have to get ashore an' wait to be rescued!' His mouth twisted with bitterness. 'What a joke, eh?'

The schooner rolled slowly on to her side, the twin booms digging into the racing water. Another breaker surged against her round bilge and struck her with the force of a giant boulder, so that she staggered still further on to her side.

They were all shouting at once, Fraser like a maniac, as he swung his whole weight against the wheel, heedless of his broken ribs and the terrified cries around him.

With something like a prayer he called out to the old schooner: 'Come on, girl! Don't go like this!'

With infinite pain she climbed back on to her worn keel, the sails billowing immediately to a fresh blast of wind.

It was Dinkila, the terrified Malay cook, who saw the island first, his fearful eyes and quavering hand directed towards the mass which, like another great wave, seemed to move towards them out of the night.

Myers clutched Kari's bar-taut arm. 'The 'eadland! We'll be sheltered there, won't we, Vic?' He imagined that he could smell the land. He did not care what happened to the ship, or anything else. Just let us get ashore, an' wait to be rescued, as Vic said. He stared with disbelief at the black mass of land as it slid past the creaming hull. Fraser had all but lost his voice, but his very desperation seemed to drive the others to do his bidding.

The Phalarope Reef was completely hidden by the madly tossing whitecaps, but the lonely pinnacle of rock which he used as an aiming mark stood out clearly against the black land mass, its base shrouded in spray.

Their fingers torn and bleeding, cursing and praying alternately, they fought with the salt-hardened canvas, and heaved desperately at the swollen ropes which seemed determined to defy every effort, until with a great scream of blocks the ship went about, and staggered rather than sailed towards the maelstrom of short, steep waves which surged across the narrow entrance.

Fraser found quite suddenly that he was able to think about finding Tarrou again. Even Blair might have managed to survive. He shied away from the thought, his red-rimmed eyes raking the seething white mass ahead of the ship. Perhaps they would be able to ride out the storm behind the reef. His father had always said that next to plenty of sea-room the Pharlarope Reef was the best place to shelter.

Myers was shouting excitedly, 'Be able to get a better idea of what's 'appenin' wiv a bit er daylight, eh?' He clung to the wheel, his round face transformed. 'God, I never thought I'd see the ruddy dawn like that.'

Fraser tore his eyes away from the reef and glanced irritably in the direction of Myers' pointing hand. With complete horror he stared at the long thin line which Myers had mistaken for the probing light of the dawn.

Across hundreds of miles of the Pacific the wave had relentlessly built itself into a mountain of water which, driven by the wind and tide, now thundered towards the reef with the speed of an express train. For as far as he could see on either side of the horizon the tidal wave extended in an impossible dimension.

With a bellow like a wounded bull he flung himself at the wheel, screaming at the petrified seamen as he did so.

Queensland Pearl seemed eager to answer the helm, as

if tired of running away. Her bilges heavy with water, and with practically every plank spouting leaks, she wallowed heavily in a deep trough. On one side lay the reef, beyond which the comparatively calm water glinted with tempting malice, and on the other, with its mile-long crest already curving with anticipation, the tidal wave thundered to the end of its long journey.

The rain, which had been falling steadily for several hours, splashed over the sides of the rock cliff in a thousand small waterfalls and gurgled amidst the countless gullies and crevasses, covering the weather-beaten floor which sloped dangerously towards the seaward side. At the far end of the cliff, some three hundred yards from their original position, the three small figures crouched in a shallow alcove, cut long ago in the solid rock by wind and weather, and which now afforded some small protection from the driving wind. The wind, deflected by the cliff and its uneven barrier of stone teeth, seemed to come from all directions at once, so that their soaked bodies were left feeling bruised and breathless, and their hearing had long been deadened by the sighing roar of its power as it lashed the sea into a frenzy of trapped anger and drove the rain into their hiding-place in short, savage gusts.

Blair had propped his back against the slippery rock and had cradled the girl into his shoulder, the small warmth of their bodies giving him comfort, and enabling him to think with surprising clarity. It had been a painful crawl along the cliff in search of this small shelter, but the feel of his arm about her waist, as they clung together beneath the pounding weight of the rain, and bowed against the mounting wind, which threatened to brush them over the side of the cliff, had made him forget the agony in his foot and all else but the fact that they were together.

As her sanity had returned, Blair had felt her tight body move against his, as if she was exploring her surroundings and still unable to believe that she was alive.

With her mouth close to his cheek she had tried to explain what had happened before Spencer had met his death, and what he had told her about Blair's sister.

Blair was even more surprised to find that he no longer felt any pain at the memory of what had haunted him for so long. He gently quietened her halting efforts to comfort him, and marvelled at the strange feeling of happiness which possessed him. To hear this girl who had suffered such terrible handling, and had yet retained the strength and courage to comfort him, filled him with humility. He had tried to tell her his thoughts, as the storm bellowed around them and their bodies glistened with the continuous rain.

Tarrou sat close to Blair, strangely silent, yet he, too, seemed more relaxed, even assured, and Blair felt strangely moved by his unaccountable loyalty.

He stared across his outstretched legs and down at the heaving mass of the sea. Viewed from above it presented a moving pattern of white and silver, which, trapped by the reef and harried from every angle by the wind, surged dementedly in a wild criss-cross tangle, thundering eventually at the foot of the cliffs so that he could feel the very rock vibrate and quiver beneath his stiff body. He strained his eyes across the dark, tossing waste at the distant semicircle of creaming surf which marked the reef, and gave it the appearance of the hanging under-jaw of a nightmare shark. The reef; which had brought him so far to discover himself. He tightened his grip about the girl's shoulders, and felt her eyes watching him through the darkness.

Gillian wriggled her body slightly and tugged away the remains of the crude kilt of water-leaves. Beneath Tarrou's long jacket, which hung down almost to her knees, she could feel her naked body still soft and pliable with its coating of scented oil. She wanted to strip off the jacket and stand out on the unprotected rock to wash away the filth and the terrifying memory which hovered in the background of her mind. She flung the broken garment over the cliff and watched it torn away by the wind.

She still could not believe what had happened, nor would she allow herself to consider the future. She had the sudden urge to cry, but instead she pushed herself closer to Blair, shutting out the storm and ignoring the desperate efforts of the sea below.

Blair noticed the movement and lifted his arm slightly as if to shield her from the storm. He was conscious of the growing pain in his chest, and the sudden quickening of his breathing. He thrust away his reserve, which he had used in the past to protect himself from ridicule and envy alike, and with gentle firmness moved his other hand through the opening of her jacket. He pressed his hand against her breast and held it there, hardly daring to breathe, and aware of the shiver which ran through the soft oiled skin beneath his touch.

Gillian moaned aloud and, unable to help herself, lay trembling against him as the warm, gentle hand caressed her aching body, and seemed to transmit better than speech the message which Blair had concealed for so long.

Blair's voice, when it came, was thick and unsteady. He spoke hurriedly, as if afraid that she would move away and exclude him.

'After this is over we'll go away somewhere together.' His hand moved tenderly across her smooth shoulder and rested momentarily beneath her chin. 'I'll get things sorted out somehow, but no matter how long it takes I want you with me.'

She nodded, unable to trust her voice.

'What a journey it has been.' He sighed deeply. 'One day we might realize just how slender was the chance which brought us together!'

She lifted her chin and rubbed her cheek against his. 'Rupert, we were a pair of fools to waste so much time.' She gripped his wrist and pulled his hand down to her breast again. 'We will be good for each other, my darling.'

Tarrou's voice broke in on them like a disturbed bird. 'Look! Look, Major!' The dark arm wavered with incredulous excitement towards the sea. 'A ship! It's the schooner, I'm sure of it!' He rocked to and fro, his arms clasped around his knees. 'Vic came back, Major! He *did* need me, didn't he?' There was pleading as well as delight in his voice.

Gillian squeezed Blair's arm. 'Sure he does, Michel! And so do we all!'

They watched in silent wonder as the pale blob, which had first appeared as another mass of foam, grew more distinct, and without daring to guess at Fraser's reasons for turning back, followed the schooner's slow but superb efforts to approach the reef.

Blair could feel a lump in his throat, and wanted to cheer the frail white shape which staggered and plunged across the tumult of the waves, and which seemed to defy even the greatest breakers which danced across the reef. He forced himself to think calmly. Fraser could have no idea where they were, nor would he even know for sure that they were alive. He groped for the discarded revolver, and without taking his eyes from the ship, felt the wet metal with his fingers and prayed that it would still fire. Gently disengaging his arm from the girl's shoulders, he crawled to the rim of the cliff and peered down at the pounding surf. Although the tide was dropping, the fury of the wind still

240

held power over the water, and retained the battering strength of the waves at the foot of the cliff face. He dashed the rain from his plastered hair and looked again. There was one small piece of beach that was visible. Steeper, and higher than the rest, it made a tiny shelf which somehow managed to defy even the highest breaker.

He spoke slowly over his shoulder. It would not do to make Tarrou more excited, and too much was at stake at this point.

'I am going down there.' He indicated the place with the revolver. 'When you think the schooner is safely through the reef I want you to fire the rifle, d'you understand?' The dark head nodded, and he hurried on: 'Down there I may not be able to see the ship very well, and I shall be depending on you,' his teeth showed briefly in a smile, 'again!'

Gillian knelt beside him, her voice anxious. 'Why must you go down?'

'I shall fire the revolver to signal our position. Up here, the wind would carry the sound away before Fraser could hear it, but on that little beach each shot will be magnified and reflected by this cliff.' He smoothed the hair from her brow with a grin. 'Simple, see?'

Tarrou pointed wildly. 'See how she comes! Vic's driving her like a bird!'

The schooner was like nothing Blair had ever seen. Small and fragile in the black waves, she never faltered. She was much closer inshore now, and he could see the hard outline of her straining sails, and the creaming bone of foam under her forefoot. It was as if the old ship was flinging herself straight at the island, and Blair imagined Fraser's impassive face peering across the wheel as he drove his ship to the limit of its endurance. It was time to go. His injured foot would not allow him much time, but it was better that he should go and not Tarrou. I'm no sailor, he thought grimly, and Tarrou'll be able to guess the ship's intentions far easier than I would.

Something moved in his pocket, and in surprise he pulled out the cigarette-case. He laughed and passed it to the girl. 'A top-ranking journalist and a captain of industry, and look at us! This is all we've got left!'

He began to lower himself over the edge, his shoes slipping in the rivulets of rain as they kicked out for a foothold.

As their faces drew level, the girl leaned over the edge. Her lips brushed against his mouth, and he could see her eyes, almost luminous, in her pale face.

'You're all I want, darling!' She had to shout above the banshee wail of the wind. 'If we had ended our lives together right here, I would have been content!'

For a short moment longer he hung there, savouring her words and her touch. Then he was slipping and sliding over the smooth rock face, his injured foot sending messages of pain to his crowded brain. Once he nearly fell, but somehow he managed to summon up the last of his strength and cling to a small niche of rock, and check that the gun was still in his belt. It was nearly over now. He felt the sand soggy beneath his groping feet, and seconds later he was leaning back against the cliff, facing the fury of the sea, and soaked by the spray as well as the water which cascaded down from above.

He sometimes imagined that he could see the schooner, and wondered what Fraser would say when they met again. He smiled inwardly. Each had nothing to fear from the other. Each had followed his own code in his own way. He thought of the girl he had just left, and shivered. She made the fury of the storm almost unimportant.

Gillian laid full length and tried to see where Blair was

standing. At first she could see only the breakers, and then she saw his small shape, pale against the glistening piece of beach. He looked so isolated and helpless that she wished she had insisted on going down with him.

Tarrou was murmuring encouragement to the schooner, like a mother to a fretting child. 'Come on there! Keep your head up!'

She smiled. How they had all changed. Blair had been right when he had said that they had been stripped of all pretence and property. They had been left to fend for themselves, as mere mortals, without the protection of their remote society.

Tarrou's voice at her side broke off for an instant, and she lifted her eyes to look for the schooner. She saw its shape lengthen as it began to broach to. Then Tarrou began to scream, his voice cracked with anguish. Over and beyond the ship the great tidal wave rode in like another giant cliff. From their position they both saw its unspeakable horror at the same moment, and were stunned by its size and power.

Like a trapped animal the *Queensland Pearl* tacked round to meet the challenge, her sails flapping in silent protest as the water raced across the wallowing bulwarks. The wave towered over her full length, so that her slim masts and arching booms stood out with sudden clarity and sad beauty. The white crest curled and broke, and even on the cliff they heard the great rumble of sound as the avalanche of water crashed down on to the unprotected deck. Then the wave had passed over her, and they saw the schooner lying half submerged on her beam ends. Dismasted, her sails and rigging dragging painfully alongside, she appeared to drift willingly on the tearing wake of the wave. She seemed to make one final effort to right herself, the curved line of her poop rising as if in defiance

243

to her destroyer, and then with a splintering shudder she struck the reef. As the next leaping line of surf subsided from the coral they saw that the sea was empty.

Tarrou tore his eyes from the place where the ship had vanished and flung himself on the girl's back, and with all his strength pinned her arms to her sides, while she screamed and pleaded and stared with horrified eyes at the victorious wave as it bore unchallenged towards the foot of the cliff.

She leaned far over the edge, kicking and tearing at Tarrou's grip, and trying to find again the small figure at the bottom of the rock wall. She cried his name again and again, her screams lost in the wind and in the roar of the approaching wave. She imagined that she could see his upturned face, and she fought still harder to free herself.

After crossing the open sea, and gathering the power of the ocean as it went, the tidal wave had all but spent itself on the rock and coral of the reef. Yet, when it reached the foot of the cliff, the very island seemed to shake, and a towering mantle of spray rose up over their heads, so that Tarrou all but let the girl slip through his arms. He realized that she had fallen limp in his grip, and he shook his head dazedly, stunned by the enormity of this final disaster.

As the sea, hissing and grumbling, subsided from the empty beach, a small gap broke through the racing clouds, and a star showed through. The storm had passed, and within the reef the water glided uneasily in the dying wind.

Tarrou pressed his hands into the girl's shoulders, and wondered how he could help. Now there was nothing left, and the dawn no longer mattered.

Epilogue

The afternoon sun hung motionless over the calm blue water of the harbour, and reflected against the pale grey sides of the Australian frigate which swung easily at her moorings. Her sharp, business-like outline clashed with those of the nodding schooners and high-hulled shape of the Burns Philp steamer, whose spidery derricks clanked and squeaked as she unloaded stores into the waiting lighters.

The frigate's captain stared down at his ship from the window of Grainger's office in the British Residency, his sleep-starved eyes momentarily softening with affection. The ensign hung quite limp over the ship, as did the flag outside the office window. A staccato roar filled the quiet harbour with sound, and Grainger rose quickly from his desk and crossed to the other man's side.

On the far side of the harbour the Quantas flying-boat shivered under a brief cloud of thin smoke, and then, as the engines settled down into a confident growl, the small boats which hovered nearby began to idle clear, the occupants waving jerkily in the relentless glare.

Grainger watched with narrowed eyes. 'It's all quite a story,' he said, half to himself. 'If you hadn't sent a landing-party on to the island I don't suppose we should ever have known what had happened.'

The naval officer grunted. 'I thought the girl was a gonner, I can tell you, but the other character soon got his strength back.'

The flying-boat started to taxi slowly across the water, a twin roll of white foam creaming away from her hull.

Below the Residency some natives paused in their work repairing the roof of a small weatherboard building. Apart from the missing corrugated iron, which had been flung fifty yards up the road, and the small launch which now lay up-ended on the beach, there was little left to show where the storm had struck and passed on.

'We did all we could for the girl,' Grainger continued slowly, 'but she hardly spoke the whole time. There was a telegram waiting for her from her New York office, but she did not even glance at it. I think it was another assignment for her.' He shook his head, unable to forget Gillian Bligh's face.

'Where's she off to now?' The captain's voice reminded Grainger of Fraser, and his heart felt suddenly heavy.

'She said she was going home,' he said simply.

The flying-boat lifted easily from the clutching water and began to bank lazily towards the west. Grainger turned away from the window and stared at his wall chart. There would be a lot to do on Hog Island before he could relax again, he considered. He tried to raise some enthusiasm, but the noise of the flying-boat's engines seemed to defy his thoughts.

On the beach, within feet of the gentle water, Tarrou followed the aircraft until its sound and glittering shape had vanished. Gently, and with extreme care, he took the gold cigarette-case from his pocket and turned it over in his hands.

When he had said good-bye to her as she had stepped down into the waiting launch, she had handed it to him without a word.

A few people passed him as they walked back towards the town. Those who noticed him assumed that he had been staring too long at the flying-boat. How else could his eyes be so wet?

Also by Douglas Reeman

PATH OF THE STORM

The old submarine-chaser USS Hibiscus, re-fitting in a Hong Kong dockyard before being handed over to the Nationalist Chinese, is suddenly ordered to the desolate island group of Payenhau.

For Captain Mark Gunnar – driven by the memory of his torture at the hands of Viet Cong guerrillas – the new command is a chance to even the score against a ruthless, unrelenting enemy.

But Payenhau is very different from his expectations, and as the weather worsens a crisis develops that Gunnar must face alone.

THE LAST RAIDER

It is December 1917. Germany opens the final, bitter round of the war with a new and deadly weapon in the struggle for the seas – the Vulcan sails from Kiel Harbour.

To all appearances she is a harmless merchant vessel. But her peaceful lines conceal a merciless firepower; guns, mines and torpedoes that can be brought into play instantly.

The Vulcan is a commerce raider. And under crack commander Felix von Steiger her mission is to bring chaos to the seaways.